Margaret J. Gray
639 Lillian Way
Hollywood 4

Oct. '54

The Desperate Hours

a novel by

Joseph Hayes

Random House
New York

For Marrijane, my wife, who helps all the way, all the time; and with a sidelong nod of thanks to Mary B. Orvis and James Oliver Brown.

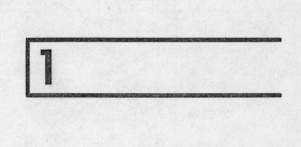

1

They emerged from the woods a few minutes after dawn, a cold, moist dawn with a mist billowing up from the fields. There were three of them, their uniforms blending with the yellowing autumn green. They paused only briefly, scanning the deserted highway that lay flat across the flat Midwestern country. At a signal from one—the tall, lean, young-looking man who walked slightly ahead of the other two, with his head tilted and his shoulders lifted at a defiant and slightly triumphant angle—they proceeded swiftly, but not running, behind a screen of trees and underbrush, in a line parallel to the highway. In a very short time, and before anyone or anything else appeared on the road, they reached a farm. In the barn lot, one detached himself from the others, moving quickly, a small young man, even younger than the tall one but without the other's jaunty manner, and began to work on the wires under the hood of the late-model gray-colored sedan parked there. The other two moved swiftly but with stealth toward the barn. Inside, they came upon a middle-aged farmer, wearing blue overalls, shifting with pail and stool from one cow to another. The shorter of the two men—who was middle-aged and slower, but powerful-looking, with the ponderous forward-leaning gait of a bear—picked up an ax handle and stepped across the straw-littered, concrete floor. Before the startled farmer could utter a cry, the tremendous arms went up once, there was an ugly sound, and the farmer sprawled. Then the heavy man lifted the handle again, but the other stopped him with a short commanding gesture similar to the one he had used on the highway. He then knelt down by the unconscious but still breathing farmer and stripped him of his overalls.

They then went out of the barn, rejoined the boy who was now seated behind the wheel of the car with the motor purring. With no eyes upon it, the sedan slipped out of the barn lot, turned south, and became lost in the thinning mist.

All this had been accomplished with a minimum of effort, no waste motion and in the most precise and machinelike manner imaginable.

Word of this incident, and all that had preceded it but nothing that followed it, reached Indianapolis, seventy-two miles to the east, less than half an hour later. Almost immediately then a telephone rang in the bedroom of a small, neat cottage in one of the newer but unpretentious subdivisions northwest of the city.

A rangy young man in green-striped flannel pajamas rolled over in bed, yawning, and then, not groping, reached across his unawakened wife and picked up the telephone. He spoke into it curtly, then listened briefly. "I'll be down," he said quietly. Wide awake at last, he replaced the telephone in its cradle and turned to the woman in the bed.

Her eyes were open now, and she crinkled her nose at him,

4

stretching with an exaggerated display of well-being and satisfaction to cover up the sharp cut of apprehension that such
phone calls always caused in her. She sat up, watching her husband climb into his dark suit. He was an extremely tall man, in
his early thirties, with extremely thin arms and legs that in no
way betrayed the wirelike twist of muscles that lay below the
surface. He was talking as he dressed, and he spoke in a laconic
sort of drawl, grumbling in such a way that she caught the
thrust of emotion he was trying to subdue.

"Glenn Griffin, his kid brother and another con, a lifer
by the name of Robish," Jesse Webb was saying. "Not more
than an hour ago. From the Federal prison in Terre Haute."
He strapped on his gun, gave the shoulder holster a quick pat,
then pulled on his suit jacket, flipping it back once, with an
automatic gesture so that the deputy sheriff's badge showed
once, briefly, a dull glimmer in the dimness. "I'll catch a shave
downtown, Kathie."

"You'll eat, too," she reminded him, and he turned to the
bed, grinning slowly, his face suddenly very young.

"I reckon I'll eat, Kathleen Webb," he drawled, "if you
say so."

But even as he spoke, the smile flickered, failed, and he bent
quickly, kissed her, and turned.

Her voice caught him. "Is Glenn Griffin the one you—" She
broke off when he paused in the bedroom doorway.

"He's the one," he said. "He had twelve years to go. I hope
he heads straight for his old home town." He was rubbing the
back of his narrow, lean, efficient hand, in that way he had, and
Kathleen rose from the bed.

She walked with him to the front door. "But isn't this the
last place he *would* come?" she asked reasonably, trying not to
betray the slow knife-turn inside.

Jesse Webb, of the Marion County Sheriff's office, himself
in charge this entire week because his superior, Sheriff Masters,
had gone to South Carolina on a combined extradition case

and hunting trip, turned to his wife in the doorway and explained why he thought, or hoped, that Glenn Griffin would come to Indianapolis. In the first place, he said, you had to bank on the homing-pigeon instinct in the criminal mind: a familiar town, even if their faces are known in it, gives them the illusion of security. They always think they know where to hide, although today all such rat holes would be turned inside out by nightfall. Then, too, there was the woman, name of Helen Lamar; she was thirty-five at least, ten years older than Glenn Griffin himself, but important to him. And Jesse had a hunch she had the money.

"There's always a woman," Kathleen said, reluctant to release the slender arm with the taut muscles rippling in it.

"Not always, but if there is, it helps. If she's still in Indianapolis, I'll lay two to one she's the beacon will lead us straight to those three——" He clamped down on his tongue because Kathleen despised what she called "courthouse language." He stopped and caught her chin in his hand and again he kissed her lips, still warm with sleep, then strode toward the car parked in the driveway, his mind almost consciously waiting for the inevitable words from the door.

They came, floating in the chill, sharp air: "Good luck, darling."

He waved with one hand, unsmiling, and backed the Sheriff's car into the street, guiding with his other hand.

At that moment the gray sedan was cruising along in farm country that had begun to have a slight lift and roll to it. Glenn Griffin, wearing the faded blue overalls, was at the wheel. The middle-aged man sat beside him, his enormous hulk of head sunk between two permanently upthrust shoulders so that it seemed almost a part of his thick, heavy body. The boy, Glenn's younger brother, lay stretched out on the back seat, his head well down, his eyes closed.

But Hank Griffin was not sleeping. He was remembering the slow flat crawl in darkness over the hundred yards of bare ground with the walls and gun towers behind them; he was remembering the headlong, reckless crash of the three bodies through the comparative safety of the dark woods. His chest was lashed and scratched and his shirt front torn and slightly crusted with blood. There was a gash across his forehead and it had begun to throb. But worst of all, he was shuddering. Now that they were beyond earshot of any shrieking sirens, insistent, shrill and blood-curdling on the high walls, he could imagine the sound as if he had actually heard it. His rather short, tight-knit and very youthful body had begun to shake with crawling vibrations in every bone and muscle, and there was nothing he could do to stop it except grit his teeth together and lie there listening to Glenn and Robish in the front seat.

"You're going south," Robish was complaining in a heavy but querulous voice. "Indianapolis is northeast."

"I'm going southeast now," Glenn Griffin said easily, and the words leaped and flickered in that laughter that now colored every word he spoke and filled the car with an exultancy that moved like warmth over Hank in the back seat.

"Didn't you say Lamar was in Indianapolis? With the dough."

"She moved away last week. To Pittsburgh. If they can't locate her in Indianapolis, it'll take the heat off. They won't locate her."

"Where the hell we heading then?"

"Indianapolis," Glenn said quietly, mocking the man beside him, with the laughter still in his tone. "I got some business there, remember? But we're not walking into a roadblock from the west, pal. We'll circle all the way around and come in from the northeast some time this afternoon."

"Then what?"

"Then we'll find us a cozy spot. And I'll contact Helen."

"A cozy spot—like where?"

"You name it, Robish. Only no hangouts, see. They'll be watching all of them. No hotels, either. Pick a nice quiet house on a nice quiet street on the edge of town, say, with no other houses close by. Make it a big place, though, with soft furniture. Comfortable, scared people—a sucker who goes to work every day, maybe a kid in the family. Some place to take the stir-taste out of our mouths."

"Then what?"

"We wait."

"How long?"

"Till Helen gets there from Pittsburgh, P.A. Now shut up, Robish, let a guy enjoy his freedom."

In the back seat Hank heard Robish swear under his breath. Hank had to hand it to Glenn: he could certainly handle Robish. First, Robish had growled that they had to ditch the prison clothes; Glenn wouldn't listen. He'd get him clothes when he needed them—good clothes. Meanwhile, stay down. And then Robish had complained about not carrying a gun: it made him feel helpless. What if they ran into a roadblock? They wouldn't, Glenn had said, because nobody ever heard of these roads. As for the gun, they couldn't afford to pull a job and tip off their whereabouts; besides, Glenn had one, didn't he? A .38 revolver, taken from the guard who was now in the prison infirmary with a bump on his head, if nothing worse. Relax, Robish, and enjoy yourself.

But Hank was not relaxed. He was looking ahead. And he was picturing a house such as Glenn had described. After the clank of lock, the smooth mechanical sound of cell doors closing, the hard stiffness of concrete floors and metal bunks, he was imagining sinking down again into a deep soft chair, his feet planted on deep-tufted carpet, the warm and intimate reality of ordinary walls with framed pictures on them. As yet even the crisp, cold air that penetrated the closed windows of the sedan had not reached the valleys of memory where the harsh iron-tasting odor of the last two years still lingered like stench from a swamp. But in a house like that, he said to himself . . .

The Hilliards had bought their house on Kessler Boulevard because it was quite large compared to the new homes selling for slightly less money in the subdivisions. It had been worth the difference in price because, while fairly convenient to shopping centers and bus lines, it was remote enough from other homes to give the family a sense of privacy. Also, it was outside the city limits by only ten blocks, and the taxes were lower. In the eight years that they had occupied the house, they had come, without any of them ever being quite aware of it, to love every corner, stairstep and shingle. It would require another paint job in the spring, true, and the furniture, purchased new when Dan was released from the Navy after the war, showed some, but not much, evidence of wear and tear by two growing youngsters. Cindy, who was now nineteen, thought they should replace the living-room suite as soon as possible, but her mother, Eleanor, wasn't just sure. Even though they received a 20 per cent discount on furniture purchases because Dan was now personnel manager of the largest department store in town, they were living, Eleanor argued, in inflationary times and the furniture *was* comfortable. Besides, as she pointed out to Dan less than a week ago, Cindy might be getting married soon. Dan had said nothing—which was his way.

As Dan came down the stairs at 7:40 on this particular Wednesday morning, he was trying to look ahead to the complicated problems of the day at the office rather than give in to the nagging uncertainty, almost anxiety, he had begun to feel about his daughter, Cindy. Not that he had anything personal or in particular against Charles Wright. Perhaps, he chided himself, only a banked-down sort of envy. Dan had had to work for everything he had ever made, every cent. This house itself was evidence of how long and how hard. Without an education past the second year in high school, he had come to this. And he was proud—a hard pride that was compounded of a personal sense of accomplishment and of gratitude. Charles Wright, on the other hand, was not the sort of young man with whom Dan could ever feel comfortable. Chuck—as Cindy had come to call him after going to work as secretary in the law office where young Wright was already a junior partner—had had it all handed to him, everything easy. Fine. He was lucky. But he was also, Dan knew from hearsay and from certain knowledge, an irresponsible young man, more interested in fast sports cars, beautiful girls, and long, wine-drenched parties than in finding a solid place for himself in the life of the community. Very well, then, Dan was acting like a typical father, or as Cindy had chided, "a conservative old fogy."

In the kitchen the day's routine had begun almost an hour before. Ralphie, who dawdled over breakfast as though it were some sort of punishment for past crimes, was glaring at a half-full glass of milk. He looked up when Dan doubled up a huge freckled fist and placed the knuckles lightly against the soft ten-year-old cheek. Eleanor, whose face was rounded like her son's and who had passed along to him also her light-colored hair, smiled and placed Dan's steaming ham and eggs before him, then sat down across from him, at the kitchen table. Without make-up, she looked like a child herself, small and still slender.

"Lucille is sick," she announced, explaining the absence of the maid who usually came on Wednesday and Saturdays.

"Again?" Dan said. "Any gin missing?"

Eleanor frowned and shook her head in swift wifely warning, nodding to Ralphie, who lifted his eyes from the milk and grinned knowingly. "She's probably blotto," he said sagely.

"Where does he learn his language?" Dan inquired.

"Comic books," Eleanor said, buttering toast. "Television. Do you know what blotto means, Ralphie?"

"My name," Ralphie announced, punctuating each word with a click of his glass on the table, "is Ralph. R-a-l-p-h. There's no *y* on the end of it."

"Sorry, old fellow," Dan said.

"And blotto means tight. Tight means drunk. Have I drunk enough milk?"

Eleanor was laughing, behind her napkin, and nodding. Ralphie was up, jarring the table, kissing his mother's hair swiftly; then he turned grave eyes on Dan and gave him a swift salute, half defiance and half apology, and turned on his heel.

"I'll ride my bike. I've got a whole half-hour, almost." He disappeared onto the rear porch, clumped down the three steps and was gone. Dan heard the garage door sliding up and was reminded again that he had to oil the runner mechanism soon.

Eleanor said, "Our son Ralph, spelled R-a-l-p-h, is too old to kiss a man—that's you—good-bye or good night."

"Well," Dan said wryly, but feeling a pinch somewhere inside, "that seems to be that."

"A milepost," Eleanor said, her eyes on him steadily now, studying him.

"We seem to be flying past mileposts darned fast, old girl," he said.

What Eleanor saw was a man of average height with heavy shoulders, the bulk of his body fitting finely under the double-breasted suit; she looked into the familiar deep blue eyes and was conscious of the mahogany-red hair above and the freckles climbing over and across the rather broad nose and the deep fine lines that added, she thought, so much character to an otherwise very ordinary but very appealing face.

11

Reading his mind, she said, "Cindy'd like to ask him for Thanksgiving dinner, Dan."

Dan downed the last swallow of coffee, stood up, yanked at his suit coat like a boy dressed for a party and determined to impress.

"Should she?" Eleanor asked.

Dan shrugged, but not successfully. "Ellie, I don't want to jump in and start opposing this thing and get Cindy's back up. But—well, Thanksgiving's a sort of family day."

Eleanor lifted her face for his kiss, then walked to the kitchen window while Dan went out the rear door, his topcoat thrown over his arm instead of over his shoulders.

When she opened the window, the gusty warning of winter swept through the kitchen. She watched from an angle as Dan backed the blue car out of the garage, maneuvering it around Cindy's black coupe in the driveway. Then, for absolutely no reason at all except that it was a ritual between them, meaning at the same time more and less than the word itself, she called, "Careful. And I mean it."

His hat pulled at its usual not quite proper angle, Dan shouted back, "Close the window," and swept out of her line of vision.

Eleanor complied, as she did every morning, five days a week. She never caught colds, and Dan knew this, just as she knew that there was no particular reason for him to be careful. Careful of what?

As she set a fresh place for Cindy, Eleanor decided against mentioning Chuck Wright this morning, especially in view of Dan's unspoken rejection of the Thanksgiving-dinner idea. All the words that occurred to her seemed stereotyped and flat, anyway—that Chuck Wright had a reputation for being wild, that he was the type that would never settle down. Cindy would only reply again, from the summit of nineteen years, that you could blame the war for that, hinting at some great tragedy and dramatic feat that, if known, would explain Charles Wright completely and utterly and make him totally acceptable in every far corner of the land.

Eleanor flipped on the radio, punching the buttons one after the other, finally settling for a news report as she prepared to drink her second cup of coffee.

After listening for perhaps five minutes—her attention not caught by the report of three escaped convicts in Terre Haute or attracted by the warning that these men were armed and dangerous—she heard Cindy descending the uncarpeted back stairs that only the family used, her heels a quick tattoo. Eleanor turned off the radio and set down her cup. As soon as Cindy was out of the house, Eleanor's own day would really begin.

In the office of the Sheriff, which was attached to the Marion County jail building in downtown Indianapolis, the day had started long before. Through the morning, Jesse Webb had kept in close contact with the state police, the city police, the teletypes, the news reports, and the local office of the FBI. They had now a very accurate description of the gray sedan, its license number, and the approximate time of its theft from a farm south of Terre Haute.

Jesse hated waiting. It went against the grain. There was a helplessness about it that worked like sandpaper on his nerves. The roadblocks had been set up on all the main highways, there were no reports of further thefts, no sports stores robbed for guns, no clothing shops or cleaning shops broken into for suits; in short, everything that could be done was being done. But Jesse was not satisfied.

His uncle, Frank Pritchard, telephoned him after the 10 o'clock radio news. Jesse listened to the tired voice he could barely recognize, nodding his lean head occasionally, his hat

13

tilted back, his feet pressed against the edge of the roll-top desk in his office. Then he said, "I haven't forgotten a thing, Uncle Frank. Go to sleep."

Afterwards, he sat with his lanky frame folded eaglelike over the desk, smoking until his cigarette burned his fingers.

"Was that Frank P?" Tom Winston, the deputy who shared the small office, had heard the conversation—what there was of it—and his curiosity finally broke forth. "Bet he'd like to be back in the business today."

"Yeah," Jesse said slowly, contemplating an invisible spot on the high, bare plaster ceiling. "Yeah. With two good hands and his gun."

"Why'd you tell him to go to sleep?"

Tom Winston started at the suddenly fierce brown eyes that Jesse Webb turned on him. "I told him to go back to sleep," Jesse said, and he was not drawling but biting the words so that they came out like bullets from an automatic, "because he's got a job he has to keep. A night-watchman job at the meat-packing plant. I don't want him to lose *that* one because of Glenn Griffin."

Winston picked up a sheaf of papers from his desk, and retreated. "I didn't know what had become of old Frank P," he said apologetically.

Jesse stared after his friend as Winston slouched down the corridor toward Records. Don't blame Winston, Jesse reminded himself, breathing hard now; blame the guy who did it. He could see it happening again, all of it. Uncle Frank had been behind the parked car when Glenn Griffin came out the bleak-faced little apartment-hotel on the south side. Even in his blue uniform, Uncle Frank had looked too small, too old and too wispy for the .38 he held in his hand. Then he shouted. Glenn Griffin had whirled, firing, and two bullets had ripped into Uncle Frank's arm, permanently injuring a nerve so that now the right arm was a hanging, limp, useless thing, hardly a part of that frail little body at all.

Jesse had blamed himself for not letting go then, blasting; but he had been temporarily stunned and surprised to hear Uncle Frank scream like a child, a terrible unashamed shriek that still haunted Jesse in dreams. Glenn Griffin had leaped back inside the doorway, graceful as a dancer, despite the roar and whine and thwack of the other guns. Then Glenn Griffin, while Uncle Frank lay writhing on the ground, had shouted for a chance to surrender, even throwing his gun into the street.

Jesse recalled the blank wall of unreason that had come smashing down on him as he stepped over the gun on the pavement and approached the unarmed young hoodlum; he had been helpless despite the shouts of the other officers, including his lieutenant, ordering him to stop, not to fire. The wall had lifted slightly then and he had not fired. But it was not until he had yanked the cowering Glenn Griffin to his toes with one thin but clawlike hand and brought his other, a twisting fury in itself, full into the prisoner's handsome but distorted face that Jesse Webb had felt a momentary relief from the grip of rage.

Thinking about it now, more than two years later, left him pale and shaken, the sweat gathering at the back of his neck. More calmly he remembered what had followed: the way Uncle Frank had been eased off the city force because of his dangling and soon-withered arm, the unreasonable way he himself had turned in his badge. He recalled, too, the trial of Glenn Griffin, with the boy smiling blandly at the jury box through the bandages that held his broken jaw in place while his attorney pointed dramatically to this "indisputable evidence of police brutality." Even after the jury had brought in the guilty verdict—it was Griffin's third major conviction—the young man had kept up his front. At the sentencing, his kid brother, captured with him that same night, had gone pale and begun to tremble. But not Glenn.

The only time Glenn Griffin had shown any emotion at all was that day in the corridor of the city jail when the Federal

Marshal was taking him away. Jesse, although he was by then with the Sheriff's office and no longer on the city force, had made a point of being present. The bandages were no longer on the boy's face, but it was white and strained and he spoke carefully, stiffly.

"You got yours coming, copper," he said—not spitting out the words, nothing dramatic or violent about it.

Finished with memories, elbowing them aside in his mind, Jesse Webb stood up from his desk. He rubbed the back of his neck with the palm of his hand; it came away hot and wet. Then he left the office and, his long lean body pitched slightly forward as usual, he walked out of the building, across the center of town, around Monument Circle, toward the State House. He could have telephoned; he could have taken his car. He needed the walk, and the sharp, pinpointed air.

Lt. Van Dorn of the State Police, ruddy-faced and gray-haired, grinned at Jesse's scowl from behind the counter. "The city can't pick up any trace of this Helen Lamar, Jess. They've ripped whole buildings apart. We can't get anything from the roads except the usual—the car's been spotted thirty-two times since 7 o'clock. North, East, South and West. But not officially. My guess is the woman's out West somewhere, maybe California, and we're beating our tails ragged over nothing around here. They're on their way to her, probably all the way across Illinois by now." Then he turned his head and peered at Jesse from the corner of his eyes. "You look like hell yourself. Bad night?"

"No," Jesse answered slowly. "No," he drawled, thinking of Kathleen.

Then something struck him between the eyes. It was only a possibility, and a very slight one at that. But he was taking no chances. He picked up the telephone from the counter, dialed his office.

"Tom," he said when Winston answered, "send a car out to pick up my wife. Bring her to the office. Tell her I'm okay. I

16

just want to see her. And Tom—don't scare the girl, hear?"

Anything was possible. You could never tell when it came to a mind like Griffin's. But if that sonofabitch came near Kathleen . . .

By selecting only the most unlikely and untraveled back roads, the locations of which Glenn Griffin seemed to have traced on the flintlike surface of his mind, he had by now maneuvered the gray sedan all the way around the city, staying for the most part forty or fifty miles south, and later, twenty miles east. By noon, however, he was approaching the city on a small road northeast of town, a road so small that the actual boundary of the city was not designated by one of the black-on-white signs reading "INDIANAPOLIS, CITY LIMITS."

It was now ten minutes after twelve. Robish slept, snoring. Hank, in the back seat, had fallen into the habit of rubbing the palms of his hands down the sides of his shirt over his ribs as though to wipe off some invisible stain or slime that clung to the rough cloth. Driving, Glenn Griffin was whistling, softly, steadily.

It had taken more than six hours by this roundabout route to reach a destination only seventy-two miles from their starting point. But they had progressed without incident, as smoothly and easily as if they had been flying a plane over the hundreds of alert and watchful eyes.

All three had begun to feel the emptiness of hunger, but Glenn refused to stop.

Kathleen Webb, at the white counter of a restaurant around the corner from the Courthouse, kept urging her husband to eat up. Instead, he sipped his fifth cup of bitter black coffee and stared into it, imagining again a scene that had not and would not occur: Glenn Griffin stepping onto the miniature porch of Jesse's and Kathleen's small home, knocking, entering, smiling at Kathleen as blandly as he had once smiled at the jury box.

But Jesse should have learned long ago, he told himself with a taut, secret smile, that the things you fear the most are those least likely to happen.

On the other hand, those scenes that are beyond the reach of a man's imagination, once he has fallen into the secure routine of a way of life, do actually occur and with more frequency than anyone is likely to acknowledge. Dan Hilliard, immersed in an interview with an applicant for a responsible position in the shipping department, sat behind his desk in his comfortable sixth-floor office of the department store and concentrated on the task at hand, all the while letting his mind wander in and around the personality of the man before him. He had a warranted reputation for being able to judge character, and the secret of how he accomplished this was hidden even from him. At any rate, he had no thought at the moment, certainly no concern about what might be happening on his own front porch on Kessler Boulevard north of the city, ten miles from his office.

Eleanor Hilliard was about to go up the front stairs to change into her gardening clothes—too many leaves had fallen on the flower beds under the maples—when she heard the step on the porch. The front doorbell rang. She pushed a strand of light hair off her forehead and sighed. It was that blissful moment after lunch when Ralphie had returned to school and she felt a certain treasured sense of freedom until 3:30. The front door was a solid panel, without window, and although there was a safety chain attached to the door frame, she never bothered to use it. It annoyed her that anyone had come to the front door. The family and tradesmen normally used the side entrance, because it connected the driveway directly with the sun porch and was more convenient.

The man who faced her on the porch, a very young man with short-cropped but soft-looking and glistening black hair, wore faded blue farmer's overalls and he was smiling almost apologetically. He looked boyish, and so miserable about his errand that Eleanor smiled, too.

"Sorry to bother you, ma'am," he said in a voice that was almost a whisper, "but I guess I've lost my way. I'm trying to get to the Bulliard Dairy. I know it's in the neighborhood, but——"

Then he stopped, and now he was looking over her shoulder into the sun-streaked front hall. The smile remained on his face, but a subtle alteration took place around the edges of his mouth, a tightening that froze the smile. Involuntarily, she turned.

After that, everything happened so fast and with such cool mechanical precision that she was paralyzed, mind and body, and that numb helplessness must have been what carried her safely through the next few minutes.

She heard the door behind her open, felt the knob hard against her ribs, then heard it close. The older man, who must have entered through the back door, turned from her and stomped up the stairs. A third man, much younger, who wore the same strange gray-green garb as the big fellow, appeared in the dining-room door, then walked swiftly, lightly through the entire downstairs section of the house, opening doors, closing them. Eleanor saw, without really comprehending, the black gun in the hand of the young man in overalls who remained with her in the hall. She thought of the small automatic upstairs, concealed in the coil of spring under Dan's bed. She felt then a scream accumulating, powerful and uncontrollable, in her parched, locked throat.

"Take it easy, lady," the young man beside her advised softly. "Take it easy. You open your mouth, your kid'll come home from school and find your body."

She could feel her mind take hold, with a sharp click in her brain, as of a switch thrown. Instead of screaming, she lifted her hand to her mouth and bit down hard on the back of it, so hard that she tasted blood. But the scream was choked off in the back of her aching throat.

The boyish man returned, not looking at her, and said, "All clear down here, Glenn." Without another word, or even a nod from the one called Glenn, the youngster turned and went through the dining room toward the kitchen.

Eleanor heard the back door open and close and then a motor grind over in the driveway. Only then, after he had left the room, the boy's voice reached her—young, casual, subdued. He might have been one of Cindy's young admirers speaking. The naturalness of that voice in the hurricane-center of nightmare filled her with an incongruous terror that not even the gun had aroused. Outside, she heard a familiar sound: the garage door descending on the metal runners that needed oiling.

Then, in the silence, the middle-aged man came down the stairs; he carried one of Dan's suits flung over one arm. His animal-like face wore an expression that might have denoted pleasure, but his yellowish-green eyes, lost between the slits in the bulbous pouches, seemed as depthless and opaque as marbles.

"Nobody home but the missus," the man reported.

Staring at Dan's tweed suit, Eleanor thought of her husband. Big, calm, reserved, never roused to anger. Even in the swift flood of panic and disgust—as she saw the older man's eyes crawl hungrily over her—the thought of Dan calmed her.

"Get in there, Robish," Glenn Griffin said, "and keep an eye open out front."

Robish, pulling his eyes from her, followed the order and went into the living room and dropped himself into the large chair half-facing the wide front windows. He uttered a huge sigh. The back door opened and closed again. All three of them were in the house, the car concealed in the Hilliard garage.

"Now," said the one named Glenn. "Now, Mrs. Hilliard. We got a phone call to make, you and me. I guess you got the idea now. I guess you know what'll happen, you let go with anything fishy while you're talking. Case not, though, listen. We're playing for keeps. We don't want to hurt nobody, specially kids. But when the little guy who owns that bike out there gets home . . ."

"What do you want me to do?" Eleanor asked.

Glenn Griffin grinned again. "Smart little lady. Hope the whole family's smart as you, Mrs. Hilliard. Now."

Leaning against the telephone table, Eleanor listened to the very explicit, low-toned directions. Then she picked up the phone, dialed Long Distance and for the first time noticed the strange bloody tooth marks on the back of her hand. She gave the operator a number that she knew she should remember but could not. A number in Pittsburgh, Pennsylvania . . .

"Pittsburgh!" Jesse Webb uttered an oath and stood up from his desk after talking to Carson, the young FBI man assigned to the case. "They've located Helen Lamar."

Tom Winston, catching the explosive note of disappointment and defeat, didn't turn from his desk. "They got her?"

"She checked out over an hour ago. Why? Nobody knows. She just came in suddenly and checked out. They're still questioning the hotel people, but as far as they can dope it, she didn't receive a phone call, anything. At least not at the hotel. She'd be too smart for that, figuring we might be watching. If Griffin called her, they used somebody in between." He was striding up and down in the office, hands jammed into his pockets, head shot forward. "But maybe he didn't have to call. They could have it all timed. Hell, they think of these things, smart rats like that. Now you know where that leaves us, Tom? I'll tell you. Nowhere. That leaves us with a license number and the description of a car. A car they'll ditch soon enough, but they're taking their time on that, too. No trail. Three eggs like that can't melt into the ground, for God's sake!" He sat down abruptly and cracked the top of the desk with his fist. "Tom, where the hell is that car?"

All through the endless afternoon Eleanor Hilliard's mind returned again and again to the dust-covered gray sedan parked in the garage.

Ralphie arrived home at 3:30, but he didn't notice the closed garage door. She detained him in the living room, speaking swiftly and firmly. She had a terrible headache, she said; she had to have absolute quiet all afternoon; she was sorry, but he would have to go out and play until suppertime and he was not to come back until then. No, he didn't have to change his clothes, not today. But Ralphie was hungry—as usual. Then he was to go to the drug store, get a sandwich; she gave him the money. Puzzled at his mother, who never before had complained of a headache, but pleased at the chance to buy a drug-store sandwich on his own, Ralphie climbed on the bicycle and went spinning down the boulevard.

"Nice work, lady," Glenn said, replacing his gun in his pocket.

She looked at him without expression, feeling nothing now but the hard stone in the pit of her stomach. "If you keep eating up everything, I'll have to shop before supper."

"I got a few more questions now, Mrs. Hilliard."

Then the process started all over again. The questions . . . This daughter, this Cynthia, what time did she get home from work? Did she drive her own car? Was she ever late? Okay then, just let her walk in.

"You won't have to do a thing but keep quiet, see."

If Cindy saw the garage door at all, she did not stop to question why it was closed. At 5:18 she brought the coupe to a halt in the driveway, leaped out, and came into the living room through the sun porch. Eleanor was sitting stiff and still on the sofa. Glenn was standing, his ankles crossed casually, by the television set; the gun was in his hand. Robish was in the small combined library-den in the rear of the house, with the door between it and the long living room standing open. Eleanor could see him watching the driveway through the side windows. She knew that the young one, named Hank, was still in the kitchen, his eye on the back yard, listening to the news reports on the small radio.

Cindy burst in, in that way she had, always a little breathless lately, her checked coat flying, her hair flowing behind her. When she caught sight of her mother, she stopped, her hazel-flecked blue eyes snapping around the room, remaining a split second on Glenn Griffin.

Glenn grinned. "Come right in, redhead."

23

Before Eleanor realized that Cindy had moved, the girl whirled and started to retrace her steps, running this time.

"Okay," Glenn Griffin said easily, but his voice lifted, "we still got your old lady, sis."

Robish burst in from the den as Cindy's step faltered at the sun-porch door. She turned, slowly, catching sight of Robish then, the big man planted in the center of the room, and, dismissing him instinctively, she faced Glenn Griffin, who had not moved a muscle.

"That's better, redhead," the tall young man said, grinning. "Now you're being real sensible." As his eyes flicked over her, the grin faded.

Cindy did not wilt, or go slack, or in any way indicate that she was terrified. She moved her feet one small inch farther apart and glared. "What do you want?"

"Spitfire, too." Surprise colored his tone. "Not sensible like your old lady." Without taking his gaze from the girl, Glenn said, "Robish, get back to the window. The old guy's going to be pulling in any minute."

"I need a gun," Robish said.

"Get back there," Glenn Griffin told him, still not glancing at him, dismissing him.

"You think you can——"

"Now."

Robish stayed only a second longer; then he turned about and disappeared into the gathering shadows of the den.

"Sit down, redhead," Glenn said, his voice hushed a little. "Sit down and let me explain the facts of life. With that hair, you might feel like getting real brave. You can do that, just about any time you feel like it. You might even get away with it, not get hurt at all. But that's not saying what'll happen to the old lady . . . or the kid brother . . . or the father. We're waiting for him now, see, so take off your coat and sit right down in that chair."

Without in any sense suggesting that she was following an

order—without, in fact, removing her coat as commanded but glancing at Eleanor with a hint of a reassuring smile that failed to come off—Cindy crossed to a chair and sat down. She even lighted a cigarette, steadily, returning the young man's arrogance by simply ignoring his presence.

"How long have these animals been here, Mother?" she asked.

Glenn laughed, a short explosive snort of sound, derisive and ugly.

"I've lost track of time," Eleanor said. "Some time after noon. Cindy . . ." She had meant to voice a warning, but she stopped herself. "There's another one in the kitchen."

"In other words," said Cindy, blowing smoke, "the house is crawling with them."

Eleanor was watching Glenn Griffin's face at that moment, and she felt a tightening of her own terror; a hand clenched her heart. The young man's face, a faint unhealthy jaundiced pallor at all times, went icy white, colorless, and the flesh around his even white teeth drew back into a stiff grin. He seemed to stand there undecided for a long time, perhaps half a minute; then, soundlessly, he turned and, in that graceful feline glide of his, he walked into the hall and through the dining room toward the muffled chatter of the radio in the kitchen.

There he remained until the sound for which Eleanor's nerves had been tensed reached her.

"Griffin!" Robish barked from the den.

Glenn Griffin materialized again. "No lights now, not a word out of either of you. Got that?"

Eleanor nodded dumbly.

"Got that, redhead?"

Cindy had her eyes fixed on the wall beyond Glenn Griffin's poised body as he stood in the hall doorway. She seemed to look through him as though he were glass, or simply not present

25

at all. Eleanor longed to put out a hand. This couldn't be. This was no time for Cindy's stubborn temper.

"He's trying to open the garage," Robish said. "You want me to grab him now?"

"Not with all those cars going by," Glenn said. "He'll come in." He lifted his voice. "You watching, Hank?"

"He's not coming in this way," the other's voice called from the kitchen.

Again Eleanor felt the scream gathering like some terrible inhuman force in her chest. She listened to the familiar footsteps, brisk and energetic even after a hard day: up the two steps, across the tiled sun porch. This time Glenn did not waste time: he pointed the gun directly at the door, directly at Dan Hilliard.

First, Dan saw his wife—a statue, pale, haggard. He stopped short. The room was filled with the fading blue-gray twilight. Then he saw Cindy, sitting straight, smoking, her small face angry and defiant. At once, he thought of Charles Wright: had Cindy announced something to Ellie? Only then, because there was the faintest sort of shadow movement from the direction of the hall, did Dan see Glenn Griffin. And the pointed gun.

He felt his breath hold, and before anyone could move or speak, although he felt Eleanor straining half out of her chair, he had the whole picture straight and clear. He recalled the news reports on the radio in the car less than fifteen minutes before; he realized he had been a fool for not comprehending as soon as he saw the gray sedan through the windows of the garage. But such a far-fetched thought would not have occurred to him. However, he wasted no time now in bewilderment or amazement or rebellion at the situation as it stood.

Eleanor saw the unnatural redness mounting her husband's craggy face, spreading violent under the tilted hat. Dan's mind, she knew, worked slowly but thoroughly, wasting no time on suppositions, moving straight ahead, but with caution, into whatever faced him. And she wondered, relaxing only a little,

26

why she had dreaded this moment more than any other of the day. Before Dan spoke, she knew that his would be the first meaningful words that met Glenn Griffin all day.

"I suggest you put the gun away, Griffin," Dan said. "If you fire it, you'll have the whole neighborhood down on you in less than three minutes. The Wallings next door are home, and they'd hear the shot, even with the woods in between. If they didn't, someone driving by would."

The only sound in the dusky room was something between a whimper of hysteria and gasp of relief and gratitude from Eleanor. Dan felt a movement from the direction of the den, but he did not shift his eyes from Glenn Griffin's.

"You try something, mister, you all get it," a heavy, dull voice said from the den. "You dumb, mister?"

"No," Glenn Griffin said, very slowly. "He's not dumb at all, Robish." The odd grin was flickering into place. "He's a smart boy, smarter than we figured, maybe." There was an edge of warning in his quiet tone.

Then, repeating his daughter's words—as Eleanor, knowing them both so well, might have expected—Dan demanded: "What do you want?"

This time Glenn Griffin was not taken by surprise. "I don't want anybody to get hurt. What do *you* want, Pop?"

Dan crossed then, despite the gun, toward his wife; he placed a hand—large and freckled and tender—on her shoulder and simply let it rest there, relaxed. "That's what I want, too."

Glenn let go with a laugh at that; he dropped the arm holding the gun. "Now you talk sense. So I'm going to talk sense, too."

The room was deep in shadow now, and Dan listened in silence, feeling the shudders subsiding in Eleanor's shoulder. He didn't increase the pressure of his hand.

Glenn, striding in that slender catlike manner of his up and down the room, spoke in the unemotional manner of one who has known for months, perhaps years, exactly what he wants to say. Dan listened while the helplessness of his position seeped into him like some mysterious benumbing drug.

All they wanted—the three of them—was a safe place to stay till about midnight, at the latest two or three in the morning. They had some money coming, a lot of money, and when it arrived, they would go. It was as simple as that. In the meantime, life in the Hilliard house was to go on normally. In every way.

"Just like normal, see. You got it straight, folks?"

He spoke like an actor who had rehearsed his words many times. He moved around the room and his brows lifted and his face worked as though some invisible camera were on him, as though he were carefully but arrogantly trying in his behavior to live up to some picture of himself that he carried in his mind. Dan recorded all this, for whatever good it might do, his own mind noting everything in that indirect but almost infallible way he had of judging people. Dan reached one inevitable, stone-hard conclusion: these were not idle threats. This boy would kill one or all of them if anything went wrong. Once Dan had accepted this, fully, he acted upon it, but he could feel his legs shaking now, his body frozen and numb with helplessness.

"We'll do whatever you say, Griffin," Dan said in a flat voice. "Only——"

"Yeah?"

"Griffin, what if I could get you the money you want? Right away, I mean. Tonight. *Before* midnight? Would you leave then?"

"You couldn't do it, Pop. I had a look at your bankbooks. You just don't have it."

"That sounds like a deal to me," Robish said from the darkness of the den. "We could get the hell out of here."

Dan noted also the urgency behind the invisible man's tone. "Maybe I could raise it. Somehow. What then, Griffin?"

"We're sticking," Glenn said.

"Yeah," the voice from the other room muttered sourly. "Sticking to wait for that babe. You'd risk our necks just to see that dame again."

Having unexpectedly created the breach, Dan stepped into it. "If this woman, whoever she is, knows where to come, how do you know the police won't be following her? It's as much to my advantage as yours now to avoid the police."

"What about that?" This time Robish emerged, planting himself at the far end of the room, his hulk of body bleak and hard in threatened mutiny. "The guy talks sense, Griffin. Hell, you can pick up a woman anywheres."

A flicker of bewilderment passed over the hard, young features of Glenn Griffin's face. He glanced from Dan to Robish. Then he whirled to Robish, the movement a dancer-shadow in the room. "I'm running the show, Robish. I thought we had that straight. We're staying, see, till Helen gets here. She's too smart to let the cops get on her tail. And she's got the kind of dough I got to have. And I got to have it here, see. Right in this town."

"You got no right to take these chances just so you can get a copper knocked off. What do I care somebody broke your god-damned jaw? That was a long time ago, anyway, and if this guy here can raise the dough——"

"No!" The word crackled. "You heard me, both of you." Slowly Glenn stepped toward Dan. "You, Hilliard, you lay off. I don't need no ideas from you. I got my own, and I got them all worked out and they been working fine."

"Ain't worth it," Robish snorted.

"I say it is, Robish. Where'd you be if it wasn't for me?" He spoke with his back to Robish, his eyes on Dan. "You'd be sitting down to that stew again, that's what, with a gun on you, and a guard breathing down your neck again. This way, *we* got the guns, and that's the way it's going to be." He was rubbing his cheek, feeling the hard ridge of tissue that now protected the mended bone. "And you, Hilliard, you're going to talk when I ask you something or when I tell you to talk. Otherwise, you're going to keep your trap closed. You love this woman of yours, you're going to play ball. Like you say, pal, it's as much your advantage as mine to keep any coppers away from here. Any red lights show in front of this joint, it's not going to be pretty."

Mrs. Kathleen Webb was smiling happily at her husband across a red-checkered tablecloth and what was left of a very thick steak. He was talking as he ate, and the ripple of excitement reached across the restaurant table.

"She left Pittsburgh at approximately four o'clock this afternoon. That much is for certain. Driving south on U.S. 19. Less than an hour later, she was spotted on U.S. 40, heading west. West, hear? That's us. That's here. I told you they were homing pigeons. She's sailing along now in her nice maroon two-door job, and they're holed up somewhere here thinking how smart they were to get her out of town so she could backtrack to them without being watched. Smart? Not so damned." He shoved the platter back and worked a napkin over his chin. "Every town she goes through, I reckon there's going to be a pair of eyes on her, clocking that maroon job like it was in a race. But nobody's going to bother her. Oh no, oh no. Along about Greenfield, they'll put a real tag on her and she'll breeze in here tonight some time and lead us right to the hole. State troopers, FBI, all of us." He clutched the napkin into a knot. "Just like that."

"Jess," his wife said gently, with a faint wonder in her face, "you want to kill that man, don't you?"

Jesse didn't answer that at once. He knew the truth, the blank and absolute fact: yes. But suddenly it seemed important

30

to explain and justify this feeling, although everything he said toward this purpose was also the truth: "Look, I don't know what makes people go bad. I grew up in a neighborhood that was worse than the Griffin boys' if it comes to that. So did the Mayor. And I don't know about all these here psychological things you're always reading about nowadays. I reckon they've got something, too. All I know is that as long's a guy like Glenn Griffin is running around free and safe, and with a gun in his hand to boot—well, it's not free or safe for the rest of us, any of us. It's like that, hear? That's the way it is." He leaned across the table. "That's why you're going to sleep on a cot in my office tonight. Or at a hotel. Which do you reckon?"

"I'll take the jail. I hate hotels and we can't afford them, and I'd like to be near you."

Jesse smiled again, taking her hand on the table; she cast an embarrassed glance around the restaurant. But Jesse held onto her hand, and she watched a scowl replace the smile on his narrow face.

She had no way of knowing that his mind had, by an accidental association of images and fears, pounced upon a picture that was true in its general outline if not in detail. Jesse Webb was imagining Glenn Griffin with that gun pointed at frightened and innocent people, and no one knew better than Jesse Webb that Glenn Griffin was capable of using it.

But where? If he only knew where . . . If only he didn't have to sit now and wait, with that picture coming back at him in different forms . . .

As Dan Hilliard stared at the gun held so casually in the hand of the young man and as his mind shied from the pictures of destruction inherent in the very fact of that gun's presence in his house, he was caught in a sickening helplessness. If the police came, it would be tragic; if they did not come, it might be worse.

"The kid's coming up the drive on his bike," Robish reported from the den.

"If you'll let me talk to him," Dan said quickly, "I could explain it and . . ."

"Shut up," Glenn Griffin said softly.

Dan could hear the sound of the single tire skidding on the gravel of the driveway. "But with the lights off like this, the boy will be scared to death. You can't . . ."

Glenn Griffin took two swift silent strides and jabbed the gun point with bruising force into Dan's ribs. Dan gasped for breath, and his hand closed down on Eleanor's shoulder.

Regardless of this, he heard quite distinctly the few short carefree steps on the back porch, the back door opening, the small cry of astonishment and sudden fear. He stiffened. As though his own insane and suicidal impulse had communicated itself through the gun against him, that point once again rammed itself with force into his ribs.

There was a brief and one-sided scuffle in the kitchen; it continued through the dining room, with Ralphie's voice mingled incoherently in it.

Then Ralphie was standing in the hall, held in the grip of a young man whom Dan had not seen before but whom he recognized immediately as Glenn Griffin's brother.

"Let *go!*" Ralphie said, twisting himself out of the short man's grasp.

"Hank." Glenn switched the gun idly so that it was directed at the hall. "Turn on the hall light, pull the blinds in the dining room and get back to the kitchen." As he spoke he stepped into the hall, out of view of the front windows.

Anyone going home from work on the street outside could see the Hilliards in their living room, facing the hall. They could not see the small straight figure of the boy in the hall,

32

outrage and not fear written on his play-streaked face. Nor could they see Glenn Griffin beside the boy.

"What's that guy doing in our kitchen?" Ralphie demanded.

"It's all right, Ralphie," Dan said quickly, but not moving despite the impulse that quivered along his legs. He saw then the alert flash of comprehension and terror leap to the boy's face as the eyes fell on the black metallic gleam in Glenn's hand. "I'll explain it to you, Ralphie."

With startling suddenness, the boy whirled, leaped to the front door, turned the knob and tugged.

"Take it easy now, kid," Glenn said in a single breath.

Still tugging, Ralphie began to cry. Then, almost as quickly as he had moved the first time, he gave up on the locked door. It appeared that he was going to turn to face them, but what he did was so abrupt and ridiculous that even Glenn seemed startled into inaction. Ralphie darted into the living room, passed Dan even as his father's hand went out, and reached the unlocked sun-porch door.

"Ralphie!" Eleanor screamed, but not loudly because her throat closed with terror.

Dan was after the boy, but before he could reach him, there was another movement, from the direction of the den, and the man Robish, cursing, grabbed Ralphie.

Glenn flipped off the lights almost as soon as Robish appeared in the living room.

What followed was pantomime and dumb show, in semi-darkness, with the big man twisting Ralphie about, the enormous hands spinning him, then slipping down to his shoulders and shaking the small body. Dan heard behind him the metal-and-cloth swish of the front window curtains as Glenn drew them shut. All he saw was his son's head snapping up and down against his chest and the heavy shoulders of the man half-turned away from him.

It was enough. Dan forgot the gun behind him. He forgot Glenn Griffin completely. In that blank moment of wildness he took two more steps, felt the lights come up on the room, saw the tear-filled incredulous eyes of the boy and the enormous hate-twisted, frustrated face of the man looming over the boy. Even as he reached for the man's shoulder, Dan knew it was madness that drove him, but he was helpless in the grip of jungle instinct.

Eleanor watched the pantomime in horror, torn between the impulse to leap at the man herself, clawing the flesh from the bone of that ugly, brutal face, and the knowledge that she must somehow dam up and control the same rage that she saw naked and terrible in her husband's whole body.

It was too late by then to do anything at all. Dan had whirled the hulk of body about as though it were an inanimate toy one-third its size. The eyes in the bulbous pouches glittered once, as much with satisfaction as surprise. Then they closed completely as Dan's fist crashed upwards, at a slight angle, and exploded in the square face.

Before, all had been silence; now the flesh-against-flesh, bone-against-bone sound of that single blow filled the whole house. The body straightened slightly, then tottered a split second uncertainly, finally collapsed into a soft heap.

What broke the silence again, and completely, was Eleanor's cry as, with Ralphie clinging against her, she saw Glenn Griffin move in behind Dan, lift the gun and bring it down full force against the top of his shoulder.

Dan didn't feel this at first, suspended as he was in the abrupt and awful knowledge of what he had done to all of them. Then the pain struck, but at first it was not pain at all but a blackness falling across his mind. Then it focused momentarily, as though a knife had severed a nerve; then it exploded. The whole right side of his body went numb and cold and he felt himself staggering sidewise.

He felt, too, the rough hand righting him, twisting his body, shoving him backwards into the enveloping softness of the sofa. The blackness closed in again.

34

When he could see again, and hear, he saw Glenn Griffin facing the man Robish, the gun directed at Robish's stomach.

". . . not going to be like this, see! Not like this, Robish!" Glenn Griffin was almost, but not quite, shouting.

Robish was muttering incomprehensible words, and his hand was across his face; above it the greenish yellow eyes were fixed on Dan. His whole body strained forward despite the man in front of him.

"Get to the kitchen, Robish, fast. Get there!"

Robish's words came through. "You think I'm gonna let him get away with that? You think . . ."

"Nothing's going to foul this up!" Glenn cried. "Got that, Robish? You got time for him. But not now. *Nothing's going to foul this up, see!*"

After that, the blackness threatened to return. Dan caught a glimpse of Eleanor's shell-white face, of Ralphie's grave stare, of Cindy's suddenly murderous glare as she watched Glenn Griffin. His next impression was of Glenn Griffin bending down to him, the words coming at him close yet seeming to make only a wild din in his ears.

He kept nodding, not knowing why, although vaguely comprehending the oath-filled warnings, the vile threats that seemed to be pouring from that working mouth before him. Finally Glenn straightened, reached into his pocket and drew out something small which Dan could not see. The young man crossed to Eleanor, and Dan felt himself stiffen. In that instant he knew, with only faint surprise, that under the same or similar circumstances he would be unable to do anything but what he had just done when Robish grabbed Ralphie. That or worse. Next time, perhaps right now, he might kill one of them.

"Read it," Glenn said. "Read it loud enough so your old man can hear it, Mrs. Hilliard."

Dan heard his wife's tight voice begin to read, after she had unfolded the yellow frayed newspaper clipping, and he had to concentrate very hard over the scorching ache in order to catch the significance of the words.

What she read was a dispassionate news-service story of an occurrence in New York State. It described, in some detail, the manner in which a convict, attempting to escape from a police net surrounding a small house in which he was hiding, had brutally killed a small girl when the police fired at him as he left the house. He had climbed into a small pickup truck, holding the girl in front of him. Even though wounded himself by police fire, he had shot the child through the stomach and she had died.

When Eleanor had finished reading the newspaper clipping, there was silence. Eleanor held Ralphie's hand. Cindy's face was ashen and it seemed to have shrunk until it was, somehow, too small and not her face at all. Dan could picture Glenn Griffin carefully clipping this from a newspaper months, perhaps years, ago—looking ahead to just this moment of his life.

Dan, who had prided himself on his coolness when he first came in, realized that he was consumed now, engulfed, by a shaking rage and hatred of this young criminal who stood carelessly letting the significance of that newspaper account sink deeply into the souls of the Hilliard family. A sharp warning twisted in Dan: no matter what, he must not let himself become the victim of his emotions again.

"Now," Glenn said, his eyes on Dan. "Now Hilliard, you got a gun in the house?"

Without hesitation, Dan nodded. His mind was beginning to function properly again: he had no choice in the world if he opposed these three. He couldn't afford to fight: too much— the lives of his whole family—was at stake. "Upstairs. In the coils of bedspring. My bed."

Glenn shouted for Hank, who came into the room at once; Glenn spoke quietly to his brother, and Hank disappeared up the stairs.

When he returned, quickly, Glenn said in a whisper, "Put

it in your pocket and forget it, Hank. Don't tell Robish." He turned sidewise to Dan and grinned tauntingly. "You agree with that, Hilliard?"

Dan nodded. He had reached the conclusion that, in addition to playing *their* game in as emotionless a manner as possible, he must also concentrate on Glenn: he was the leader, sly, cruel, cynical, but the one to watch and to fear and to depend on.

"One thing, Griffin," Dan said when Hank had gone again.

"Yeah?" The scorn edged his voice; a challenge glittered in the word.

"One thing. I'll handle my family. We'll string along."

"You have a choice, do you, Pop?"

"Yes," Dan said slowly, the pain steady and knifelike down his side. "Yes, we have a choice. As long as nothing else happens—nothing similar to what just happened in this room when that man grabbed my son—we'll all do anything you say. Anything within reason. But if one of you touches one of us again——"

"I don't go for threats, Pop."

"Griffin," Dan said, his breath paining him, "you're not as smart as I give you credit for if you think this is a threat. I'm stating facts. If one of you touches one of us again, you're done for. So are we, but that's just the way it'll have to be. There's a limit, Griffin. Next time I won't stop by taking a sock at him. I'll kill the man. And before you can shoot me."

Glenn laughed then, softly but uncertainly. "Pop, for a guy with so much to lose, you sure talk tough."

Despair threaded itself down Dan's body. "I'm not talking tough, don't you understand, man? I'm saying we'll help you if you can take care of your men."

When he saw the eyebrows lift slightly in the darkly handsome face, Dan knew that he had struck pay dirt. This was the sort of appeal, and challenge, which Glenn Griffin was capable of comprehending. Perhaps the only kind.

"I handled Robish, didn't I?"

"And very well," Dan said. "I think we understand each other, Griffin." He glanced at Eleanor. "I think we all know what we have to do, don't you, Eleanor?"

Eleanor could only nod her head and wonder in silence why she had never known her husband before tonight. . . .

2

2

The night was dense and full of wind beyond the windows. The curtains had been drawn open, but the headlights passing occasionally on the boulevard seemed remote and unreal. Dan Hilliard held his evening paper in its usual position and by lifting his eyes from the photographs on the front page under the blazing headlines he could look across the hall into the dining room and see two of the faces reproduced there: the Griffin brothers bent over road maps at the table. Although he was not able to see it, the third face—heavy-jowled and sullen—was in the darkness of the den beyond the open door at the end of the living room.

Cindy, on the sofa with Ralphie, who pretended to be reading a book, was also conscious of the third face because every once in a while she would twist her slender young legs farther up under her body and arrange her skirt with care; her back was turned purposefully and contemptuously on that door. Eleanor was seated in her usual chair, too, so if any casual passer-by should glance in, he would see a perfectly normal family group.

It was all very ordinary, very carefully arranged, and un-nerving in its theatrical cleverness. From the slit in the blind on the front windows in the dining room, Glenn Griffin com-manded a view of the street, the lawn, the driveway. From the den Robish could keep watch on the back yard and the garage and the driveway along the side of the house.

Dan was stiff, and wracking pains traveled up and down his right side; his rib was bruised and aching, and with each breath the ache sharpened into a stab of pain in his lungs. The two and a half hours that had passed had filled him, inch by inch, with a slow, banked-down fury—not the blank, violent rage that had hurled him into his attack on Robish but a steady, slow-burning hatred and rebellion. It was not directed only at the three men themselves, but at something larger and less tangible: an incredible fate, or accident, that had caused these men to choose *his* house. Because they had seen Ralphie's bicycle in the driveway? Because the closest neighbors, the Wallings, were two city lots away, beyond a heavy grove of masking trees? Yes, but why *this* house? There must be others as ideally situated for their purposes.

He saw Glenn Griffin throw an arm carelessly over his younger brother's shoulders at the table: a gesture of warmth and friendship. This was the same young man who, behind the theatrical façade of his personality, had known from the start exactly how a man like Dan Hilliard would behave under cer-tain circumstances and had then created those circumstances.

Dan glanced at his watch again. 8:34. Three hours and twenty-six minutes until midnight. He had made it so far; he would get through the rest. He would behave like a man whose will has been broken. He would, in fact, do anything, anything within reason, to get those men out of his house—anything so long as the three persons now around him remained safe and uninjured.

The evening had been more or less without incident. They had eaten supper, first the three men—Glenn, now wearing one of Dan's sports jackets, in the dining room, and Hank in the den and Robish at the kitchen table. Cindy had served them while Eleanor cooked. It had been shortly after that that Robish had demanded to know where Dan kept the liquor. There was none in the house. Robish had muttered that Dan was lying; he had crashed about in a fruitless search, snarling threats of what would happen if he found any. Through this Glenn remained detached: the issue was not large enough, or threatening enough, for him to intervene. In this way, Dan guessed, Glenn held to his cunning control; in small matters, let Robish think he was his own boss. In large matters—as when Robish might have killed Dan—Glenn stepped in. Glenn's behavior followed a certain pattern that Dan found he could comprehend, even deal with. Hank Griffin, on the other hand, remained an enigma—a boy obviously devoted to his older brother in some strange, dependent way. But that was as much as Dan knew. Robish—well, Robish was emotional, twisted, ugly and unpredictable. He represented, in some ways, the greatest danger; dealing with Robish was like trying to talk language to an animal.

The telephone shrilled. In the shock of silence that followed, the house came alive. Dan rose. Glenn Griffin came into the hall, gun in hand, and his brother Hank went up the stairs as though at a given signal; Dan surmised that he was going to listen on the extension phone in the bedroom.

"Okay, redhead, you get the pleasure. Answer it, and be careful. If someone asks for a Mr. James, that's me. If it's for anyone in the family, let 'em talk. Quick now."

On the third ring, Cindy picked up the phone, her dignity untouched, her back turned defiantly to Glenn Griffin.

"Hello . . . oh . . . Yes, Chuck. I'm . . . well, I'm not feeling very well . . . Oh, a cold, I guess. You know . . . I can't . . . No, I just can't, that's all. I told you I'm sick." She listened a long moment, finally turning helplessly with an exaggerated shrug to Dan and Eleanor. "No, Chuck, but please understand. You do, don't you? . . . Tomorrow, then. G'night." She replaced the telephone and then she did face Glenn Griffin. "Do I pass, teacher?" she inquired, her tone acid and scornful.

Glenn looked up the stairs as Hank descended, nodding.

"You pass, sis," Glenn said. "Maybe you got more sense than I figured. Who was that, the boy friend?"

"It was Anthony Eden," Cindy said and returned to the sofa where Ralphie reached out and placed his finger delicately against his thumb in a gesture of congratulation.

The grin came up automatically into Glenn's face. "Have your fun, redhead. No skin off mine."

Cindy's plea with Chuck to understand, the note of fear that she might offend him when in the past she had always been careless, sometimes even a bit ruthless, with her young men— the significance of this attitude worked into Dan and rubbed against his tense nerves. Surprised that he could let this matter at a time like this, Dan covered his annoyance and said, "Ralphie. Bedtime, pal."

Without protest, Ralphie rose and kissed his mother, threw one in Cindy's direction, and went into the hall to mount the stairs. Dan followed, according to ritual. Glenn didn't object, watched them both unsmiling. Dan happened to glance at Hank Griffin then, caught a strange expression lurking in those dark eyes. Perhaps he imagined it. The boy was slouched over the table, his head back a bit. He wore a pair of Dan's slacks and a coat-style sweater, a sports shirt and no tie. The expression, as Dan saw it or imagined it, was one of longing, or envy. Or both.

In the bedroom, with the model airplanes dangling from the ceiling and surrounded by the miniature ships, Ralphie was un-usually quiet, grave. He undressed, donned his pajamas, went into the bathroom, brushed his teeth quickly—while Dan sat on the side of the bed, in silence. How could a man explain a thing like this to a ten-year-old boy? Was he being a coward by trying to spare the boy the haunting and gruesome pictures that clogged his own mind?

Climbing into bed, Ralphie spoke. "They don't look so tough."

"They're . . . tough, Ralphie. Don't you fool yourself."

"You're scared." Although there was a slight rising inflection in the sentence, it was not a question but a statement—an accusation.

"Yes, son," Dan said softly, "I'm scared. And you should be, too."

"You licked the big guy."

"No. I lost my temper, that's all. I can't do that again."

"Mother's scared, too. But Cindy isn't. And I'm not."

There was nothing else to do then but to speak the truth, fully. So Dan leaned forward on the bed and whispered steadily and firmly for a few moments while his son's eyes, fixed on him, narrowed with a growing disillusion. Dan saw this, helpless, perhaps at that time not really caring how Ralphie felt toward him if only he could make the boy comprehend what was at stake. When he finished, he met the disillusion head-on, rising.

"Whatever you think I am, Ralphie, you remember what I say."

"Why'd you have to tell them where your gun was?"

The blank wall he faced—still another one!—stirred a slow anger, but Dan fought it down, clenching his fists at his side.

"I could sneak down the back stairs," Ralphie said. "That guy Robish is in the den, but he wouldn't even hear me open the back door. Nobody's in the kitchen now."

"Now listen, Ralph," Dan growled. "Listen, you want me to call you Ralph, don't you? You want to be considered a grown boy in this house. Then you've got to act like one, and *think* like one. Beginning now. If you went running out of here and got the police, do you know what would happen? They'd shoot your mother and your sister. You'd be the reason they did it. Can you understand that, Ralph?"

45

The boy's face clouded; then suddenly he turned away and stretched out, his head face down. He muttered something unintelligible into the pillow. Dan stooped over him, his hand on the boy's back.

"What did you say, son?" he asked.

Dan felt the back twist under his hand as Ralphie lifted his face. There were tears in the corners of the boy's eyes. "I don't want them to take me along," Ralphie blurted.

"Take you . . . ?"

"You heard what Mother read. That newspaper thing about the little girl. What's going to happen when they go, Dad? You know, don't you? You know."

"They're not going to take you," Dan said slowly, his clenched fists straightening into stiffness along his legs as he stood up. The fear in his son's eyes lashed knifelike at the rational control. Perhaps he had known all along and had been afraid to face it. Well, he was facing it now. "They're not taking you, or anyone, Ralphie. I'll see to that. You go to sleep now. And don't worry. Trust me, Ralphie."

"But—what can you do? Now you don't even have a gun."

"You heard me!" Dan took a breath and reached for control of his voice. "I said not to worry. Go to sleep. You ought to know I wouldn't let them take you along, Ralphie. Don't you? *Don't* you?"

"I'm not afraid," Ralphie said, but a bitterness was in his voice, in his face as it turned away again. "I'm not afraid at all."

Dan stood motionless and stunned. Somewhere in the back of his mind he must have known all along. Was the human mind able to hide the unpleasant simply by ignoring it? Yes.

Dan reached out and took hold of Ralphie's shoulder and held it a brief moment; then he went into the hall, turning off the light, closing the door.

The back stairs, his mind reminded him in panic. You could

get down them easily. They might not miss you for five minutes, perhaps ten.

Yes, but what then? What then?

Dan descended the front stairs slowly, the fierce new hatred choking him. He kept seeing Ralphie's small face with the disillusion written bitterly in it. In the living room again, he looked at Eleanor, sitting quiet, her face wan, paler than he had seen it since that time in the hospital the night Ralphie was born. He saw Cindy whose head was resting on her arm along the back of the sofa, her face hidden, her hair tumbling.

You can't let rage force you into action, he warned himself violently. You can't.

He sat down again. Three minutes to 9. He stared incredulously at his watch, then lifted it to his ear. It was still running.

The electric clocks in the jailhouse and Sheriff's offices had large round faces with stark lettering. The minute hand did not move until the full minute had passed, then it clicked, the sound first, then the black hand jerked forward, stopped and waited for another sixty seconds to pass. Jesse Webb, his long legs stretched out, his ankles crossed on the desk-top, found himself watching the clock so steadily that the intervals between the clicks grew into hours instead of minutes. He had to sit with his head twisted at an angle to see the face of the clock and his neck ached.

Although he had been waiting for the telephone to ring, the sound echoing in the night stillness startled him. He couldn't believe that, finally, something had sounded in the room beside the maddening, spaced clicks of that clock.

He spoke his name into the phone. Then he listened. In less than one minute, he said "Check" and replaced the phone.

Then he stood up, tense but with a high running excitement released at last. He took one step, and it was then that the excitement, which was only the reaction created by the waiting, left him like breath itself.

He had nothing to do. He could do nothing. And, from now on, even waiting was a foolish waste of time.

Helen Lamar had disappeared.

Jesse Webb smashed his right fist into his left palm and thought of Uncle Frank who had telephoned again at 7:30. He could picture the man standing at a wall telephone in the stench-filled meat-packing plant, the night watchman's mechanism around his neck. He could see the tension in the frail body as the man asked his quiet-sounding questions. At that time, an hour and a half ago, Jesse had assured his uncle that everything was going as expected; if Helen Lamar continued at her present cautious rate of speed, she would arrive in town around 11.

Now she was not coming. Uncle Frank, having been a policeman for nearly twenty years, might understand the reason; but Jesse was damned if *he* could! It was rank carelessness. Worse. His mind roved over the scene that had been described to him by the FBI man who had just received the story himself.

Helen Lamar, in the maroon two-door sedan, had been sighted east of Columbus, Ohio, approaching the city. It was quite a proposition to follow her progress through a large city, especially when there was always the chance that she might swing north toward Toledo or south toward Cincinnati. But as it turned out, all the precautions, all the hard tedious work had been unnecessary and useless.

Helen Lamar had made one single, simple mistake. She had exceeded the speed limit on the outskirts of the city. And a traffic patrol car had attempted to stop her.

She must have grown panicky then—Jesse could see it clearly—and she stepped on the gas. The patrol car gave chase. But, damn it, they had their instructions, all of them: DO

NOT ARREST REPEAT DO NOT ARREST. The order was on every teletype between Pittsburgh and Indianapolis.

"Speeding, for God's sake!" Jesse said bitterly in the silent office, tasting the sour irony on his tongue.

She gave the pursuit car the slip. How had she? How could she? Well, she was taking no chances, this Lamar woman, because, unless Jesse missed his guess, she was hauling money, and a lot of it, and she couldn't let herself be stopped. She couldn't answer questions, and how did she know—how could she ever guess—that the fools only wanted to give her a traffic-violation ticket?

She careened into the downtown area, charging into the 8-to-9 o'clock traffic, reckless now, desperate, determined. She whirled into a side street, brought the car to a crazy halt half on the curb, and leaped out. The police had found the car, but not soon enough. Helen Lamar was gone. Swallowed up. Presto.

There you have it, Jess. She's gone. She had slipped somehow, mysteriously, in that snakelike way of the criminal, down a hole, into hiding, protected somewhere by others of her kind. Right now she was probably trying to think of a way—a safe way—to contact Griffin.

And when that happened? What would Griffin do then? No money now, no means of escape in the clever manner he'd planned, all his neatly laid calculations gone haywire—what would he do?

He would have to get money. Maybe this would force him to pull a job. And he would have to devise a new way of escaping now. He couldn't lay low in any one place too long. If he did, he knew he was asking for it. But to try to imagine what Glenn Griffin, his back abruptly shoved against a solid wall, might do—this was beyond Jesse Webb's powers but was the problem with which he was faced.

It might take Griffin some time to learn what had occurred. In the meanwhile, what? This also was Jesse's problem, although there was nothing he could do about it. All the known hiding places had been searched and searched again, all Griffin's friends in town had been questioned at length and without results. Where the hell *was* the man?

Glenn Griffin remained in the Hilliard house, but Dan was now out of it. It was fifteen after nine.

His mind was on the house as he sat behind the wheel of the family car while a service-station attendant filled the gas tank and checked the oil and water. He was following orders now. The car was needed for a quick and safe getaway. That much Dan understood. Robish had called Glenn a fool for letting Dan leave the house, but when Glenn had suggested that perhaps Robish would rather go on the errand himself, the big man had subsided with a surly growl. Glenn was confident that Dan would do what he had to do, simply because the others— his wife, his daughter, his son—remained in the house.

Glenn was right, as usual. But Dan's calculations were running ahead of the young man's cleverness this time. He was staring at a telephone on the wall inside the lighted service station. He could speak to the police now in less than thirty seconds. What if he explained the exact circumstances in such a way that they would realize, too, that it would be irresponsible murder of innocent people for them to attempt to move in at once? Could he make them understand this fact?

Perhaps. But even if they did, what precautions would they take? They would have to set up roadblocks in the neighborhood in the hope of stopping Griffin in his escape later, after he had the money and the woman. Their job was to capture or kill the two Griffin boys and Robish. His was to protect his family. And certainly Glenn Griffin had not overlooked any possibility, any danger inherent in letting Dan leave the house. He had certainly looked ahead.

He knew that he couldn't take the dust-spattered sedan in the garage; he needed the Hilliard car. But Glenn must have realized already that, as soon as he had gone, leaving the Hilliards behind, that blue car would become as well known and as dangerous as the gray one—once Dan had notified the police. How did Griffin hope to prevent this?

Dan tore his gaze from the telephone and swept the idea, or temptation, violently aside. Glenn hoped to prevent it in the same way that he was now making sure that Dan did not telephone the police: by keeping a member, perhaps several members, of the family with the three men in the escape car. For as long as he needed them.

I don't want them to take me along, Ralphie had said.

Dan was shaking with an intensified sense of futility. If he brought the police into it, he was running a risk; if he did not, he was no better off and perhaps even more at the mercy of Glenn Griffin's design. Now, instead of looking forward to the time when the money and the woman would arrive, he dreaded it. Only three hours. Less than three hours; perhaps much sooner if the woman hurried. His mind wrenched away from the scene. It was a long time away. It was not inevitable. Nothing was inevitable. Perhaps, in the interim . . .

Perhaps what?

In the interim, he told himself grimly, you will do as you have been told and you will hope that, by the time the moment of departure arrives, you will have thought of some threat to hang over Glenn Griffin's head that will make him change his plans. Right now you don't have time to think of that. Right now you can only do what you have been told to do.

Dan paid the attendant, with whom he was not acquainted because Dan had made a point of avoiding the station in the neighborhood where he had an account. The car purred easily. A fine car. Solid, perhaps a little more expensive than they could afford, a luxury: efficient, fast. Just the kind of a car that could do the job Glenn Griffin had in mind. Dan knew that he was taking his last ride in it, cruising now toward the Broad Ripple shopping district. He had to concentrate very hard on the project before him in order to avoid imagining the stellated holes that bullets would make in the rear window and perhaps the windshield, the dark ugly stain that blood would leave on the upholstery.

If only it was the blood of the men, and not . . .

He concentrated on the high whine of wind around the stores. Not many were still open. But there was a light in the window of the liquor store. He brought the car to a halt at the curb.

The old man behind the counter was counting money, in preparation of closing. He looked up when Dan entered, and he frowned.

"What can I do for you?" The voice was not cordial.

Dan bought a fifth of Old Grandad—Robish had insisted on bourbon—and noticed that the old man did not turn his back when he reached for the bottle. As he paid, Dan caught a glimpse of himself in a mirrored sign behind the counter. His face was ashen-gray, his tie slightly askew, the hat pulled far down over his forehead. He glanced at the man who was still studying him suspiciously. Dan didn't blame him. The broad and craggy face that, under normal circumstances, gave the impression of strength, of pleasant but distinguished restraint, now appeared sick, furtive, perhaps even dangerous to the old man.

Dan tried to force a smile; it didn't come. He saw in a swift final glance, as he turned away, that his eyes were red and inflamed.

When he was in the car again and turning it in the direction of his house, bearing down on the gas in his abruptly renewed anxiety, he wondered whether he was playing the fool. How could he ever be sure, if disaster ultimately struck, that he was not partially responsible himself? How could he be positive that by giving in to their demands, he was going to save anyone?

He couldn't be positive of anything. Perhaps he should have given in to the impulse back there at the gas station. Or perhaps he should have explained hastily but thoroughly to the man in the liquor store. Afterward, after the tragedy, if tragedy came, a man could be haunted forever, if still unmercifully alive, with the cutting realization that he might have, by some sly or bold cleverness at just the right moment, prevented it all.

The man in the liquor store probably had a gun. With the thought, Dan automatically relaxed his pressure on the gas pedal. Should he go back and get it, by whatever means? He would not hesitate, not for a second, to kill. If it were possible to step into the house now, to blast swift and successive bullets into the three bodies without any peril to the others, he would do it. In fact, it might be the only thing *to* do.

In less than four hours they had brought him to this.

As he caught sight of the yellow flare from the front windows and the bulky shadow of the house itself, he gave up the idea. He didn't dare. He couldn't be quick enough. They had two guns now, and he could not be sure that they would turn them on him. No. He could take no chances. A wave of futility broke over him, smashing at him. Then another—heart-stopping blows that broke over him, washed him under, then lifted him, helpless, and thrust him back again into the void of his own impotent rage. He could only fall back on one certainty: that now, at this moment, he was doing what he considered right from the clouded vantage point of this moment. What more can a man do? What more is there?

He parked the car as he had been instructed to park it: nose pointed toward the boulevard, clear of Cindy's coupe, the side doors unlocked, the key in place. He cut the motor and climbed out, feeling eyes upon him, crawling over him like obscene insects from the primordial slime. But he was not sick now, or faint. He was filled with the knowledge that he, by some

53

miracle, had to find a way to keep them from taking anyone along with them at midnight.

He uttered a few words that he knew, vaguely, were not blasphemous although tinged with fury; they were the opposite: humble prayer of some sort, incoherent and mumbled, addressed to the darkness around him.

He went into the house through the side door, crossed the sun porch and then the living room toward Glenn Griffin waiting in the hall, out of sight of the front windows. It was not until he was standing there in the hall and after Robish had clumped in from the dining room and snatched the wrapped bottle that Dan realized that there was something odd about the living room.

"Didn't get any ideas, did you, Pop?" Glenn proceeded then, while holding the gun, to search Dan, touching every pocket with that thoroughness and arrogance that Dan had come to despise.

Dan permitted this, standing rigidly, his eyes returning to the living room. He must have been behaving and reacting in a dreamlike manner, his mind told him, or he would have asked at once the question that now surged up in him, hot and choking: "Where's Cindy?"

"She's gone out, dear," Eleanor said, from her chair. "It's all right. She'll be careful."

"Out?" His voice was only an echo.

"With Charles Wright. He came anyway. Don't ask me why. And they saw him drive in, so they let Cindy go out with him before he could get inside."

"I talked to her, Hilliard," Glenn Griffin explained easily. "She's a smart gal. She won't make any mistakes. I told her what would happen if she did feel like talking. Robish now, he's jumpy, see. He thinks I'm a fool. What about you, Hilliard? You don't think I'm a fool, do you?"

"Not a fool," Dan said slowly. "No."

Glenn laughed. "Pop, you know what? You're all right.

You're a real funny guy. Now you can go in and sit down while I have a little drink with Robish. Wouldn't want him to kill the whole bottle, would we?"

Dan felt himself moving into the living room; vaguely he saw his reflection in the windows as he sat down—a slow stiff old-man way of sitting, holding the arms of the chair against the pain that still climbed up and down his side and burned hot in his shoulder.

"Cindy won't take any chances, Dan," Eleanor said, trying to smile. "You're not worried about that, are you?"

"Of course not," Dan lied, recalling the defiant contempt in his daughter's eyes. "Cindy's too smart for that. Trust Griffin to know."

"Dan . . ." Eleanor lowered her voice to a whisper. "Dan, you didn't . . . ?"

Dan shook his head.

Eleanor relaxed slightly. "Because it's only such a short time now, dear. Till they go. Just think how we'll laugh about this at breakfast, darling."

Dan stared at her. Her face told him that she would never laugh at it. She could laugh at nearly everything, but she would never laugh at this. Besides, she still clung to the hope that when the men left, all would return to normal. Dan had accepted the fact that this was not possible; and he knew he was right.

And what if Cindy, herself free now, moved by that deep anger that, in her, seemed to be without shock, perhaps even without fear—what if she made some foolish desperate attempt to get help? What if she decided to confide in Charles Wright?

Certainly she would go over all the possibilities that Dan had struggled with, while away from the house; Dan had conquered the abortive temptation. But what would Cindy conclude? You could never be sure that someone else, even your own daughter, might not examine the same set of facts and arrive at the opposite conclusions.

You could not, really, be sure of anything. This, too, Dan Hilliard had learned since coming home from work at a little before 6 o'clock . . .

There was a cold glint in Cindy's eyes—very puzzling to Charles Wright, who had always thought of those eyes as soft and, if not exactly merry, at least unclouded and hinting at gaiety. Sitting beside her in the small seat of the sports car in the parking area of a drive-in restaurant—where he had brought her finally, after suggesting almost every place else in the city, including the country club—Chuck sipped at his coffee and let the evening's silence gather around again.

Over and over she had assured him, finally with some impatience, that she was fine; everything was fine, it was just this cold nagging her. But Chuck had known Cynthia Hilliard for nearly three months, and he had never seen her behave like this before. Even at the office, where she was brisk and business-like, she managed a secret smile occasionally. And tonight, her eyes were clear and hard, with *no* evidence of a cold in them.

Chuck himself had been involved in a problem of his own, that problem being Miss Cynthia Hilliard: what exactly did he feel about her? She wasn't the sort of girl Chuck normally chose for a playmate. That much was granted. Since coming home from the Marines, he steered clear of the ones who might want to turn a nice thing into a permanent and therefore, in his book, a not so nice thing. Chuck had worked out for himself a very neat little philosophy, not very original perhaps but congruent with his nature as he saw it: life is short, marriage is long, and love is something no one can depend on, ever. If this was, as his father irascibly suggested, only the fashionable cynicism of youth, so be it. He, Chuck Wright, was stuck with it.

But with this Cindy Hilliard, things had been different from the beginning. This fact bewildered him and continued to fill him with an odd high-running excitement, night and day, whether he was with her or not. What did it mean? And why was he sticking around to find out since, along the hazy edges of his thinking, he already suspected that she could not, in any conceivable way, fit into the pattern of detachment from the ordinary and conventional that he himself had decided was for him.

Tonight now, she had lied to him on the telephone and she had been lying ever since—since she had leaped out the door of her house before he could so much as touch the doorbell and had brushed past him and climbed into the car. In the hour he had been with her, she had allowed him to park, then she had thrown herself into his arms, clinging to him for perhaps a minute in a startling and rather desperate sort of way; afterwards, she had drawn herself away, insisted on a cigarette and then fallen into a silence that shut him out completely. He had explained that he came by to bring her the novel she had remarked on at lunch, thinking she might enjoy reading it while in bed. Cindy hadn't heard this at all. Her eyes had been then, as they were now, fixed on some horizon that he could not see.

"Look, I don't mind being ignored," he lied, twisting his tall, athletic body about in the small seat, "but you might give me a hint. I can't say I know anything, being only a poor lawyer who spends his young life writing briefs that any college sophomore could write, but I'm not the town moron. Or am I?"

"I'm sorry, Chuck." Just that. Flat. With a period.

Chuck shrugged, offered a cigarette which was either not seen or ignored, then lighted one for himself. "Okay, okay. Then I'll talk. Look, Cindy—here's a fellow. He was walking along a street. The sun was shining. He was whistling. He hadn't paid much attention to the sun for a long time, this

57

fellow, and when he whistled, it was usually because he was kidding himself into thinking he was a happy guy. But this time I'm telling you about, nothing in particular or stupendous had happened. Oh, he was running around with a girl, a very pretty girl, but he'd run around with girls before. Anyway, he was whistling, just because he felt like whistling. He was even kind of shocked at himself underneath—in a darned pleasant sort of way, though. Then he turned around a corner and wham! Something hit him in the face. A door. A blank door. Locked tight . . . Now the question is, honey, was this fellow kidding himself all along?"

Slowly—very slowly then—Cindy turned to him. For a split second that hard gleam was gone. Then it happened. The small face trembled, but only a moment, a quivering along the delicate jawline; then the face fell apart, twisting oddly, going all wrong. She was lowering her head, her lip shaking, and before he could speak around the sudden bulge in his throat, she was against him, full against his chest.

His heart tightening, Chuck held her. Under his hands and his arms he could feel her flesh leaping and shuddering. The questions surged in him, but he said nothing. He caught the fresh scent of that lovely deep red hair, and waited.

But when she didn't speak, or cry, his mind leaped to its own conclusions and froze around them, the suspicions of the last few weeks hardening into words: "They don't like me, do they?"

"What?"

"Your people. Mr. and Mrs. Dan Hilliard. They don't think I'm worth much, do they?"

Cindy, with her head buried against his chest, her mind battering like a trapped wild bird against the stiff helplessness that only added to her anger, decided that she had to tell him. Chuck would know a way, find a way. She had gone over it all, all evening long, and she could find no way out. But Chuck would know what to do. There had to be a crack in the wall if only a person were free enough and detached enough to see it; if only a person weren't tied up in this blind terrible anger that made you want to act, not think; kill, not talk.

"Chuck, I have to tell you. Chuck——"

But then, just then with the words already forming in her throat, she remembered Glenn Griffin whispering hastily into her ear as he half-led, half-shoved her toward the door an hour ago: *You tell anyone, we'll take your mother along on our little ride after while, redhead. Maybe the kid, too, in case the cops get wise to when we're blowing out of here tonight. Any shooting, you folks get it first, see.*

"Yes, Cindy?" Chuck prompted.

"Take me home."

"What?"

"Please, Chuck, no more talk, no more questions. Take me home."

"Not now. What were you going to say?"

"Please, please, please."

She was sitting up straight again, in her own corner, and he caught again the hard flatness in her blue eyes—almost as though she would like to strike him, as though she hated him.

He took her home. What the hell, he was thinking, with the irritation erupting through him. She had slammed that door again, harder this time. He whipped the miniature car northward, hit the boulevard, driving fast. What the hell. Mr. Hilliard looked upon him as reckless, restless, irresponsible. Okay. Fine. That's what he had been the last few years; that's what he was. The law office bored him. What do you want, Chuck—another war? No. No, thanks, no more of that. Among a lot of other things, he didn't want the dull routine of life such as his parents and the Hilliards lived. There had to be more to *his* life than that. And he was not going to be pushed into it, not by anyone, including the lovely red-haired girl who had just shut that door in his face. Why had she? Probably Papa Hilliard had had his say: Chuck Wright isn't going to marry you,

Cindy, you or any one else. And she had believed him. This was the brush-off.

Anger curled in Chuck Wright. What else do you expect? Mr. Hilliard was right, wasn't he? You don't intend to marry her, do you? That much was for sure. Then why the balled-up, bitter-tasting resentment?

He turned into the Hilliard driveway, and he noted a small but, to him, interesting fact: Mr. Hilliard had failed, for the first time within Chuck's memory, to put his car in the garage for the night. Tsk-tsk, he thought satirically, tsk-tsk, Hilliard —what will happen to our little world if we start breaking with our trivial little ironclad habits?

The house was dark except for a hall light upstairs.

Chuck jumped out, came around to open Cindy's door. She still sat there. She looked unable or unwilling to stir.

He felt a strange melting sensation in the pit of his stomach. His pride forgotten, youthful anger gone, he touched her arm. For a split second he was sure that she was going to crumble against him again. Her gaze still held the look of stolid hatred. And, no matter how he figured it, that didn't jibe with the other, with his own conclusions about her tonight. It seemed almost distinct from her, an impersonal force.

"Chuck," she whispered suddenly, "do you have a gun?"

He couldn't speak. There was no answer to that question that seemed to come from nowhere, staggering him, taking his breath.

"Cindy, can I help? What do you mean? *Cindy!*"

But she was already up and out of the seat, running toward the house, her breath sounding above the click of her heels. He followed her to the rear door, the one she always used because there was no key to the side door and her mother carried the one to the front door. She turned there, while her hand fumbled at the lock. "Forget it, Chuck. Can you forget everything?"

"No," he said and took the key from her trembling hand

and inserted it and unlocked the door. "Cindy, you can't go in now, like this. Let me come in with you. We've got to——"

"No!" The whisper threatened to grow loud. "No," she hissed. "Leave me alone, Chuck. Just stay away and leave me alone, that's all!"

She slipped into the house, closed the door. Chuck whirled about, strode to the car. He discovered, without really noting the fact, that he still held the key to the back door of the Hilliard house in his palm. He shoved it into his pocket, stepped into the car, maneuvered it in reverse past Cindy's coupe, past the blue sedan, onto the boulevard which was now dark and totally deserted.

This time the door was slammed and locked. Bolted tight. But Chuck couldn't say what the hell. At least he knew he couldn't make it stick. Not now. What would a girl like Cindy Hilliard want with a gun? If nothing else, he'd have the answer to that one. He'd get the answer tomorrow morning, first thing.

Dan heard the back door open and close. He had come up to bed at 11, following orders, of course. Since then, he had lain there with his hand stretched between the twin beds, holding Eleanor's closely but without pressure in his grasp. In the darkness he imagined the minutes passing. As yet, although his mind had worked its way into, through and around the problem thousands of times, he had not decided what he would do if Glenn Griffin insisted upon taking any of them along when he left. He dared not rely on impulse when the time came—it was well after 11 and the woman should arrive any minute now—and yet he could not devise any threat strong enough to prevent Griffin's doing exactly what he pleased then, as now.

Young Chuck Wright was driving as Dan always suspected

he drove; he heard the angry screech and spin of tires, then the receding motor. Dan realized that he was sitting up in bed. Why?

There was a low indistinct rush of voices in the kitchen. Dan stood up and went into the lighted upstairs hall. "Cindy?" he called.

Behind him Eleanor inquired with taut concern, "Dan?"

"Stay in there, dear," Dan warned her, then called down the stairwell again: "Cindy?"

The dining room light clicked on, and a flow of light reached the downstairs hall.

He was moving then, carelessly, quickly, going down the stairs, when he heard: "What's it to you, Hank?" Robish's voice, blurred with whisky, rougher than usual, harsh with intensified venom.

Dan paused in the front hall and looked into the dining room. He heard Glenn Griffin approach from behind him, and he knew the gun was on him. But what he saw before him made him forget that. Cindy was backed against the buffet, her arm upraised before her face and her eyes hard and brilliant, glittering. Robish was in front of her, his head twisted on the almost invisible neck, his small eyes on Hank Griffin, who sat at the table. The room reeked with the whisky, and the table was scarred by the glasses on it. Dan took in everything in a sickening and terrifying flash. His mind clicked: *Now it's happening; now it's going to happen.*

"What's the matter with you?" Robish demanded again of Hank. He was standing in such a way that Cindy, who might or might not have seen Dan appear, could not move past Robish. "Got to search her, don't I? Searched the old man, didn't we? You trust a dame, do you, kid?"

Dan could see Hank's profile as the boy stood up at the table. He had been drinking, too, or at least Dan surmised he had; his dark eyes were sharp and bright and filled with expression for almost the first time. "Get up stairs to bed, miss," Hank Griffin said, each word clipped off and distinct.

"Oh no, oh no," Robish said hazily, and Dan cursed himself wrathfully for following Glenn's order and bringing the whisky into the house; it could be something this small that would ignite the dynamite. "Gonna search her, might have a gun, got to search the pretty little redhead."

Then Robish turned to Cindy. Dan felt the pressure inside rising, and he said, quietly, to Glenn: "You going to let him get away with this, Griffin? Because if you are——"

The boy's words, still soft, still quiet, almost chiding, cut across Dan's warning to Glenn: "You're drunk, Robish. Let her by."

Robish turned fully, a slow massive movement. "You giving orders, too, Hank?"

"This time."

Robish uttered an obscenity. Ignoring Hank, he turned again to Cindy. But Hank moved before Dan could. He reached Robish in two steps, whirled him about, and then, his arms flashing in two successive movements that Dan could not see, he stood very close to Robish, his back to the hall. Dan saw Robish's head snap back; he saw the sudden blood; he heard the faint, almost plaintive groan.

Hank stepped away then. "You going up to bed now, miss?"

Cindy slithered past Robish and joined Dan in the hall as Robish shook his head twice, his eyes blinking.

Then there was a low roar from that broad working throat. The jaw hardened, the eyes disappeared in the bloody contorted face. One arm went out to Hank, but Hank stepped easily aside. Glenn ran toward his brother as Robish took one bearlike step.

Out of nowhere the automatic appeared in Hank's hand.

"Hank, you damn fool," Glenn Griffin breathed harshly.

Robish was blinking at the gun in Hank's hand. Dan's automatic, the one Robish didn't know existed. He didn't move.

Then, very slowly, he turned and stared owlishly from one to the other of the two brothers. He lifted a hand to his face, pulled it away. All this was very slow and silent and dreamlike in the sudden hush.

"Turning on *me*, huh," Robish muttered at last. "All of you. Turning on your old pal." The drunken maudlin words, filled with surprise, seeped from between thick, moist lips. He was staring at Hank. "Prize fighter, I could tear you apart. You better stay away from me." He took a tentative step toward the hall; his eyes flicked over Cindy. "Should've known better. Couple brothers. Stick together. Should've pulled it on my own." He was apparently trying to smile: the attempt was grotesque. "Kid going soft. Likes this joint. Told me so. Likes it fine. Likes the pretty little red-headed gal, too."

"Crazy talk," Hank snapped. "Loony!" He glanced from Glenn to Dan, avoiding Cindy's eyes.

"Okay, you wait," Robish was saying, rocking in front of Dan who felt his nerves clench in anticipation of some new violence. "Second time I been pushed around here, ain't it, mister? Okay."

Still muttering, Robish crossed the hall, his step unsteady, and disappeared into the dimness of the living room. Dan watched Hank slip his gun back into his pocket. Glenn glared at his brother.

"What's it to you?" Glenn demanded.

"It ain't safe to touch the women."

"Yeah," Glenn said skeptically. "You want to have to use that thing? You know what happens if one of these heaters goes off, don't you?"

Hank frowned under his brother's steady, accusing gaze. He glanced toward the hall. "Get the hell to bed," he said, his tone hard and resentful. "What you think you're looking at?"

"Thank you, Mr. Griffin," Cindy said then, her eyes on Hank.

She held Dan's arm. They turned to the stairs. Eleanor was

halfway down, halted on the steps, facing down, her face waxen.

It was at that moment, while Dan's mind was still struggling to assimilate the conflicting impressions of the last few unlikely minutes, that they heard, from the living room, the sound of a door closing. It took several seconds for the significance of that sound to reach them.

Glenn understood first. "Stay down here," he barked to Dan. Then to Hank: "Cover 'em."

Glenn ran across the dark living room, through the sun porch, cursing as his leg struck furniture twice, delaying him.

Robish was outside. Glenn was outside. Dan, frowning, realized that for the first time he was in the house and two of them were not. The pressure of her hand on his arm told him that the same thought had taken hold of Cindy.

He looked at Hank. The boyish face was passive again, very quiet and pale above the fixed black automatic that he held upon them, not casually as his brother held a gun, but pointed, certain and direct.

The idea in Dan's mind took shape completely and fully, all the details sharp, racing. Robish might get away. If so, nothing in the world could keep the police from arriving, sooner or later, at this house. Nothing. If all three men were in the house then, and armed—this was the disaster that Dan most wanted to avoid. If Glenn caught Robish outside now, the big man was still useless to him drunk and unarmed. The time for the arrival of the money was close, so there might be the woman to deal with, but that was one of the chances. If Dan did nothing now, he knew that Glenn would not risk leaving the house later without taking one or perhaps two of the family along. He had already decided that this was the way it would be, and he had not yet hit upon any device strong enough to prevent it. He could depend on Cindy's acting fast now; he could depend on Eleanor's getting upstairs to the telephone. He hadn't shot a gun of any description for six or seven years, but in the dark, and inside, he had as good a chance as Glenn who was outside and unprotected.

His first and immediate problem was to get hold of Hank's gun, in whatever way he could without risk to anyone else. If the boy should shoot him, neither Glenn nor the boy would waste time wreaking revenge on a dead man by murdering his family. They would go, and fast. Very fast. Dan had to depend on that assumption.

All this, in less than half a minute, went through his mind, and he made the decision.

In the house, all doors locked and the family safely huddled upstairs in one room out of range of Glenn's gun, Dan had a chance to hold off Glenn and Robish, perhaps to force them to get in the car and leave. A slight chance, perhaps, but he had no other.

It came to him then exactly how he would get hold of Hank's gun.

"Faint," he whispered to Cindy.

Cindy, not questioning, not waiting even a second, collapsed on the floor with no sound at all but the rustle of her clothes . . .

3

3

As Dan Hilliard reached his decision, it never occurred to him that he was taking advantage not of the evil of these men but of the one decent impulse he had glimpsed in any of them. But if he had thought of this, he would not have hesitated. He could afford no fine moral distinctions.

He uttered a small breath of surprise as Cindy fell, as was expected of him, and stooping over her, he watched Hank Griffin out of the corner of his eye. The boy looked bewildered, as Dan had hoped, the dark eyes flashing after his brother; on his own, even with the gun in hand, he seemed uncertain, poised for action or flight.

"Give me a hand, Griffin," Dan said, attempting to lift his daughter.

Still the boy hesitated, straining to hear whatever sounds Glenn and Robish might be making outside the house.

"Dammit," Dan said, "can't you see this child is sick?"

Hank made up his mind then, and seeing this, Dan was forced toward still another decision: he couldn't kill the boy. The others, yes, but not this child who was no older than Cindy.

69

Hank, with the gun in one hand, came forward, bent down, placed his other arm under Cindy's shoulders.

The gun was directed toward the front door. It was the second Dan had hoped for, anticipated. He struck out, fast and smoothly, his fist catching the boy's wrist. The automatic clattered to the floor. Dan made a dive for it.

The metal felt moist and warm in his hand. Behind him he heard a small cry of astonishment and pain and turned to see Cindy sitting up now, her mouth clamped over the boy's wrist, biting hard. Hank's face writhed in pain, and over it fell the awful sense of betrayal that even then sent no shame through Dan.

"Get out," Dan said curtly. "Cindy, lock the other doors and get upstairs. Ellie! Ellie, get on the phone up there, fast, and keep Ralphie with you, away from the windows."

Cindy was already up and moving, flipping off the dining-room light. Dan heard the click of the side door lock and watched Hank, dazed, his face mean and ugly now, stepping toward the front door.

"Hurry it up," Dan said to young Griffin.

Hank opened the front door. Dan reached and shoved him, wondering in the instant whether this might not be a mistake; perhaps he should have shot the boy at once. Dan locked the front door and he was turning toward the stairs when he heard, from above, Eleanor's scream. He bounded up the stairs as Eleanor appeared from Ralphie's room, still screaming, with her hand over her mouth.

"Ralphie . . . Dan . . . Ralphie's gone!"

Cindy came up the stairs behind him, flipped off the hall light, plunging them into blank total darkness. They seemed frozen there then, the three of them—not the four as Dan had seen it happening—mute figures, caught, trapped.

"Maybe he got away," Cindy said at last. "Maybe he——"

But Glenn's voice, caught in the low whine of wind outside, reached them then.

"We ain't going, Hilliard. Open up the back door and throw that gun out."

Dan automatically dropped down, out of window range in case Glenn should decide to shoot anyway. Cindy pulled her mother into the bedroom and they crouched low.

"Should I phone the police now?" Eleanor asked.

"Hilliard," Glenn cried outside, and there was a note of cruel desperation behind the call. "Hilliard, listen!"

Dan tensed, listening. At first he couldn't believe the voice that reached him. But Eleanor recognized it and uttered a faint cry of defeat that worked its way into Dan's bones, sending a coldness through him. Cindy stood in the bedroom door.

"Dad?" The one word. It came from outside. There was no bravado in it, no outrage, no childish valor; the word was high with terror. "Dad."

"If we go, Hilliard," Glenn Griffin's voice said, "we're taking the kid. Open up and we'll forget the whole business."

Dan glanced at Cindy's dim figure in the bedroom door; it had gone slack and limp against the door frame. Dan's hand closed convulsively over the handle of the automatic. He could shoot; a shot would bring help. He could telephone. He could keep the three out of the house.

But Ralphie was also outside the house.

Dan flicked the safety latch on the gun and stood up. "Don't yell out there," he warned Glenn Griffin. "I'm coming down to the back door."

It was not a shout that reached him then from the darkness in the rear of the house, but a laugh, a thin and arrogant gust of triumph.

"Lock the bedroom door, Cindy. If you hear a shot downstairs, make the call anyway. If you don't, keep Eleanor up here. No matter what else you hear, don't call."

Cindy didn't move at first, but as Dan descended the uncarpeted back stairs, he heard the bedroom door close and the lock turn. He walked blindly through the tiny pantry at the

71

foot of the stairs, paused only a second, listening to the sound of the wind; then he threw open the door.

"Toss the gun first, Hilliard," Glenn Griffin advised.

Dan tossed the gun. Again he had no choice. He was a man without a choice, over and over. He stood waiting numbly for whatever was coming: a bullet, a blow, the men, or his son.

Glenn appeared first out of the darkness. Then Ralphie. Dan felt the boy's hand on his arm, heard the stifled sob as the boy leaned against him.

"Go upstairs, son," Dan said.

The boy obeyed quickly, running on bare feet up the back stairs. A door opened above, and Dan heard Ralphie taken in with the others.

Now Glenn was standing before him, tall and angular, a dim, shimmering shadow. Behind Glenn, Hank Griffin appeared from the darkness, stiff and small-looking.

"We got Robish, too," Glenn Griffin said, pushing Dan backwards out of the door into the pantry. "I had to put him on ice for a while, Hilliard. So he'd learn who was boss around here." The young man spoke coolly, without passion.

It may have been this calm lack of emotion that caused Dan to relax slightly before the blow struck. It was a vicious swipe and it came at him from above, the barrel of the revolver catching him on the forehead just below the hairline.

He went down. That was the first blow.

He had no idea how much later it was that he awakened on his own bed in his own bedroom in the darkness. He stirred with a groan and heard the sound with some distant surprise. Then he felt Eleanor's hand on his face, over his mouth, gentle and cool and incredibly soft. He struggled to sit up but she held him.

"Dan," she whispered, "Dan, don't talk, don't move, darling. Dan, you hear me?"

His head nodded under her hand. The darkness threatened to close in again, not the darkness of the room with the windows outlined in some pale outside light, but the darkness in which he had been lying for some time, without awareness, without pain.

"Dan, I gave you some pills to make you sleep. It's almost morning. If you can hear me, listen to me."

"Ralphie?"

"He's all right, Dan. Sleeping."

"And . . . *them?*"

"They're still here. Cindy's with Ralphie and one of them's in her bedroom up here. The other two are downstairs. Listen, Dan. I've been thinking all night. You did a foolish and terrible and wonderful thing, and I love you. No, that isn't what I want to say. Can you hear me, darling? I want to say that you must never do anything like that again. You cannot try ever again to do what you did. You might have been killed, Dan. They would have killed you last night if they didn't need you. Hear me, Dan. This is important. You can't save us if you die. We aren't saved if you die, do you understand! You must understand that, Dan, please you must, because if you don't, something terrible is going to happen. Nobody knows anything about what's happening here, nobody in the world. It's only us. Dan, I'm pleading with you. Promise me. Promise me, Dan, darling, promise me. Never again."

"I promise," he whispered, dully, not knowing completely, from her words, what she had meant to convey, but forced by her tone to nod his head. "Yes, darling. I see that."

"Don't be brave, darling," his wife said, lying beside him now. "We don't want you to be brave. We want you well and alive and with us."

There were things that Dan knew vaguely at this moment, but he couldn't arrange them in his mind and he couldn't explain them. "Didn't the woman come?"

"Telephoned," Eleanor said softly. "A collect call to a Mr. James, after midnight some time. She's not coming, Dan. I don't know what it means. I was so busy, I couldn't ask. She's

73

not coming but they're staying. Now try to sleep again. It's not a serious cut on your head, dear, but you'll need your rest. Please."

He felt then her lips closing over his, soft and full and a trifle moist, and he felt his love for her stirring deeply, more deeply perhaps than ever before. He could hear her breathing close to him and her hand lay against his face. He slept.

It began to rain at 5:30 in the morning, just before dawn. Jesse Webb had been dozing, his head down on his arms, when Carson, the FBI man, came briskly into his office, smiled a little, stirred the young Sheriff with a nudge.

Jesse blinked up at the young man, recognizing him only vaguely: a studious-looking fellow in a double-breasted brown suit, wearing dark-rimmed glasses, carrying a brief case. Carson removed his raincoat, sat down straddling the back of Tom Winston's chair and offered Jesse a cigarette.

"Looks like we're about the only people in town awake," he said.

"What is it?" Jesse demanded, alert now, recalling the disappointment of the long, dull night, but pushing it behind him.

"It's a telephone call," Carson said. "It's not much but it has its promising aspects. Sit back, friend. Take it easy. Nothing we can do now, not for some time, so just listen to my little story and maybe it'll get light outside. Lord, don't they heat this place? It's almost winter."

"A telephone call?"

Carson related the story, as it had come to him through the Columbus office. He spoke easily but carefully, his trained mind not missing any detail; Jesse Webb listened without interrupting because Carson filled in the whole picture.

Three plain-clothes men and two uniformed policemen had closed in on an apartment in Columbus; this was at about 1 o'clock. They had reason to believe that Helen Lamar was there. She was not. They found another woman, though, name unimportant, who, after about an hour of intensive police questioning, admitted that Helen Lamar had been with her. The woman claimed, of course, that she had no idea Helen Lamar was in any trouble, but if she was there was no cause for the woman to get involved. She would be co-operative, she said. Helen Lamar had left the apartment at least an hour before the police arrived. She had to make a telephone call, she said. Also, she had to buy a car. The woman swore that she had no idea whether or where Helen Lamar had done either. It was the last she saw of her.

This information set in motion a vast, swift but complicated series of investigations in the Columbus area, but Carson himself was inclined to think that only one of these would prove fruitful: that telephone call. She would have to contact Griffin, wouldn't she? She was too smart to place the call from a friend's apartment. What then?

"Pay station," Jesse Webb said.

"We'll soon know. God knows how many long-distance calls are placed at that time of night in Columbus, but there's a record of all of them."

"The Indianapolis calls——"

Carson grinned, blowing smoke. "You'll get them, Sheriff."

Jesse was thinking of the myriad number of reasons a person in one city picks up a phone and places a midnight call to a person in a city 175 miles away. Working his way through that list would, he realized with a slight lifting of his spirits, occupy a great deal of time; it would be action, of a sort. But— and his legs ached, his neck was stiff—in that time, in all this time that had passed and was passing, what was Glenn Griffin doing?

Carson read the thought in the tall man's eyes. "It's none of my business, Webb, and stop me if I'm out of line. You've got something personal at stake in this, haven't you? It's not just a job for you."

Jesse managed a smile. He could lie to himself: there was a way of twisting the truth, as he had twisted it for Kathleen's benefit, in order to justify his motives. But neither his personal reasons nor his job explained the way he felt, one exclusive of the other. "It's pretty complicated," he said. And then he added, for Carson and for himself, still another element: "I've got a hunch, though, that Griffin's after me just as much as I'm after him. It's just a hunch. I broke his jaw once. He probably could have forgiven me if I'd shot him, wounded him. But there's a crazy sort of quirk in a mind like Griffin's. I guess we all have our own twists more or less, but guys like him have more of them and they're stronger. He's a handsome boy, you know. I reckon maybe kind of vain, too. Gave a real show at his trial. You can bet, wherever he is now, he's putting on quite an act."

Carson nodded, relaxing into the conversation that might help kill the time till another report came through from Columbus or from the telephone company. "There's a quirk, as you call it, in all of them. The criminal mind's not like other minds. Odd you should be interested in that angle. The show-off type's fairly predictable, I think, once you get the hang of him. He's shrewd but no imagination, really. Always acting, as you say, but the pattern's pretty old stuff. He's tough enough, but he likes to look and talk even tougher . . ."

Glenn Griffin was at the head of the table, tilted back in his chair, one of Dan's hats pushed back from his face. A cigarette dangled between his lips. This morning he didn't bother to make the gun evident. It was there. And Hank's was back in his possession, too, but concealed. Hank stood in the corner of the room, his young face showing none of the resentment that Dan guessed he must feel after last night. Dan studied his own large freckled hands as they lay on the whisky-ringed table top. Beside him, Eleanor pressed her leg against his; Dan couldn't bear to look at her. It was as though, in a period of thirteen hours or so, her soft oval of face had hardened, aged. Cindy was across from Dan, her eyes no longer contemptuous or angry, the blue darkened until they looked black. Black and hard and determined. Beside her, Ralphie was alert, his gaze soft and bewildered as he stared at the gash on his father's forehead.

"Things've kind of changed, folks," Glenn was saying. "My friend who was coming can't make it like she thought. It seems some coppers tried to pick her off."

Outside, the rain hissed and gurgled in the drains and, caught in the gusts of wind, hammered against the windows, against the sides of the house. It seemed, somehow, to soak through the walls and into the aching crevices of Dan's body.

"Now we don't want to stick here any more'n you want us to, see. But I got things to do before I can go. We're going to be your guests just a little longer."

"How much longer?" Dan heard his own voice, without recognizing it.

"Now Pop, is that any way to start talking? Just because you got a wild idea last night and had to take your medicine. Hell, you don't have any worse a headache than Robish. I had to put him out for a while, too. And he's got a hangover to boot."

"How much longer?"

"Until I get a certain envelope in the mail, Hilliard, that's how much longer."

"When will that be?"

"It might get here today. It ought to."

"Meanwhile——?"

"Pop, I like you this morning. You act real interested in co-operating."

"Meanwhile——?"

"Meanwhile, Hilliard, everything goes on around here just like normal. I guess you know how important that is. You and the redhead go to work, just like usual. Only Junior here's too smart a boy. He stays home. He's sick today. Junior hates my guts, so he's going to miss a day at school. That won't hurt him. I missed a few myself. And look at me." He laughed. It was the only sound in the room above the rain.

"I'm sorry, Griffin," Dan said then, slowly. "I'm not going to work today. I'm sick, too."

Glenn's laugh died. "You could be a lot sicker, Hilliard."

"I can call my office. There are a lot of colds around. No one will think anything of it."

"Then how'm I going to get the envelope, Pop? With the dough in it." He was grinning faintly. "That envelope's addressed to you at your office, see. We wouldn't want any coppers following it right in here, would we?"

Dan considered this, feeling the pressure increase along Eleanor's leg; he considered it in that emotionless way that he was thinking this morning. Then he shook his head. "I can't leave my wife in the house with that drunken friend of yours, Griffin. Not after what happened last night."

"You don't have much to say about it, do you?"

"I think I do," Dan said. "Yesterday it looked as though you held all the cards, Griffin. Today I know better. Every minute you have to stay here, you're taking that much more of a chance. You can kill me, yes, or beat me into unconsciousness again. But you'll have to do it quietly. There are people awake now. I'll force you to make some noise about it this morning. I'll make you shoot me, Griffin. Then where'll you be?"

Dan recalled his promise to Eleanor, but he was not breaking it; he was judging Griffin and working on that judgment.

Glenn stood up, strolled to the curtain, placed his eye against the slit he had cut there. A poisonous silence hung over the room.

Without turning, Glenn said, "Mrs. Hilliard can stay upstairs all day. I'll keep Robish down here."

"I can't take that chance. After last night."

"*Goddammit,* Hilliard, I said I'm making a promise! Don't push, Hilliard. Don't push too far, Pop." Glenn was facing them again, his chest heaving. "I took orders all my life from smart-eyed bastards like you. Now. You're going to that office of yours, Hilliard, and as soon as that dough comes, you open the envelope, take it to your bank or some place and get it changed into small bills, nothing over twenty, and then you call me and tell me you're on your way home. Just that, Hilliard. Only listen and listen better this time: I been in touch with a pal of mine, see. And this guy's going to do a little job for me, something I can't do myself. Before you come home, I'll think of some way for you to pay him off for me. You think you want to try something different, we won't bother to open that cut on your head next time. The kid and the wife'll be here." He stopped and threw his shoulders up and began to grin. "Pop, you're a tough old guy and I give you credit, but you be careful, see."

Eleanor reached for Dan's hand, covered it on the tabletop. She said, quietly, "Dan, if one of them starts up the stairs all day, I'll scream so loud they'll have to use their guns, and that'll be the end of it. Do you understand me, dear? It's only a little time now." She stood up. "I'll get your raincoat. Isn't it an awful day?"

Dan happened to be watching Hank Griffin's face when Eleanor went into the hall: the boy stared after her with a strange expression of admiration flickering in the glance he turned, questioning, on his brother. Glenn still grinned.

"Whole family's getting tough," Glenn said slowly. "Just so you don't get brave, too."

79

In the hall, Dan climbed into the coat she held, then turned around and took his wife into his arms. You can live with a woman for more than twenty years, he was thinking, and not really know her. He drew her to him, remembering her palm against his face last night, and kissed her, unmindful of the eyes.

Glenn's mocking laugh reached from the dining room, raucous and coarse, and Dan tightened his hold. He saw Cindy rise and come toward him.

It was then that Hank Griffin spoke—Hank Griffin whom he had betrayed last night, whom he had tricked and made a fool of. "What's so funny?" the boy demanded of his brother.

The laughter broke off jaggedly.

"I don't see anything so damn funny you should break your neck laughing, that's all," Hank said in reply to the questioning glare. But his voice was shaky now.

"I laugh when I feel like it, Hank," Glenn said evenly, in hollow tones. "You got nothing to say about it. That right, Hank?"

A moment passed. Dan wished he had gone; he didn't want to witness this.

"That right, Hank?"

"That's right," Hank said, but a sullen growl of rebellion sharpened the defeated words.

Hank crossed into the hall, passed them there, his face blank, but his eyes challenging and dull with hatred and confusion. He reminded Dan of fighters he had seen: having been beaten in the ring, they defied you disdainfully afterwards, their faces reading, *Could you do any better? Want to make something of it, chump?*

"Wake up Robish," Glenn called after him with a laugh that might have carried his forgiveness in it. "I need some shut-eye. And you, Hilliard—what are you waiting for? Wouldn't want to be late and get docked down there at that store, would you?"

Dan was looking past Glenn; then he took a step toward his son. It had to be said. Impatience rose in him and the cut on his forehead beat hotly. "Ralphie, you heard what Mr. Griffin said. You stay with your mother. And mind her. Stay upstairs and out of trouble." He heard the firm but inadequate words and suddenly he wanted to shake the boy, to force by pressure his own years of experience and knowledge into that ten-year-old body and mind. Beneath the weariness and blankness, he felt a twist as the words came up in him: "Ralphie, you've got to understand!"

Ralphie only nodded, and of a sudden Dan wondered whether it was sheer terror that held the boy or whether he was still blaming Dan for not acting against the impossible. Dan's throat tightened. His heart cried: What else can I do, Ralphie?

Abruptly he raised a hand in brief salute and went out into the bone-chilling rain, giving his hat a tug as he crossed sloshing through puddles toward Cindy's car. Cindy joined him at once, sliding under the wheel, shooting the coupe forward and down the driveway and away from the house. Dan didn't look back.

He was struggling with too many swift and formless impressions. What, for instance, had that brief clash between the brothers meant? And did that young one, that Hank, fancy himself in love with Cindy? If so, it would explain what happened last night when Robish stopped her in the dining room. If there had been any room in him for pity, Dan might have felt sorry for the boy. God knows what sort of life might bring a kid to this.

He pulled his mind away from that. He was only glad that he hadn't shot Hank last night when he had possession of the automatic. Why hadn't he? Too civilized? He didn't feel civilized, not in the least; throbbing below the numb, sleepwalking deadness in him was the aching impulse that he had felt before: the need and desire to kill. But something had held his hand last night. And if it had not, what?

Ralphie. He hadn't known Ralphie was out there, gripped between Glenn Griffin's hands. What if he had shot? What had held him back?

The jagged end of memory cut and sickened him.

The coupe followed a familiar route, along the curve of creek, under the maples, into the traffic.

Robish would wake up now. Drunk, groggy, with a hangover —then what? Would he turn on Glenn? Could Glenn control him?

And some time during the night another fear had slipped into Dan's mind, vague, formless; he could not bring it into focus then and it hovered now, elusive and shadowy.

"Don't worry about Chuck, Dad," Cindy said. "I'll take care of him, I guess I acted a little funny to him last night, but I'm better this morning. I don't want you worrying about that, too."

Dan had not been worrying about that; he had not thought of Chuck Wright. Perhaps another slip. You never knew where the loose chink was, the one uncertain stone that could bring down the whole structure of lies and deceit.

Today's mail, he was thinking; there's one at 9:30, another around 2:45. Let the envelope arrive in the first mail. Let it come soon.

Then the drugged blankness of the night returned momentarily, and in it hovered the disturbing thought that had been evading him: the telephone call. The woman had telephoned.

It seems some coppers tried to pick her off.

Then she telephoned. She called the Hilliard number. What if the police caught her then, perhaps while telephoning or immediately after? If they had the number, what would they do, how proceed? Dan was ignorant of police procedure, but in his mind he could picture them approaching the house with caution, guns drawn, shouting. He could picture Eleanor and Ralphie inside, Glenn turning wrathfully from the window, satisfied that Dan had sent the police; he could picture the loutish, dull-witted Robish not waiting, leaping, his hands going out——

And what could Dan do about that? What power did he have over something like that?

He heard a deep groan in the steamy interior of the car as it stopped along the curb by the side entrance of the department store. It took him a moment to realize that the sound had come from his own chest.

The black sedan with a siren perched on the roof and two red lights on the fenders, the word "Sheriff" printed in block letters along its sides, was north of the city limits, and only five blocks from the Hilliard house. Behind the windshield wipers Jesse Webb had begun to sense that the day would be a waste. At first, several hours ago, he had been sure, or had at least convinced himself that the long list of names, addresses and telephone numbers would turn up something. But now he had worked his way through the first half dozen, all but one of the collect calls that had been placed at pay-station phones in Columbus, Ohio, to Indianapolis, Indiana, between 10 last night and 3 o'clock this morning. He had narrowed down the time in his office while his mind leaped ahead to the activity involved. Now, however, he had only one name, address and telephone number left of the first group: not many people placed collect calls. If, by some chance, Helen Lamar had paid for the call at a pay station, he had two more numbers to investigate. Then, if all this failed, he would check with the deputies and city police who had been making inquiries at the numbers in the city where prepaid calls had been received from private numbers in Columbus. This group seemed the least likely of all to turn up anything, but Jesse was plugging all the holes from this end.

He had to remind himself over and over, because of the twists of disappointment, that he was only stabbing about blindly in the dark, anyway. All he had to go on was the statement of the woman who had hidden Helen Lamar in Columbus; as far as that woman knew, Helen Lamar had gone out to buy a car and make a phone call. She hadn't bought a car in any legitimate sense, from any dealer: that much was easily checked. And she hadn't made the call from a phone in the neighborhood: that much had been even more quickly established.

Of course it was more than possible that if she *had* telephoned Glenn Griffin—and even this was a guess—she might have called New Orleans or Denver or New York or Chicago. Why Indianapolis? How can you be so sure?

Jesse Webb was not sure at all. It was only an idea he had, one that he held to with bulldog tenacity because he wanted Glenn Griffin to be in his home town. Even Kathleen, at breakfast, had shaken her head at the irrational theory, or hope. But at that time Jesse was remembering Uncle Frank's withered arm and even more withered spirit. He was picturing again the arrogant way the boy had shot first, *then* tossed his gun into the street and demanded mercy. He was remembering, too, the words, spit at him in the bare jail corridor: *You got yours coming, copper.*

But great God, Jesse told himself irascibly as he whipped the wheel and began to crawl to his stop, you can't bank on some wild hope, or flimsy intuition! You're a trained policeman, man. Stick to the evidence at hand.

All right, he was sticking to it. He was doing all that was in his power to do. He pulled the car to a halt, reached under his jacket, touched the gun with one hand, and started to climb out. There was always a chance, although it appeared slimmer now, that he would walk up a sidewalk or driveway directly into the ambushed gun of Glenn Griffin behind a window. That was a chance he had to take. Better that than to alert Griffin by making inquiries on the telephone. You had to figure the odds and then work from there. The odds were certainly in his favor: there was little likelihood of an ambush simply because there was damned little likelihood of finding Glenn Griffin.

His narrow head shot forward, the water pounding and dripping off his hat brim, he started toward the house. It was not until he was almost on the front porch that he saw what he should have noticed from the car: a floral piece, lavender in color, hanging on the glass front of the door. He stopped. The folding chairs of an undertaking establishment were leaning in neat stacks on the porch.

The explanation of a midnight telephone call was too obvious. Jesse retraced his steps, clambered back into the front seat, and after touching his pencil to his tongue in a schoolboy habit he had picked up, he crossed the number BR (for Broadway) 8470 and the name Reilly, James, off the list.

Then, glancing automatically at the clock on the dashboard, he started the motor. Twenty-seven minutes after 9. It was going to be a long day.

The mail arrived in three large canvas bags at 9:31. The mail clerks worked fast, faster perhaps because Mr. Hilliard was standing in the door of the mail room. He remained there, square and still, until all of the mail had been sorted and dispatched by messenger to the various departments. Handing him all the envelopes addressed to Personnel Dept. or to Mr. Daniel Hilliard personally, the elderly senior mail clerk was unable to guess from the taut and drawn face with the adhesive

85

strip across one corner of forehead that Dan Hilliard had begun to give in to despair. Memories still crowded sharp and broken through his mind; it was not memory but the recognition of the return addresses on every envelope in his hand that caused Dan to turn away abruptly, his whole body packed solid with defeat.

The next mail was at 2:45.

Five hours and ten minutes away. And no power on earth could hurry it.

He rode to the sixth floor on the employees' elevator. He tossed the mail to his secretary's desk, went into his office, sat down behind the familiar desk and considered slowly and with great anguish all the things that could happen in his home in five hours' time. Of one thing he was certain: they would not leave under any circumstances, without taking along Eleanor or Ralphie or both. So even when they had the money, he would be faced with that.

But there had to be a way around that. If not to prevent it, at least to make certain that when it happened, the police would be aware of the facts of the case. But how? Without bringing them into it sooner than that time.

Acting without thought after that, working on some calculating impulse that he dared not take time to question, he reached for a blank piece of paper and his pen.

To Whom It May Concern, he wrote in a back-handed scrawl. *Innocent people will be in the automobile with the three escaped convicts you want. If you shoot, you will be responsible for taking the lives of people who have done no harm. To attempt to trace this letter will endanger these same people and will not accomplish what you hope to accomplish.*

He sat back and studied what he had written. Then he folded the paper without signing it, drew a plain envelope from his desk drawer, sealed it over the note and addressed it: *Police Headquarters, South Alabama St., City.*

He picked up the phone, dialed 9, waited for an outside line, then dialed his home number.

"Ellie? Where are they?"

"Downstairs. I'm with Ralphie. Are you all right, dear?"

"Anything happen? Anything at all?"

"No. Only Mr. Patterson came to the back door. You know, the little man who collects our trash. He wanted to get in the garage, but I told him we'd lost the key and not to bother. He seemed awfully disappointed in a funny way, but that's all."

"He didn't notice anything odd?"

"No. I'm sure not. But Mr. R. thought he did. I was worried for a few minutes."

"That's all?"

"That's all, Dan."

On the other end of the line Dan heard a familiar taunting laugh: Glenn Griffin listening on the downstairs phone.

"Nothing in the morning mail," Dan said. "Perhaps this afternoon. 2:45. It'll soon be over, Ellie," he lied. "Don't think about it."

"Good-bye, dear."

Click. Then another click: the downstairs phone at home. Dan replaced the instrument on his desk. He sat bent forward, longing for a return and deepening of the blank, sleepwalking mood. At the same time he recognized it for what it was—his enemy. Like sleep, inviting but fatal, to a man lost in a freezing forest. He listened to the rain driving against the windows. Almost gratefully then, he felt the tugging insistence in his muscles: every nerve cried out for him to stand up, to go home, to murder those men. Quickly. No more of this. Efficiently. Get it over with. But all he could do was sit trying to devise a way to have that anonymous note delivered to the police without answering any questions about it.

Then his phone jangled. His heart stopped and he picked it up. The metal was still warm and moist from his palm.

"Dad?"

"Cindy!"

The cold blue gleam was still in Cindy's eyes this morning, but farther back, less immediately apparent. Chuck Wright sat at his desk and looked through the open door into the outer office where Cindy was talking on the phone, the instrument pushed hard against the delicate line of cheek. She held the phone with two hands. The light from above caught in the mass of mahogany hair.

What the devil is the pitch? What does it all add up to?

She had smiled at him and apologized for last night.

"You still want a gun?" he had asked.

That did it. She turned away. And for the rest of the morning she had stayed turned away.

Chuck was not angry now, only baffled.

None of your business, Chuck, he told himself. This is the brush-off. It was never in the cards, anyway. Look at the way she's talking on that phone—no silence there, no withdrawing and twisting away.

A gun, a gun, a gun: that was the part that made no sense whatever. He could have added up the rest: the brush-off, the intensity now on the phone with another fellow, the decision to follow her father's good advice. But what did any of this have to do with a gun? And what exactly was she saying on that phone? If he knew that, perhaps . . .

What Cindy was saying to her father on the phone was direct and, to her, simple: the idea had just come to her, so please listen and don't interrupt. Suppose she and Dan, no matter how, found some way to raise the money, quite a lot of money, perhaps five or six thousand dollars. Then, if the money Glenn Griffin was expecting didn't arrive this afternoon, rather than have them around another night, she would take this other money to them, in the house. She, not Dan. What about it? Didn't it make sense? They weren't waiting for the woman now, only the money. Then they could leave and go to wherever the woman was—although Cindy devoutly hoped they wouldn't get that far.

"How much money, Cindy? Even assuming we could raise that much, how do we know *he* doesn't know the exact amount that the woman mailed to him yesterday? If ours was too much or too little, he'd know it was a trick. And if you took it to him, not me, he'd be sure it was."

"Oh, but that's part of it. We wouldn't have to pretend it came from her. But listen. Suppose I explained to him that you were in the woods, out of pistol range, with a rifle. That all they could do was go. And if they tried to use Mother or Ralphie or me as a shield, you'd be there, waiting for them, ready to pick them off. Would they risk getting shot, any of them, if they thought they had the money and could get away without trouble?"

"Cindy, Cindy," Dan's voice said faintly, almost sadly. "Yes, they would risk it." He sounded patient and tired. "Why? Because they don't have any choice. They know I wouldn't shoot, no matter how good a shot I was if there was a chance of their killing any of you. So they've got us there and we'd better face it. Even after a man's been shot himself, he can pull a trigger. That's why they had Ellie read that news story to us—to impress us with that fact. And, Cindy, on top of all this, they never figure they're going to be killed. Not them. So far they've been lucky and in their own eyes they have a sort of immortality. They always figure it'll be the other fellow. They *have* to figure it that way. It's the way you think in a war. It's one way of getting through." He paused and took a heavy deep breath.

"You've thought of it all, haven't you?"

"I'm sorry, Cindy. No one can think of everything. That's the thing that can——" He broke off. "I'll call you when the next mail comes in."

"Yes."

"Eat some lunch, Cindy. You had no breakfast."

"Yes."

When she replaced the phone, Cindy sat staring at it, but seeing instead the house ten miles away. In five hours the money would arrive. Would or would not. Until then, she prayed silently, please God make them all stay away. Everybody. The police most of all, but also peddlers, salesmen, insurance men, everyone, everyone.

"I saw him snooping around those damn windows," Robish said, and he was trembling. "We got to grab him, Griffin. Listen! He was up on his toes, looking in the garage. Just before he got back in the truck. Don't you believe me?"

"Mr. Patterson?" Eleanor said, still seated at the kitchen table. "He just came to collect. He picks up the trash every Thursday morning and then he comes back just after lunch every other Thursday to collect."

"You always pay him with a check, Mrs. Hilliard?" Glenn asked, speaking first.

"Yes. Almost always. It prevents my having to have a lot of cash around the house, and being out here like this——" She had almost said it was safer not to have cash in the house, but a giddiness rose in her and she stopped herself.

"I know what I seen," Robish said, his voice murky. "He saw the car. I'm going to get him. Let me have your gun."

"Hank," Glenn shouted into the dining room, "where'd the old guy go?"

"House next door. Behind the trees. I can see the back end of the truck at the curb down there."

"Calling the cops!" growled Robish.

"No," Eleanor said hastily. "The Wallings aren't home. I know."

"Then maybe I can catch him, Glenn."

"Glenn," Hank called from the next room, "why take any chances anyway? Let's just blow."

Eleanor's eyes were fixed on Glenn's face, which was locked in indecision.

"Mr. Patterson wouldn't be suspicious. He . . . you saw him . . . a man like that."

"Shut up," Glenn Griffin said and extended his gun toward Robish. "Mrs. Hilliard, you want the old guy to bring the cops up on your lawn? Use your head. What else can we do?"

Robish shoved the gun into the side of Dan's gray jacket. He took a step toward the back door. Glenn's voice halted him.

"If you get into trouble, don't come back here, Robish."

"Me? I don't know what trouble is."

Just before she collapsed over the table, Eleanor thought that she had never heard Robish's voice so light-hearted, so pleased and excited and not in the least menacing or——

At approximately this time—which was the peak of the noon hour in the downtown area—Dan Hilliard stepped into a hotel where he was not likely to be known, asked for a messenger, then spoke quickly but quite distinctly and directly to a middle-aged man who wore a maroon-colored uniform with brass buttons; the man nodded, showing no surprise but taking a closer, longer look at Dan Hilliard as he accepted from him a white envelope and a five-dollar bill. Then the messenger went to put on a raincoat and Dan Hilliard walked briskly out the side door into the steady but now windless downpour. In less than a minute the messenger was walking west on Washington Street toward Alabama, toward the offices of the city police department, directly across the street from the Marion County jail and the offices of the Sheriff.

The Wallings were not at home, which was no surprise to Mr. Patterson because Mrs. Walling was an active clubwoman, pictures always in the paper, that sort of thing. Mr. Patterson returned to his truck and started to climb in, a little stiffly because this rain raised merry hell with his arthritis; then he saw the man sitting in the cab of his truck.

"Just get in, Jack," the man said.

Mr. Patterson saw the revolver, and he frowned as he lifted himself up.

"Drive, Jack, and no hurry. Drive out east."

Mr. Patterson started the motor and glanced sideways at the huge man slouched down in the seat beside him. The man wore an expensive suit that didn't fit him. Mr. Patterson recognized the face, after perhaps ten seconds, and then he remembered the car parked in the Hilliard garage and the radio reports and the pictures in this morning's paper.

Why did I wait? he asked himself. What was I waiting for? Why did I stop at the Wallings'?

"Good Lord," he said aloud, in a cracked breath. "Good Lord, those poor people."

The man seemed pleased by this; he even chuckled heavily. "I was right, wasn't I, Jack?"

Mr. Patterson had forgotten everything but Mrs. Hilliard's face as she wrote out his check a few minutes ago at the kitchen table while he waited, as usual, in the small back hall. The gun had been pointed at her then, from the next room. Why hadn't he guessed that? Why was his mind so slow nowadays?

If he'd gone straight to a drug store and called Jesse Webb, he might have helped them. Those poor people. Mr. Patterson had even jotted down the license number on a scrap of paper that was now in his pocket; he meant to ask Jesse Webb, who would remember him because many was the night he'd played pinochle with young Jesse's father, whether the license was the one Mr. Patterson suspected it might be. Being deputy sheriff now, Jesse'd have that sort of information; and if Mr. Patterson had made a mistake, well, he was an old man, getting crotchety, getting suspicious.

But it was no mistake. And he had done nothing. If anything happened to those people, he'd never forgive himself.

It was then that he realized that what was going to happen now was to happen to him. His breathing became irregular and the arthritis pain clenched in his right knee. In the drafty cab of the truck, behind the steady swish-swash of the windshield wipers, Mr. Patterson heard a strange sound: the man beside him was humming, softly, a blurred sort of tune, but with a mounting excitement in it, a pleasure-filled anticipation. Mr. Patterson even guessed the meaning of the excitement.

He didn't shudder. He didn't grow panicky. He made a silent plan.

They were east of the city now, on a country road. With his left elbow, but very quietly and cautiously, he pressed his weight down on the door handle. Timing the click, he spoke simultaneously with it, and in a loud tone: "Mister, I swear to God I'm not going to say a word to anybody! I'm an old man. I didn't do anything to you."

The man beside him laughed then. "Why don't you get down on your knees and pray, Jack?"

Mr. Patterson had not liked saying those words, but they seemed the ones a man might say under the circumstances. The door was open now. Ahead, he saw two blue gasoline pumps set alongside the road, fairly close to the edge. There was a weathered, clapboard service-station building, too. He gauged his distance carefully, tried not to take the deep breath that his lungs ached for.

Mr. Patterson waited till he was almost abreast of the pumps, then in one movement that was co-ordinated through his frail old body, he whipped the wheel to the right, trounced hard on the accelerator, and fell from the truck just as its nose struck the first pump. He hit the gravel and rolled, twisting, with the stiffness of his right leg forgotten, hearing the metallic crash above and behind him. He kept his body crouched low and ran toward the building, feeling the rain cold and pleasant against his face, wondering why there was no explosion, no burst of flame.

He was within two yards of the weathered wood when the first bullet reached him; then he heard the cracking, ear-bursting sound. He knew he had been hit; in his mind he could see the big man standing back there, legs planted apart in the gravel, leveling the gun. But what surprised Mr. Patterson, in the only moment he had left for surprise or any other emotion, was that the bullet did not burn or sear or scorch. It was more like a paralyzing but painless blow against his back. He didn't feel the second bullet at all. Nor the third.

No one but the killer and the killed heard those shots, and as a result almost an hour passed before the report of the murder, which was thought to be an accident, reached Deputy Sheriff Jesse Webb. He kept asking for more facts on the two-way radio in his car, but he could learn very little, only that the truck had, apparently, gone out of control in front of the old deserted and boarded-up filling station, had plowed into the pumps which were no longer in use; there had been no explosion. The body, evidently, had been thrown clear. As yet it had not been identified, no police officer had reached the scene, and perhaps it wasn't worth his time to drive all the way across the city to make a personal investigation.

But Jesse had worked his way by now through the important telephone numbers on his list, with no results, and he was coming to the conclusion, reluctantly, that Helen Lamar had made no telephone call to Indianapolis from Columbus, Ohio, last night. Even more reluctantly he was concluding that Griffin was not in or near the city.

In his office, Dan Hilliard received a phone call from home. He listened, frowning, a coldness climbing his legs.

Then he said, "How can I do that, Ellie? The money should be here in less than an hour now. It's almost 2 o'clock."

He listened again, this time gripping the phone until a spasm of pain shot up the clenched muscles of his arm and reached his neck. He swore without realizing that he had spoken. He couldn't believe what his wife told him; the incredibility of what she said smashed into the tension of his mind that had been straining toward 2:45 for endless hours now.

"You will do it, won't you?" his wife said, with urgency.

"I'll pick up Cindy right away," Dan replied.

When he replaced the instrument and stood up, Dan Hilliard did not know what had happened, or why he was being instructed by Glenn Griffin, through Eleanor, to do what he was now going to do. None of it made any sense at all, but what brought the sour choking rage up in him now was the realization that he had been tricked. The money wasn't coming today. Griffin had known all along. The money had not been mailed until after Griffin had talked to that woman on the phone last night. It could not arrive and be delivered until tomorrow.

Glenn Griffin had lied in order to get him out of the house today, in order to make it appear a normal day, without incident.

Now, however, there was an incident of some sort, and Dan refused to think what it might be. In half an hour he and Cindy were to be parked in an area in front of the stores that formed a shopping center on the far east of the city. That was all he knew. Why they were to be there, for whom they were to wait, what would happen—Glenn Griffin had not told him. And very likely Eleanor didn't know or had been commanded not to say on the phone.

In the employees' elevator Dan pushed a button and rested his burning forehead against the cool metal grating and felt a scalding behind his eyes. You can only push a man so far, he warned Glenn Griffin in his mind. A man can only take so much. Any man. Any man in the world. He was approaching the edge of something and he knew it, without being fully aware of what it was; but he did know, as he tugged at his hat brim and squared his shoulders before leaving the privacy of the elevator, that he could not step over that edge, or precipice. If he took that step, everything he had already done, all that the others had been through, would be wasted effort. By playing their game—whatever it was now—he had a chance, however slight.

It's as simple as that, he told himself savagely. Remember it! He stepped out of the elevator.

Robish was unable, at that same moment, to step from the cubicle that held him. The panting was over now, the wild animal terror was behind him. Back there a bit, crashing through the woods after he realized the truck wouldn't start and he would have to go on foot, he had been scared. Sure, scared. And sore. Mostly sore at that old guy with his wise ideas. Thinking he could pull a fast one on Robish. Remembering the old guy sent a warm pleasant flush down his massive soaked body in the woods: the way the old guy'd tried to run, stifflike, and then the way he stopped, kicking up the gravel with one foot, those skinny little arms going up, and then the way he sprawled while Robish pounded the other two bullets into the jerking body. That memory had caused Robish to grin. They'd all get it just that way, wise bastards.

Glenn thought he was dumb. Oh, Robish knew what Griffin thought. But was he? Hadn't he come out of the edge of the woods, picked the shopping center, found the telephone in the service station, made his call? Wasn't he waiting here now, cozy and tight in the men's room, until the little redhead's car came for him?

From the window he could watch the parking area. His clothes were soggy, his body wet; his breath was getting back to normal; and all he had to do was watch the women climbing in and out of their cars, skittering across puddles, clutching their kids and their groceries. He liked the secret feeling it gave him —the small hot room, the still damp coldness outside, the thought of three bullets left in the gun. He had those bullets earmarked. One for Hilliard, the guy who had slugged him; one for the kid, that brat that caused it. Let Hilliard watch the kid get it first. That'd pay him off. And if Griffin objected— that damn young fool risking their necks just so he could get at some copper who'd busted his good-looking jaw—well, there was a third bullet, wasn't there? He was going to hold the gun from now on. That third bullet could just as easy be for Glenn Griffin.

Robish was feeling great.

Glenn had said a half-hour. Robish had no way to estimate time, but he figured maybe ten minutes had passed since he talked to Griffin, maybe twenty.

Then, in the distance, he heard, very faintly, the wail of a siren. A long way off. It made him grin.

But the grin twisted and left his face sagging. A lot could happen in half an hour. Maybe those cops'd try to surround the woods, figuring that was the way he'd run. He had no idea how long he'd spent plowing through them. Maybe in a half-hour the cops'd work their way through them, out onto the street.

Where was that redhead, *Goddammit!*

"Cindy'll be back in a minute or two, Mr. Hilliard," Chuck Wright said. "Why don't you wait in my office?"

"Where is she?"

Chuck stood back as Dan Hilliard entered his office. He hadn't missed the sharp note of demand in the normally easy-going voice. Nor had he missed the sleepwalking aspects of the man's appearance and manner.

"She's taking dictation from Mr. Hepburn right now," Chuck replied easily and offered cigarettes.

Dan Hilliard either did not want one or did not see them. "How much longer?"

Chuck felt a twitch of annoyance at the man who still stood, hat on head, eyes staring hollowly from under the dripping brim. "I couldn't say," he said, the irritation roughing his words. But he felt it ebb. Why? He could not have said. But the stolid way the other man stood, the slope of those heavy shoulders, and the lined, tired face with the freckles clear on the pale skin, all sent an odd start of alarm through him. "You look——" He started, then stopped himself. "Won't you sit down, sir?" he said.

The *sir* had slipped out, surprising him. He never addressed anyone, even Mr. Hepburn, or his own father, as sir. Point of honor. Pride. Whatever it was, there it was, that was Chuck Wright, take it or leave it.

"Could you interrupt her, Chuck?" Dan Hilliard asked. "It's —important."

"Mr. Hilliard." Chuck took a deep breath. "Is something wrong?"

"Why do you ask that?" The words licked like lashes of a whip.

"I mean—with Cindy. Or you? Someone." Chuck shook his head in a bewildered way and leaned against his desk crossed one ankle over the other. "I don't mean to pry. Perhaps it's none of my business. At first I thought maybe Cindy was just giving me the brush. Some other fellow. Something like that. Now——"

"Now what?"

"I'm damned if I know."

And there it rested. It stayed there because all Dan Hilliard would say was what Cindy had said earlier in the afternoon, after she'd come wandering in ten minutes late after the lunch hour, looking haggard and very tired: "You're imagining things, Chuck." Her father used the same words now.

"It started last night," Chuck said stubbornly, his teeth in it now and very little to bite them into. Then, while Dan Hilliard stood, dripping and unmoving, a raincoated statue in the office, Chuck Wright went over it all for him, what little he had to go over—the way she'd leaped out at him from the house, the way she'd insisted on being taken home after sitting in silence all evening, the abrupt and disturbing tears in the car, and the question about a gun. He watched closely, narrowing his gaze, when he mentioned the gun.

"It doesn't figure, sir. That's all."

"It's not your business, Chuck."

"Maybe not, but——"

"No *maybes* about it. This is not your affair. Stay out of it."

Chuck had not been spoken to in this manner, or with that

much force behind the order, since his days in the Marines. He hadn't liked it then, but it had been part of a pattern that he had to accept. He didn't have to take it now.

"It's my business if it concerns Cindy, Mr. Hilliard."

Then the hat tilted sidewise slightly; the blue eyes snapped to immediate attention, and some of the dazed hardness left them. "So. So it's like that, is it, Chuck?"

"It's like that," Chuck said evenly, "whether you like it or not."

"I don't. I haven't, that is. But I've no time to talk about it now. Or to think about it." The earlier urgency returned to the man; he stepped to the door. "Where's Hepburn's office?"

"I'll get her," Chuck said, moving around the blocky figure, angry and confused but a new kind of suspicion troubling him, a feeling, as he tapped on Mr. Hepburn's door, that whatever this thing was, it was bigger than any feeling Mr. Hilliard might bear toward him. It was, somehow, beyond that, more urgent and vital and desperate.

He spoke a few brief words, saw Cindy rise without so much as turning to Mr. Hepburn, and watched her as she ran out the door. He followed. He saw Cindy join her father; there were a few muttered words between them. Cindy reached for her coat. Dan Hilliard was moving toward the corridor and Cindy, with only one intense but hazy glance over her shoulder, her eyes very much like her father's, followed.

Chuck stood staring at the closed door. All right. Now he'd have to find out on his own.

It's my business if it concerns Cindy. His own words echoed back at him. There you have it, Chuck. You said it yourself. There go all your firm intentions. You're *in.*

That's the way it came to him. He loved Cynthia Hilliard, and where that left him, he didn't know. But he had to find out.

He grabbed his own raincoat and, without a hat as usual, he strode from the office without a backward glance.

4

4

On the street, after he had seen the figures of Dan Hilliard and his daughter, Cindy—the man stiff-legged, solid, grim; the girl swift and graceful at his side—turn into the parking lot where Cindy kept her car during the day, Chuck Wright had a quick moment of panic. Would he lose them before he could get, unseen, to his own car, the low-slung sports job in the same downtown lot, and onto the street behind them? Cindy, he saw, did the driving, and she was not wasting time; the mystery of her urgency worked like a soreness through him. She didn't pause in the thin mid-afternoon traffic, but swung right, north, and shot out of sight before Chuck could ease his way out of the parking lot.

In the midtown area no turns were permitted between noon and 6, and it was this accident of timing that allowed him to pick up speed and narrow the distance until he saw, two blocks ahead, the black coupe make a right turn, bearing east. He followed. It was not difficult to stay behind Cindy's car, but he was careful to keep a fair distance and, as much as possible, to stay out of line of her rear-view mirror.

She was not going home. Chuck tried not to conjecture as to what business she and her father might have at this time of day on the east side of town.

A siren was such an ordinary and expected sound on a city thoroughfare that, at first, Chuck felt no surprise when the Sheriff's car whizzed past. But when others followed—three, perhaps four, and an ambulance—he began to think of an accident east of the city. Had Mr. Hilliard heard of it? Then he had come and picked up Cindy, refusing to talk, brushing aside everything else, and they were now on their way to the scene. But, of course, that didn't explain last night, or the strange silent morning, or the long intense phone call Cindy had made; above all, it didn't explain her startling tears and the question about the gun.

When, not twenty minutes later, Cindy's black coupe edged itself into a parking space in the paved area before a block of stores, one of those new shopping centers that had sprung up on the edges of the city, the siren wails were distant, well beyond the woods to the northeast. Chuck dismissed his questions about these and drew to a halt behind the sleek white service station on the corner; he waved the attendant away and worked with the air hose at his rear wheels while he watched.

Almost at once, a man emerged from the service station itself—a ponderous bulk of man in a rain-soaked gray suit, sloshing through the puddles—and at first Chuck made no connection between his direction and the coupe. Still, Mr. Hilliard and Cindy remained seated behind the steady swish-swish of windshield wipers. It was not raining. It had not been raining since they left the downtown office building. But apparently Cindy had not even noticed.

Before Chuck could let the surprise of this observation reach him fully, he found himself clutching the air hose and staring. The man approached Cindy's car, spoke through the suddenly lowered window to Mr. Hilliard, waited while Mr. Hilliard climbed out of the car; then the man in the gray suit slid his great body into the seat beside Cindy. Mr. Hilliard, still without speaking, with not so much as a nod of recognition, stepped back in and closed the door. The car backed up, shot forward, returned to the street, splashing and shooting water like a jet spray from the angrily spinning rear tires.

Chuck didn't wait. He was behind them then, well behind but with the coupe in clear vision on the north-south highway-like street that skirted the city on the east. The square mass of the strange man's head was between the other two, and well concealed from both sides. Chuck considered passing the coupe, twisting to get a full look at the man, but the little sports car was conspicuous, and Cindy would recognize him at once. He didn't want her to know he was doing this. At least not yet. But something more than this held him back: the memory of the shambling walk, the furtiveness of the big man as he shot a quick suspicious glance around him back there before he climbed into the seat. And now the way he sat safely between them, low in the seat, only the top of his head visible from behind. The man wore no hat. This in itself was worth noting, Chuck decided; he wore none himself, but most men of middle age, especially on rainy days, would not think of going out without a hat. And the man wore no topcoat, either.

Who was he? What could a man like that have to do with the Hilliards? The black-sheep uncle? The family drunkard, threatening social disgrace? He'd probably find the explanation that innocuous and simple in the end.

Then what about the gun? What would a gun have to do with it?

Chuck trailed the coupe all the way north, hardly surprised at the complicated route Cindy followed, aware that it was not the shortest but the least populated way to Kessler Boulevard. On the open countrylike stretches, he remained far behind, knowing that if Cindy glanced into the rear-view mirror she would recognize his car at once.

In the end, Chuck had no answers: the coupe pulled into the Hilliard driveway as he knew it would. He stopped, far down the boulevard, out of sight.

Well, now what have you got? Where does this leave you? Dead end, blind alley.

"Where does it leave us, Jess?" Tom Winston asked, moving delicately on his fat legs away from the frail outstretched body of the dead man.

Jesse Webb strode even farther away from the sodden lifeless thing lying half in a puddle by the corner of the ramshackle gray building; Jesse stepped to the two uprooted blue pumps and half-leaned against the red truck. Sudden and violent death, of which he had had a certain amount of experience both during the war and after, invariably drained him, at least for a short time, of all respect for his kind, for the human race in general.

"Funny thing," Jesse said, one hand against the high fender, "I knew him. Not well. He was one of those old fellows used to play pinochle with my old man." Although it had stopped raining, the fender of the truck was still wet. Jesse wiped it dry with his handkerchief. "Lucky for us these tanks weren't loaded, huh?" He spread out on the flat top of the fender the few pitiful belongings he had taken from Mr. Patterson's pockets: a dog-eared wallet with the usual papers, a driver's license and $25 inside; four single dollar bills that had been folded in another pocket, a chewed-at stub of pencil, odd scraps of paper, a squashed package of cigarettes and a paper of matches, and nine checks, each made out for $2 payable to Floyd Patterson.

"Not so lucky for him, maybe," Tom Winston conjectured mildly, unable to pull his eyes away completely from the various official-looking figures now bending over the sprawled dead thing. "Maybe he'd rather a-gone that way."

"Who gets to choose?" Jesse said, unfolding the scraps of paper, flattening them out: a grocery list with the words "razor blades" circled heavily, a garage repair bill marked paid, and one other.

"Shot in the back. Three times. Why, Jess?"

Jesse rubbed the back of his neck, feeling the heat there despite the wet, winter-edged chill in the air. "It's a good question, Tom. He was a sweet guy. Why'd he try to smash into those pumps? Or was that an accident? You tell me, Tom."

"The state police are making a circle, starting at Arlington. The truck won't go, so they figure—and I'm with them—the killer had to take off on foot. They've got ten men in those woods and more coming. But hell, it happened so long ago now. Hardly nobody uses this road now that Twenty-first Street is paved all the way. My hunch is——"

"Hold it," Jesse Webb said, and very, very quietly—so that, hearing the words, Tom Winston felt a slow, odd shiver moving up his back. "God," Jesse breathed. He was holding between his long fingers, fingers that were beginning to shake just a little now, the last small scrap of soiled paper from Mr. Patterson's pocket. "God, Tom."

Winston bent over, studied the figures printed in pencil on the paper, then straightened and looked up into the thin, expressionless face of Jesse Webb.

Far off a siren wailed. The sound cut through Jesse, cut to the bone.

"He might've got just a quick glance," Winston said, beginning to breathe a little tightly himself. "He might've been in a hurry, y'know. That'd explain the 3."

"Maybe he heard it on the radio," Jesse drawled in a thin voice that said he knew better—or hoped. "Maybe he jotted it down from the radio, just in case, the way an old man might."

"People do that," Winston conceded, but he couldn't get

enough of the thin cold air into his lungs. "But if you change the 3 to an 8, you got it. I reckon he was in a hurry, y'know, and his eyes not what they once was. If you change that 3, you got it."

"Just for a while," said Jesse Webb slowly, eyes squinting, "just for a while now, Tom, we're going to change that 3 to an 8. We'll just kind of pretend Mr. Patterson doesn't have a radio in that little old house he lived in alongside the dump out west. We're going to pretend he saw that license, hear? And then we're going to locate that car. First, these checks. Are they all from the same neighborhood? How many other houses in that neighborhood that Mr. Patterson might have seen today, huh? Or maybe in some woods around there. I'm going to find out where he's been today, Tom, and I'm going to scour it all down with a wire brush." He was beginning to speak faster now—no drawl, no thoughtful hesitation. "And you're going to start working backwards on those checks—and all the rest of Mr. Patterson's customers—names and addresses and telephone numbers, kind of people, where they work, what they've been doing. The works. That might include a hundred, two hundred people."

"Go ahead, Jess, say it."

"I don't like to say it, Tom."

"Say it, Jess. This is it!"

"God, Tom—it might be. It might be. We got the license again. Right here in town like I said all along. I *said* it, Tom!" He was moving toward the Sheriff's car, in long swift strides. "We got the license. Now we're going to get that car. Get on it, Winston. If they pick up anybody in the woods, give it to me fast. Tell 'em who we're looking for now, Tom. Let's get on it, hear?"

Behind the wheel, he felt the hope thrust aside the nagging apprehension, overpower even the outrage and disgust. You can't stretch coincidence too far, he warned himself; on the other hand, you can't overlook a single alley. Alleys were where rats hid. He trounced on the accelerator and flipped on the siren. Something very like joy, very like hope, was ripping through him.

That car had been seen in town. Today! It might still be in town. Glenn Griffin would be capable of pumping three slugs into the back of that poor old man. The District Attorney would work all the other angles. For his part, Jesse Webb was sticking to the original tack. It all figured. The telephone angle had played itself out. Every call from Columbus to Indianapolis last night had been checked. Nothing doing. But this——

He was going to find that gray sedan with the license number that was imprinted on his mind like a steaming brand.

"The car's hot now, Pop. Not like it was before, see. But our pal Robish here, he got jumpy and he didn't go through the old guy's pockets way he should——"

"I told you he wrecked the——"

"Shut up, Robish, let me talk. I got important things to say to Hilliard now."

Hank Griffin leaned against the paneled wall of the den and, casting a glance every once in a while into the back yard or driveway on the side, he listened to them in the living room. Glenn had something in his mind; if you watched him and listened, you could almost see that motor clicking, purring along in there. Hank had always admired his brother's mind, the quick sharp way it worked, the way it made decisions. That mind was the reason he, Hank, was here now. And free.

A slow, ironic smile curled inside him without reaching his face. Free. He had never been less free, not even in the cell.

"See, Pop, it's like this. Robish here has got hold of a gun and he won't let go. He's not going to use that gun again because I'm not going to let him. You heard my little brother Hank a few minutes ago. He won't let go his gun, either. Not while Robish hangs onto his. So you might say, Pop, I'm helpless as you are. There's only one difference. Hank in there and Robish, they haven't got half a brain between 'em. Without me, they're cooked, and they both know it. Now. What are we going to do about that farmer's car out there in the garage?"

Dan Hilliard did not answer. Since he came in with his daughter and Robish some time ago, he had said nothing to Glenn, not a word; he just sat bent forward in his chair like that, staring, looking almost dead himself except for those dark hot coals in the eye sockets. Hank knew that nothing made Glenn more furious than to be ignored, and he could feel the way the man's continued silence was rubbing along his brother's nerves.

"I asked a question, Hilliard."

Dan Hilliard shifted his head, glanced from his wife, who didn't move at all, to his son, who sat curled up on the sofa watching him, to his daughter. Hank followed the moving gaze, already feeling the tight anticipation rising in him as he looked at the girl. She was a little apart from the others, standing in a certain aloof way that made Hank go all sick and faint inside. It wasn't the same kind of sickness he had felt when he heard Robish tell about killing the man; then, seeing Robish's light-hearted mood, almost gay, and sensing that under it lay something else, something uglier and more terrible—a kind of relief, relaxation, calm—Hank had been actually, physically sick. Then, seeing the girl's face twist with disgust, he had gone faint and empty, too. But this now was different. This was like looking in the window of a store, one of those fancy stores, and seeing a fine table all set up, with odd-shaped glasses glistening and silver with that high gleam on it, and the wood of the chairs all smooth and shining, and being able to picture people coming into that room, in their crisp-looking clothes, the women with their shoulders bare. A sick longing hollowed you inside, took everything away, left you weak and knowing. Knowing you'd lost something, something you'd never had and never could have, to hear Glenn tell it. But knowing that only made the hunger worse . . . This is the way it was every time he looked at the girl. And he couldn't fight it.

"Hilliard, you speak when I talk to you. Got me?"

The harsh, demanding growl wrenched Hank's attention back to his brother. For as long as Hank could remember, Glenn had told him, one way or the other, that if you wanted something, there was only one way to get it in this world: take it. Take it, Hank. Get a gun if you have to, but take it.

Hank didn't have half a brain. Glenn had said it. One minute Glenn was joking with you, kidding along in that low-voiced way that made you feel he was thinking about you and taking care of you; next, he was making some crack like that, showing he thought you were a damn fool. But this was the first time Hank could remember that Glenn had said a thing like that straight out in front of other people.

Especially in front of *her*.

"Griffin——" Hank relaxed slightly, a wire letting go somewhere inside, when he heard Dan Hilliard's voice. The man sounded tired, and old. "Griffin, by helping Robish to get back here after he'd shot a man, I've already placed myself in the position of being accessory after the fact."

There it was; that was the phrase Hank had been reaching for ever since he heard Robish telling about it. Accessory after the fact. Only, in Hank's case, maybe it was worse; he remembered hearing once, somewhere, that even if you didn't pull the trigger——

"So if you think I'm going to do any more of your dirty work for you, you're wrong." Hilliard's voice was level and empty and dry.

Glenn thought this was funny; he laughed; he even threw an arm over Hilliard's wide, thick shoulders. "Pop, you're a smart cookie, and you got guts. But you got to be reasonable. Look at my position. The kid's been yammering at me all day to go. I can't go, I tell him—throw all this over just cause we run into a little guy who can't mind his own business? You know what'd happen then, Hilliard? That dough'd come to your office tomorrow morning and I'd be miles away, and no chance to get my little job here in town taken care of. I worked for that money, Pop. Me and Hank. We can't throw any of it away. We pleaded innocent, see. That means we didn't get the money in the first place. Now you follow me, Pop?"

The money wasn't worth it. Paying off Jesse Webb wasn't worth it. Nothing was worth sticking here now with a man dead and the cops liable to close in any minute! Another part of Hank's mind also cried, *These people have had enough!* His muscles throbbed with the certainty that they should go, move, get out. But Glenn was making the decisions. Glenn always made them. And he was usually right.

Dan Hilliard was shaking his head. "I don't know what to tell you. The car's safe enough in the garage. No one else is likely to come and if you try to take it out——"

"I'm not going to take it out, Hilliard. *You* are."

The words silenced the room, stopped Hank Griffin's heart. *You're crazy, Glenn,* he said in silence. *Crazy.*

"Soon as it gets good and dark out, but not too late, see, cause you don't want any prowl cars spotting you after all the other cars're off the street. You're going out there to the garage and you're going to take the license plates off it. Tell you what, put the ones on from the redhead's coupe. You wouldn't want to get pinched for driving without plates, Hilliard. Ruin your reputation."

"Griffin——" This time it was Robish's voice, and he was pushing himself into the room from the hall. "Griffin, they pick up this guy, he'll start talking. Let the car alone."

"Is that right, Hilliard? *Would* you start talking?"

Dan Hilliard shook his head slowly, no expression on his broad face.

In the den Hank, who had writhed and blistered for years under the stinging mockery of his brother's tongue, felt that thin wash of pity in him again. He hated it. He clenched his fists to kill it: what the hell did he care about these people anyway? Hilliard—just another sucker living a sucker's life, going to work every day, getting old fast, for peanuts! Dumb bastard.

"See, Robish? Hilliard's too wise to start talking even if he is caught. Me, I trust Hilliard. He'd pull a fast one if he figured he had a chance, but he knows now he hasn't got a chance, so he's going to play ball. I got him where the hair's short, that's why I trust him. You listening, Hank? That's the only time you ever take a chance trusting anybody."

Lesson noted, Hank thought bitterly, a constriction in his chest. Same lesson. He had it. He had to admit the truth of it, too. Glenn was reminding him that the last time he'd pleaded with his brother to go, Glenn had warned him that Hilliard couldn't be trusted once they didn't have one of the family right alongside. This was why Glenn planned to take the wife and the girl along when they did leave. Hank had balked; not the girl. But Glenn's smile had withered his rebellion; the taunting, knowing look had stomped it down, even as Glenn had agreed with a shrug: *Hell, we'll take the kid then, it make you feel any better, Hank. Only don't go soft on me, see. You go soft, you're licked.*

Hank wasn't going soft. Not now. This time they'd really let him have it; this time he was a murderer. He hadn't killed, but that ape Robish had, and that meant the chair for all three of them. Life, anyway. *If* he was caught. He wasn't going to be caught. But if Glenn kept running these damn-fool risks, they'd all be shooting it out, or feeling the 'cuffs hard and cold over their wrists. Only not him. Before that, he'd get out on his own. He didn't like the idea of Robish's gun at his back anyway—after what happened last night.

But he was still glad he let Robish have it; without knowing it until then, he'd been wanting to do that for a long time. And he knew he could. He could use his fists. If Robish got close enough to pull him down, to get that weight working—well, maybe then he couldn't handle the big man. But with his arms free, hell, he could rip the man apart without Robish's even seeing what was happening. It was the one thing he could do well. The one thing. He realized it. He had always thought it was something, quite a lot. Now——

His eyes drifted again to the girl. She was watching her father. Hank remembered the way, last night, she'd said, *Thank you, Mr. Griffin.* That memory and the expression of pity on her beautiful face now caught Hank like a double blow to the stomach; he felt the breath leave him.

As Dan Hilliard said, "I'll dump the car in the river for you, Griffin, I know just the place," Hank felt the sick hollowness return. He was aching with it, empty. And he couldn't take his eyes from the girl's lovely face even though that was the source of all his pain. It was almost, he realized, as if he wanted to suffer; it was almost as if he had never had a chance to suffer in just this way before, about a girl, and he needed it. That need was part of the hunger.

"You play square with me, Pop," Glenn was saying, "and I'll play square with you, see."

Square? *Square!* When you plan to take his wife with you, to use his child as a shield! Not for the first time but for the first time in this cold and single-minded way, Hank hated his brother. Glenn was the only person in the world who had ever shown him any real kindness or had taught him anything about the world. Glenn had protected him from his mother's drunken disdain, from his father's brutal violence. Yet Hank hated him now; under all the twisted trust and love, he hated him. Facing that fact made Hank Griffin forget everything else, even the eternal prodding fear that perhaps the police were, by some combination of circumstances beyond his imagining, moving closer even now . . .

Working with the city directory and several maps, Jesse had, by 5 o'clock, located the exact sites of the houses that Mr. Floyd Patterson had visited, or probably visited, that morning. At least he had now the locations of the homes of those people who had written checks to Mr. Patterson in payment for trash removal. It was safe to assume that those who paid by cash were nearby. He had drawn a red-ink marking around the neighborhood, consisting of approximately ten square city blocks—perhaps two hundred homes, three stores, several vacant lots.

"I don't want those cars up there prowling around, Tom. Hear?" He shifted the map about on his desk. "I don't say they're in there. I don't even reckon it's reasonable to think they are. It's a nice high-toned sort of neighborhood. And if they knocked off Mr. Patterson, they'd be damn fools to stay. One thing Griffin ain't is a damn fool. But three human beings can't disappear into thin air. It don't stand to reason."

"What about that bank job up near Peru?" Tom Winston inquired mildly.

"Yeah, that's good. I just got a final report on that one. Two guys stick up a bank in a one-horse town named Denver nobody ever heard of. Two people, including a cashier who ought to know better, swear it's the Griffin boys. They were willing to swear on their family Bibles they recognized them both—till three hours later a scared young farm boy moseys into the police station in Peru and confesses. His conscience hurts. Meanwhile, half the country lets go with a sigh of relief, thinking we're finally on those boys' tail. Don't tell me that's the way it always goes, either. I *know* that. But it doesn't help."

"Take it easy, Jess," Tom Winston advised, studying the map.

"And don't tell me to take it easy."

"I'll tell you what," Tom Winston said then, "let's you and me go outside and fight. That won't help locate Griffin, but it'd let off steam, maybe."

115

Jesse laughed then; he liked the sound. He liked the way it made him feel, all down his long frame. He returned to the map. "We got four cars up there, right? Tell 'em to park. Put one here, another here, and here and here. That covers the main roads out. My hunch is they won't have any particular hankering to go through the city to get away." He straightened and took a breath. "Where's Kathleen?"

"She went to a movie. She said we keep the offices too hot in the daytime, too cold at night."

Jesse laughed again.

"Sorry to intrude, gentlemen," a voice said from the doorway, and young Carson entered. "The city police for some reason that I don't get—maybe out of resentment at you, Webb—have been sitting on this since noon." He handed Jesse a sheet of white paper with a few words written on it in ink. Carson took off his glasses and rubbed the steam from them. "It came in at the station some time during the noon hour. A bellhop from one of the hotels brought it, and he gave four different descriptions of the man who paid him a five-dollar tip to deliver it. I was privileged to get the fifth and sixth descriptions just now."

As Jesse read, the laughter died out of him. Then he passed it over into Tom Winston's fat fingers. Reading, Winston softly whistled, a cool note in the lone sound.

After that, the three men stood looking at each other in silence.

"Now we know," Tom Winston said, at last.

"The idiot," Jesse Webb muttered.

"The man's on a spot, friends," Carson said.

"But he ought to know! God, doesn't he know?" Jesse asked no one in particular. "Can't he guess that he can't play ball with savages like that?"

"Easy now," Tom Winston said.

"Don't keep up with that, Winston! I'm *taking* it easy!

116

Think of that poor guy, trapped in his own house probably with those——"

"Let's find out where he is, Jess. That's more important than——"

"Lay off! Let me do this my way. Whole damn FBI on the case, city police sitting on evidence, letting us sweat——" He stopped when he saw Winston's mouth open; then he rushed on: "You tell me to go easy once more, Tom, and I *will* take you outside!"

"Speaking of evidence," young Carson put in swiftly, "what's this?" He picked up the map.

"That's not evidence," Jesse Webb said, slumping into his chair. "That's guesswork. Plain and not-so-fancy guesswork by Deputy Sheriff Webb. Look, Carson, isn't there some way to get word to that guy, whoever he is, that he can't play their game with them?"

"How?" Carson asked.

"Tell me," Jesse challenged. *"You* take a stab in the dark this time, Federal man. They'll tear that poor guy to ribbons before they're done. Inside and out. You can't co-operate with scum like that."

"No?" Carson lit a cigarette. "What would you do, Webb? Put yourself in his place. I think he was smart to write this thing, the way he did. It might keep some itchy-fingered young cop from shooting a woman or a child."

"Itchy-fingered like me, Carson?" Jesse asked testily.

"You got more sense. That's all that's eating you, friend. You know what a spot the man's on. What would you do, Webb, under the circumstances?"

"He'd play ball," Tom Winston told Carson, touching Jesse Webb's shoulder with his balled fist, then pushing at him again, fondly.

"Yeah," said Jesse slowly, the probing fingers of hatred moving in him, opening scars. "I'd do just that, Tom. Or I'd try."

117

Dan Hilliard was trying. The steel-hard shaft of frustration and helplessness was driven deep in him now, so deep that ordinary thoughts, even the fears that had once been sharp in his mind, were shadowy, distant things. What was important was the immediate, the exact moment now and the one to follow. He was aware that he drove a car that was wanted by the police; the license plates from Cindy's coupe might throw off a questioning policeman, if, by some evil chance, a state patrol car should notice him. Also, his own appearance behind the wheel —although he had good reason to believe that this was far from normal—would perhaps mislead them. He had already disposed of the license plates that were on the gray sedan. *I'll leave that up to you, Hilliard,* Glenn Griffin had said before he left the house. *You won't take any chances. Hell, it's as important to you as it is to me.*

More important, Dan told himself grimly. Much more.

He had tossed the plates into a thicket along the side of a small street on which there were no houses; the street ran only two city blocks and was intended for a subdivision development, with the realtor's sign on the corner. He had then turned around and flooded the thicket with headlights: there was not so much as a glint of metal. He felt reasonably sure that he had not been seen.

Now he was driving, careful to use the small, narrow residential streets, to the west, avoiding all major intersections, crossing principal thoroughfares by way of obscure side streets. With nightfall a gusty wind had leaped up again, and the penetrating cold left the streets more deserted than usual at this hour. He was within the city limits, his mind informing him that in this manner he could work his way more inconspicuously toward the river. His eyes shifted back and forth from the wet pavement ahead, scanning the sidewalks and cross streets automatically for any sign of danger, to the rear-view mirror.

He was within three blocks of the river bridge, in sight of the ghostly-looking frames of the Riverside Amusement Park, which was dark and shuttered, when he realized that a pair of headlights had been following him around two seemingly directionless turns. This was not the first time that he had experienced this suspicion in the five or six miles he had come, but it brought his aching muscles to taut attention again. He made a sharp left turn down a shabby street, then a right. He slowed then, carefully.

The twin lights swung into view in the mirror.

Dan felt no panic; even fear seemed a useless and rather pointless emotion; he had passed beyond all that now. His job was to lose those following lights. Yet he couldn't speed. And any other out-of-the-ordinary action on the part of the car might call attention. There were only the two beams of light, still fairly far behind; as yet no red gleam of a third, although he fully expected this now and had no idea how he would behave if or when it appeared. The thought that he, Dan Hilliard, was afraid of the police flickered ironically in a far corner of his brain. He was in a neighborhood that he did not know at all: squat and ugly, weathered old frame houses. A few lights glimmered behind misty windows.

Only by the gusts of steam bursting from between his own lips was he made aware that he was breathing too fast. He made another turn, into a narrow street with no overhanging street lamp. The shadows of trees fell dark and flat across his path.

Then it came to him: he knew exactly what he would do, and how he would do it. And now, now before his pursuer turned the corner! He chose a driveway that ran close alongside a dark house; he judged the turn carefully, then flipped off his headlights, whipped the wheel, cut the motor, and let the gray sedan glide to a quiet stop hugging the side of the house and under the deeper shadow of a small frame garage.

He twisted about in the seat, every muscle protesting with stabs of anguish, his head heavy and bursting; he waited, trying to hold his breath, looking out the rear window. Down the street—he had no idea how far away—a door banged shut, a man's voice rose, died. In the house at his side, so close he could reach out a window and touch the rough clapboard, there was no stirring.

Then light flooded the street as the car that had been following picked up speed; the motor roar reverberated through the neighborhood. After the car had passed, Dan could hear the motor slowing into a purr, pausing, hesitating. In that moment that it passed, he could see nothing but its shape: it was a huge convertible, the outline of the soft top fairly clear in the reflection of its own headlight beams.

Without stopping now to puzzle this out, feeling only a sharp relief that it was not a police car, Dan turned on the motor but not the lights, eased the gray sedan backward; when the convertible made a turn—Dan was tensed, hearing only the sound of that distant motor—he backed into the narrow street, careful not to give the carburetor too much gas, and nosed away, in the direction from which he had come.

Only when he was crossing the river bridge, confident now that no lights followed, did Dan Hilliard begin to wonder again about the identity of the huge convertible and its driver. Here was a whole new unlooked-for element, and his mind could not quite bring it fully into the picture. It was his conviction that no policeman, at least while on duty, would drive a car like that; also, not many police officers, if any, could afford to own one like that, either. But if it was not a policeman who had recognized the gray sedan, who could it be?

Dismissing the conjecture, again concentrating on the immediate moment at hand, he turned north on the far side of the river, following a wide road that hugged the low river-cliff. The whole area here had a park atmosphere; soon he was under high trees with the dark gleam of water on his right. The river along here was, he knew, deep enough. But it was too close to the city proper, perhaps even within the city's limits. And there were people.

120

Cars approached occasionally, their headlights lowering when he automatically flipped his own; only once in a while did a set of lights appear in the rear-view mirror. Dan had, each time, to make the decision: should I let this one pass or should I try to outdistance it? Is this the convertible? Or perhaps a patrol car? And each time he decided to hold to his original plan: appear inconspicuous. Each time they whipped around him, usually filled with young people on dates.

But as Dan approached the place that he had in mind—a high cliff perhaps a hundred yards beyond the point where the smooth wide pavement curved left and became only an ordinary country road—he couldn't rid himself of the questions about that convertible back there. An ordinary citizen who recognized the gray sedan from the police descriptions on the radio? Someone who only wanted to get close enough to catch the license number, perhaps?

He knew no one personally who drove a long locomotive-type convertible like that. Then it could not have been simply a friend who had recognized him. That didn't make sense, anyway. No one has the slightest idea of the situation you're in, he reminded himself. You imagine everyone suspects, just as you become suspicious of every car that approaches or passes, simply because they have brought you to this criminal state of mind where the most normal things take on menace. It's a world they live in all the time. Now it's your world. In that sense, you're one of them.

He was searching now for a place where he would turn off the road. He had only the vaguest impression of the area. As a boy he had swum in the river along here, but then, at the top of the bluff, there had been only a narrow dirt road, rarely used. Now, after the curve of park drive had become narrow country road, everything looked different again, not the way he remembered it at all. He had swum and picked berries and even now he could taste the sun-heated juice of them as they burst in his mouth. The city lay far south of him now, several miles away. His own house, if he could cut straight across the river instead of backtracking to the bridge, was not too far, perhaps four miles, perhaps five. As yet, though, he had not faced the future hours or that return home. He had warned Griffin that this would take time if he was to do it properly, if the car was not to be found at all; he had even told a little of his plan. Griffin had whistled, in awe. "You got a walk in front of you, Hilliard." No, it was Dan's idea that Cindy would follow in her car and pick him up. When Griffin had only moved his head in a slow negative and said, "Not a chance: the more Hilliards there are around here tonight, the better," Dan had caught, in young Hank Griffin's face, a surly rebellion—that may or may not have been directed at his brother.

No time for all that now, Dan told himself harshly; no time now for all those unlooked-for cross-currents that in themselves might prove more treacherous than anything the police or the family could do. He decided to turn around: he had passed the deep part, the hollowed-out pool that he had known as a boy. But when he stopped, nosed into a clump of trees and underbrush that lay between the road and the river's high edge, he saw that there were car ruts penetrating the thicket. Did they lead to the edge of the bluff?

After he had satisfied himself that he could maneuver the car through the wet and black-shadowed grove, Dan climbed back into the seat and sat for a split second behind the wheel. He was breaking the law. He, Dan Hilliard, was guilty of committing a crime. The thought had no meaning to him, and he was not even surprised. He edged the sedan into the trees, the branches scraping and crying against the metal. At the edge of the bluff, he set the brake and clambered out again, stood listening in the silence, with the headlight beams stabbing the darkness over the water. Down below the river was almost soundless. Far downstream he caught the occasional glitter of other headlights striking across the water's surface from the highway he had just traveled. He studied the grassy and bush-tangled shelf; there were no obstacles. Then his eyes came upon a wiry-looking sapling that jutted out angularly just below the drop-off. He cursed himself for not anticipating this; he should have brought along a saw from the garage. Clinging with one hand to the roots of a bush outjutting from the black earth, he climbed down the muddy bank a few feet and tested the tension of the small tree. Would the sapling deflect the car's downward plunge? And in what way?

But he was helpless without a tool of some sort; the thin tree was securely rooted.

The car had to go all the way down. It had to reach the water. The crash would be loud and there was the chance that it would attract attention. But Dan Hilliard, at this point, had grown accustomed to calculating risks; he knew that a certain recklessness, backed by careful consideration of the odds, was necessary. This recklessness seemed to have become a part of his life. He even wondered, pulling himself up onto the level ground and standing upright again, whether this recklessness had been a part of his nature forever.

When had the men come? Only last night? Impossible! The intervening time had taken on an endless quality. Sliding into the seat, his body wet and his shoes clogged with mud, Dan wasn't able to look ahead to tomorrow morning, to the 9:30 mail tomorrow morning. The past and future did not exist now. He threw the gears into reverse, backing into trees and stumps three times before he felt that he was far enough away from the edge of the cliff to gain the necessary momentum on the wet grass to shoot the car out and over the sapling.

He didn't hesitate now. He plunged into the moment heedlessly, his mind working in that automatic way again: he threw the car into forward gear, tapped the accelerator experimentally, racing the motor, his left foot holding down the clutch. He felt with his left elbow to make sure the door was open and warned himself that his left hand must let go that door handle at the same instant that his right hand tore itself away from the steering wheel. He bore down on the gas, released the clutch, held the wheel steady, saw the black void rushing toward him and in it Eleanor's face floating toward him. His ears filled with the crackling of the tree limbs and roar of motor and the angry grind of tires in soggy earth.

Then he plunged sideways, throwing himself violently as the void reached for him, feeling a thorny prickling against his face and the jolt of hard earth under his body. Then the whole world filled to bursting with the thundering descent of the car. Dan lay curled in the underbrush as that sound echoed and reverberated, gnashing, crushing and ugly. He knew that the car had rolled, and it seemed now never to stop rolling. The splash was abrupt—first, the solid slap-sounding smack, then a series of gurgles and gasps, as though some living monster were battling for life below the edge of the bluff. Finally the bubbling slackened into utter stillness.

Dan rolled onto his back, breathing shallowly.

Had it gone under? He crawled to the precipice. The sapling quivered with a faint rusty crackle of leaves. Below, there was nothing. Sheer dark.

Dan stood up unsteadily, shaking. He couldn't know whether the car had gone under. He couldn't tell what daylight—and perhaps some hunter in the surrounding woods—would discover.

He was faced now with the hours-long walk back to the house. The trick now, he knew without thought, was to keep from thinking, from wondering. The trick now was to get away from this spot as fast as possible and to make one leaden foot follow the other over those miles, all the while forcing his mind ahead, all the while peering forward to that inevitable moment tomorrow when they would leave. What was he going to do then? How was he going to prevent their taking anyone along in the car?

Perhaps, before he arrived home, he would have the answer to that.

"Supposin' you're right then," Lieutenant Fredericks of the State Police was saying to Jesse Webb. "Supposin' this guy's in the fix you think he is. I agree with that much. But why then are they stickin' around? And when they're ready to take off, is he going to be any better off? He says it right here in his letter, doesn't he? If those sonsabitches take his wife along, f'instance, how's he going to be any better off'n if we start searching all those houses right now? And stop shaking your head that way. You're givin' me the fidgets."

Jesse hadn't known that he was shaking his head, but he made a conscious effort to stop it. This Lieutenant Fredericks had already given him the fidgets, if that's what you called them. He didn't like being called into a man's office, in the first place; Fredericks had no authority over him and he was taking a lot on himself to question him about his procedure. Co-operation was one thing; this superior-speaking-to-underling was something else again. Jesse had to admit that, on the face of it, it didn't look as if he was accomplishing much. He'd answered the questions civilly enough, sitting hunched forward in the State House office, trying to explain, over and over, to the short, crisp elderly man in uniform just why he was not trying to close in, that as yet he had no house to close in on.

"Maybe he's not going to be any better off," Jesse drawled. "But that's a decision I reckon the man's got a right to make on his own now."

"The hell he has! This is police work, son. Nobody wants to see innocent people hurt. But we can't sit on our cans forever waiting for them to make the move. You got the list of that trashman's customers——"

"Mr. Patterson," Jesse suggested.

"Sure, the old garbage collector. Hell, son, it was your deduction that the old boy had seen the car, not mine. But you got to follow through. The garbageman's dead——"

"Mr. Patterson," Jesse corrected again.

"What's the chip on your shoulder, Webb? It ain't becom-

125

ing, son. We got to work together on this. So you got cars planted up there around the neighborhood. You know how easy it'd be for that gray sedan to slip out of that? I'll tell you. Any man with reasonable intelligence could do it if he never had any experience, that's how. For all we know they've done it already. Up and gone. Your telephone hunch played itself out, didn't it? Maybe this one will, too. But son, we'll never know unless we try. Let's get men moving up there. Knock on a few doors, ring those bells, ask about the car—about this Mr. Patterson. Innocent questions. What can we lose?"

"We can force their hand," Jesse said with slow patience running thin.

"Now you're talking!"

"And they can jump to the idea that this guy, whoever wrote this letter, tipped us off. They can plug him, or his wife, or his kid or kids."

"You can't put off a showdown, son."

Jesse stood up. "Look. Nobody wants a showdown any more'n I do. Not you or every trooper in Indiana. But by all the rules, with my superior out of town now, I reckon this comes under my jurisdiction—unless the FBI has other ideas. Carson doesn't—because we've talked about it. It'd take us all night and part of tomorrow to work our way through that whole damn neighborhood, *ringing doorbells*. No thanks. I want 'em flushed, Lieutenant, but not if they're going to shoot up somebody's family just because I can't wait."

"While you're waiting," the lieutenant said testily, "an old man gets three in the back. Nothing I can see's going to stop that happening again."

Jesse stopped in the office doorway; he was shaking his head again. "We weren't waiting when that happened, Lieutenant —I mention that just for the record. We didn't have anything then, remember?"

"Webb, let me tell you something. Let me give you a little advice. How long since you've had any sleep?" And as Jesse waved a hand, he nodded. "Okay. It might be a dead-end guess and it might pay off. I'll get you as many men as you want on this, Webb. Put 'em all over the streets, anywhere. But I tell you, Webb, this slob that wrote this don't have the chance of a snowball in hell and I, for one, thinks he needs help, and plenty of it. Don't take it personal, what I just said, Deputy. I'm a sour old man and I hate to see you young punks make fools of yourselves. If they are up there and they slip away, you'll be looking for work, son."

"I'll take that chance," Jesse Webb said, feeling raw all through. "But I could use some men. Thanks."

Lieutenant Fredericks stood staring after the young lanky deputy. He spat into a brass cuspidor alongside his desk. Raring to go all day, he thought, and now he's stopped dead in his tracks. Hell, he was ringing doorbells himself this morning!

Jesse emerged on the high State House steps. It was a dull night, with a few ugly clouds drifting pale gray against the bitter dark sky. He felt a little faint. Not enough food and too much coffee and too many blind alleys, he thought; and the thought brought to mind Kathleen. She was in another movie now, her third today; then one of the deputies was to take her to Jesse's mother's house on the south side for the night. Remembering his own curled fear about Kathleen, Jesse was reminded again of the unidentified man's pitiful, pleading letter. For a moment, as he paused there staring into the city streets where only a few people moved, secure and unafraid and not even conscious of the Griffin brothers and a man named Robish, Jesse Webb thought, with envy of them, that maybe it would be a good idea to get another job, anyway. But by the time he was in his car again and cruising northward to the area that had become *the neighborhood* in his mind, an area defined on the surface of his brain by the same red mark he had drawn on that city map in his office this afternoon, he felt a slow return of the banked-down excitement.

Griffin was in town. Jesse's hunch on that had been right,

he'd swear to that much. Then this other guess, that they were hiding in *the neighborhood,* might not be too far-fetched. It was amazing, when you came to think of it, how big a part plain hunches played in police work. Oh sure, you have hints and clues—the license number scribbled in an old man's blocky writing before he was shot, a carefully worded anonymous letter from a worried husband and father. But you put the two together and the connection was slight, really. Damned slight. Yet it was all you had, and on the basis of it, you lost another good night's sleep.

The sour taste that had been in Jesse Webb's mouth since the telephone number list had played itself out on him was now a poison all through him. He was tired, but it didn't matter. All that mattered was that he had a slim chance, but a chance, to reach Glenn Griffin before morning. Somehow. The hatred he had felt all along, remembering the shapeless hang of Uncle Frank's arm, had swollen in him each time he recalled the look of death on the face of harmless little Mr. Patterson; now, with the desperate unsigned letter in his pocket, he felt the hatred expand, choking him, till he could hardly breathe.

Nothing mattered but finding Glenn Griffin, his brother and another man named Robish, and wiping the earth clean of their slime. That and nothing less.

That same need, more aching hunger than savage rage in him now, kept recurring to Dan Hilliard as he walked; it clogged his mind, averting his thoughts from the one decision he had to make before morning—how to tie Griffin's hands if the young hoodlum attempted to carry anyone along in his escape. Dan was crossing the river bridge, returning on foot by the same route he had traveled an hour ago in the gray sedan. He had made up his mind not to try to estimate the number of miles he had walked, how many more lay ahead of him. He wasn't sure, though, that he would make it. Griffin, grinning, had been cruelly specific: "No cabs, Pop. Walk it. Do you good."

All along, from the first few minutes when Glenn Griffin had brought the barrel of his gun whipping down on his shoulder, Dan had been aware of the sadistic strain in the young convict. This ugly warping was deep in him, stronger even than his judgment or his need to escape. He wanted revenge; he was going to have murder committed by paying for it with the money that was in the mail, on its way to Dan's office. This held him in town, kept him in Dan Hilliard's home. Some police officer, who was probably unaware of Glenn Griffin's general whereabouts, who had perhaps forgotten Glenn Griffin completely, had been marked for death because of some old twisted grudge in the boy's mind.

The whole idea of revenge had been foreign to Dan Hilliard, not a part of his nature at all—until now. Now he comprehended, even while loathing, the twist in the young criminal. He understood because he himself had begun to feel the same dark urge. While it was still uppermost that he get those men out and away from his family, Dan Hilliard, his chest aching and each step driving shocks of pain up his legs and into his groin, became acutely aware for the first time that he wanted to see Glenn Griffin dead—dead for death's own sake as well as for the safety of his family.

It was this realization, as he forced one leg forward, planted it, then lifted the other, that added the last tightening to his unreal, walking nightmare. Whether it came an hour from now or ten years, he wanted to see Glenn Griffin dead.

Then why not now? Why not tonight and get it over with? Get a gun, conceal it, walk in the house, draw it, shoot.

Eleanor's pale face drifted at him across the blackness again. *Dan, I'm pleading with you. Promise me, Dan, darling, promise me.*

129

He sagged against the stone buttress of the bridge looking ahead, picturing the dark wet miles ahead, asking, in a whisper, "What can I do, Ellie? I promised, but you don't know, dear. You don't see what I see."

He was under a garish street lamp that cast his shadow before him. He caught a glimpse of the slump-shouldered figure of himself, outlined darkly on the wet pavement, small-looking and shriveled. He frowned and, with great effort, twisted his head to make sure that he was staring down at his own shadow. He was. He was alone on that bridge.

He straightened, his breath a turning blade in his chest, and plunged forward again. At this moment headlights swept toward him, approaching from behind. A car careened by, a young girl's face appeared in the rear window, and a boyish voice echoed back at him as the car gathered speed and continued on: "Have another drink, old man."

Dan missed a step. They thought he was drunk. He didn't blame them. He wanted to smile. He envied those kids; he even loved them. All the safe people, unfrightened, living their unknowing lives.

He hit the rhythm again: one foot, then the other. He found that if he swung his legs forward, attaining a certain balance, he didn't drive the shafts of burning pain so high up into his body.

Without warning, then—he didn't even see the flash of headlights—a car screamed to a stop across the gleam of dark pavement. It looked familiar in a misty sort of way, as Dan stared at it. The police? A giddiness rose in him. They might lock him up for being drunk. *Drunk!* But when the door opened and a man stepped out and strode across toward him, he thought only that he must run. He had no strength or breath in him, but he knew that he should turn and run through the streets, down alleys, behind garages, anything, anywhere, rather than let this man reach him. He couldn't move.

"Mr. Hilliard. Let me take you home."

Dan recognized the voice, and finally, by peering through the three feet of dimness that separated them now, he put the voice to a face. Chuck Wright.

Incredibility struck him; he went hollow and empty, staring.

"Come on, sir, I'll give you a lift."

Dan didn't reply. The impossibility of the encounter still held him and he was without will as he crossed the damp pavement, opened the door of the car and slid into the seat. The leather was cold, penetrating to the chill inside him; but the seat was soft, incredibly soft and giving, and he lowered his body into it with gratitude only slightly edged with the knowledge that somehow, in some way, he had made or was making a horrible mistake.

He closed his eyes then, and for a long time—he had no idea how long—he gave himself over to the luxury of softness and the close warmth of the car. Blankness.

The young man's voice lifted him from it. "I'll have to know now, you see," Chuck Wright was saying.

Dan opened his eyes reluctantly. Chuck Wright drove a miniature sports car of foreign design. This was a larger car.

"I'm going to take you home and go inside, Mr. Hilliard, and one of you—you or Cindy—is going to tell me what gives."

Behind the level flatness of the boy's voice, even while he heard the words, Dan felt this other, somehow more vital question working its way up in him.

"I'll do anything I can to help, sir. You're in some kind of trouble, aren't you?"

Then the question took a double-shadowed shape: Why was Chuck driving this car and where had Dan seen it before?

"No trouble," Dan said, and his voice, in the canvas-enclosed interior of the car, sounded normal, absurdly normal. "Is this your car?"

"My father's. I borrowed it."

"Why?"

Chuck shrugged. "Carburetor on mine's acting up."

131

A lie, Dan Hilliard's mind cried, with renewed alertness. He had it now. This large car, a convertible, was the one that had followed him earlier, the one he'd eluded back there before he crossed the river in the gray sedan. Chuck Wright had been following him then. Why?

"If you don't want to talk, sir, it can wait till we get to your house."

The significance of the young man's intention struck Dan for the first time then. What did the boy know? How much had he guessed? And what would it mean? Of one thing Dan was staunchly certain: Chuck Wright must be prevented, at all costs, from taking him all the way home.

Dan was tempted to close his eyes again, to stretch his knotted muscles, pushing aside everything. He had done his part. He had done everything within his power. Wasn't it only fair now that he should have these few minutes of blankness?

But even as he thrust the temptation aside—with an effort summoned from some deep recess of his character that he had not known existed in him—a slyness took over his thoughts. The boy wanted an explanation. He had to have one. He was stubborn and he would go into the house and demand to know what this was all about. Very well, then Dan would give him an explanation.

The idea came to him from nowhere. "You haven't got a little drink on you, have you?" Dan asked.

He heard the abrupt catch of breath; he watched covertly the young man's rather blunt-looking profile as the lips opened, then closed, then opened again.

"Not a drop," Chuck Wright said quietly.

Dan was careful not to let his words blur. "Damnation," he said. "Thought you were the drinking type, Chuck. You never know, do you? Can't make snap judgments, can you?"

"No, you can't," Chuck agreed thinly, an incongruous disapproval replacing the surprise in his tone.

"Shows to go you," Dan said. "Tell you what, Chuck, old

fellow—now that you're into my little family secret, y'see, you can skip taking me home. Just drop me off at that liquor store in Broad Ripple and I'll walk rest of the way."

"Anything you say, Mr. Hilliard."

"Not shocked, are you, Chuck? You won't hold it against Cindy, will you, fellow? Man in my position . . . discreet. I'm always discreet about it. Notice the neighborhood I was in tonight? Nobody knows me there, of course. Nice people, though. Can't afford to be snobbish." He halted himself, for fear of going too far. He had made his point; the effect was in young Wright's set face and manner.

But what had he forgotten? His mind wasn't working properly. Something——

Then it came to him, in the long silence, and he spoke again, minutes later: "Lost my car tonight. Parked it in front of a bar. Thought I did. Gray car." In what he vaguely hoped was a man-to-man manner, he lowered his voice: "Own private car, y'know. For own private pleasures. You sure you don't have a drink?"

"Positive."

After that, more silence as the corners rolled by, the blocks, the miles. Had he covered everything now? Did Chuck believe him?

The stiff and unnatural silence held until Chuck brought the long convertible to a stop along the curb in front of the lighted store in which, only last night, Dan had bought the whisky for Robish.

"It's a long walk from here to your house," Chuck said at last as Dan opened the door.

Long walk? Dan looked back in his mind over the miles he had already walked and those that he had thought he would have to walk, and he choked down a wild giddiness.

Was he making a mistake? Would this competent-looking young man make an ally? If he loved Cindy, as he had practically admitted he did in the office this afternoon——

133

"Wouldn't want to embarrass Cindy, would we, Chuck?" he said in conspiratorial tones, standing on the sidewalk. "Cindy already embarrassed enough about her father. Worried sick. Poor Cindy. Don't hold it against her, Chuck."

"No," said the boy bleakly.

"Won't mention it to her, will you, Chuck?"

"No."

Standing unsteadily but not drunkenly on the sidewalk, hearing Chuck Wright's "Good night," clipped and short—no *sir* now—Dan felt the weakness clamp down on him again. The torture of those miles and the activity of the night clutched at his legs, dug at the backs of his knees. When the red taillights had blurred in the distance, he stepped from the curb, crossed the still-damp street, feeling the sharp bite of wind against his drained face.

A cloud of astonishment filled his brain: Where had the cunning come from? How had he thought to make up that story? And, more important, had he been believed?

Even though he stayed on a dim and untraveled street, walking east, he saw a police car halfway down the second block. He made a turn at the corner and quickened his steps. But the possible meaning of what he saw didn't strike him fully until, three blocks later, he saw another, this one parked alongside a dark ice-cream parlor. A wide white stripe ran down the side of the car, and he made out the words "State Police." This time he almost broke into a run, the impulse a shooting sensation down his legs. The boulevard itself looked deserted.

An awesome urgency drove him forward. Now he had forgotten all physical pain, the gray sedan, the long tormented hike, Chuck Wright. A leaden anguish weighed him down. He pulled his hat lower with a vicious wrench of which he was not even conscious. Bent forward at the waist, lips tight against the compulsion pulling at him, he warned himself, over and over: Don't run. Remember, if they stop you, you're tight. Walking home from the bus. Don't run.

Then, after a moment of blankness, he was, by some miracle, turning into his own driveway. There was a light in the living room. Cindy's car and the family sedan remained in the driveway. The garage door was closed. Nothing moved, inside the house or out. The profound quiet sent him charging the last few yards to the side door.

The living room, beyond the dimness of the sun porch, was deserted. What did it mean? He rattled the door handle.

Silence. Then, in the distance, a train whistle hooted forlornly on the wind.

The hall was only partially in view. He heard himself calling in a whisper. Cindy appeared then, coming across the living room swiftly. He heard her words: "It's Dad."

Still, when she faced him, the door open, he knew that it had not been his approach that had caused the electric tension, the terrible silence.

Cindy was white. Not pale. White. "It's Ralphie," she said, her voice quivering for the first time.

Dan pushed past her, the run breaking through his legs like a wave. . . .

5

5

For possibly five seconds Dan Hilliard stood motionless in the hall, held rigid in the shock of stark terror over the nightmare scene before him. He had been expecting something like this for so long that now that it was before him, he had to fight his way briefly through a cloud of stunned incredulity.

He saw Eleanor on the lower steps, her eyes unrecognizable with fright. He heard Cindy pause behind him on the edge of the living room. Glenn Griffin lounged in the dining room doorway across the hall. Dan saw Robish then: the savagely parted lips, the jaundice-colored skin of his face a blackish red now. The big man had been staring up the stairs, but he turned the revolver on Dan as Dan felt a movement go through his body, an impulse that Robish sensed before Dan knew he had moved a half-step.

"Where's Ralphie?" Dan asked.

"Upstairs," Eleanor said quickly. "Sleeping."

Glenn Griffin's dark eyes glinted with mockery. "This time I ought to let Robish handle him, Pop. That kid's going to foul up everything."

"Put that gun away," Dan said in a dry whisper, remembering the parked police cars.

It might have been the whispered tone, or it might have been the squared hulk of Dan's body, very still, very tense; or it might have been the terrible shimmering blackness in Dan's eyes—whatever caused it, Glenn recalled something about this man Dan Hilliard and he took a step toward Robish.

"Forget it, Robish," Glenn Griffin advised, his gaze still on Dan with a narrowing caution—no derision now, no sardonic grin. "The old lady covered it on the phone. That dumb teacher don't suspect a thing."

It occurred to Dan to ask what all this meant, but everything was happening too fast. He saw Robish lower the gun then, almost automatically; but the downward arc broke. Something came over the brute face; bafflement trembled there, and then there was a hardening of his jaw muscles that spread rigidly down the immense body. "You don't give the orders any more," the heavy voice said. "I got this now." Not so slowly then, he brought the gun up again, and this time it was directed at Glenn Griffin's belt.

The inevitability of this—for Dan had known somehow that this also was coming—left in Dan no place for surprise. Robish had forgotten Ralphie now—and whatever Ralphie had done to rouse that murderous instinct—and Dan could see the slow grinding of that dull and unpredictable mind behind the massive forehead. Glenn Griffin saw it, too. He, also, must have watched Robish's thoughts flash to the waiting car outside, to the possibility of what he might do. Uncertain rebellion turned to flat decision across the bleak face. Robish could kill them, one or all of them, and be in that car and on his way in a matter of seconds. No more nerve-eating wait, no more following Griffin's orders.

The stupidity of the man's thinking also failed to surprise Dan in the least. In that instant he knew that, any second now —and he must not wait too long—he would have to act.

With the gun inching toward his stomach, clutched in the dark hairy hand of the big man, Glenn Griffin began to laugh. At first it was a defiant crackle of sound, but staring at the intensity on Robish's face, Griffin seemed abruptly to lose control and the laugh died in a series of odd gurgles. His hands came up to his face, fluttered there, and then his jaw was working without sound.

Dan felt himself take a step toward Eleanor; then his muscles locked as Robish growled, "Don't move, Hilliard."

Glenn Griffin uttered a long but broken breath that sounded like, "For Chrissake, Robish——"

At this Robish bellowed—a wild animal cry, vast and awesome and hollow, the cave of mouth open.

Glenn Griffin's terror-stricken words caught and reflected Dan's immediate thought: "You're nuts, Robish." But as he heard the words, Dan knew at once that Griffin could not have said anything more dangerous.

Robish brought the point of the revolver against the young man's stomach in a vicious jab that doubled Griffin over with a cry of pain. Then, his back against the door frame, he began to slither toward the floor, his hands still fluttering in that odd terrified way at his chin. He was beginning to utter a low sighing sound, all breath and high-pitched plea.

Should he move now? This was it. He was in the midst of it now, everything gone, all his efforts ruined. Should Dan Hilliard act now?

"I'm nuts!" Robish bawled. "Yeh, I'm nuts, Griffin. Doing your dirty work. You, you bastard, you're the general, ain't you?"

Dan judged the distance. Immediately after the explosion, if he could leap fast enough in the confusion, if he could hit Robish hard enough the first time——

"I konk the guard, I plug the old guy, I——"

Then, from above, from the darkness of the upper hall, another voice cut across Robish's low snarl: "Throw it on the floor, Robish."

Robish turned his head, peered unseeing into those shadows above Eleanor's body, blinked. Without volition, Dan moved then, but not in the swift way he had been calculating. He stepped carefully and cautiously toward his wife, reached his right arm around her waist, and he was drawing her away from the stairs when Hank Griffin, still invisible above, spoke again.

"Throw it on the floor, Robish. Now."

Under his arm, Dan could feel small shivers passing up and down Eleanor's body.

But he was watching Robish, wondering. He saw the temptation to whirl firing; he saw that slow, prison-broken mind tearing its attention from Glenn Griffin who half-lay, half-sat slouched against the door frame. Griffin's eyes were wide and glassy, as though he still had not comprehended what was happening, until he saw Robish toss the gun to the rug.

It lay there, black and deadly, between Glenn Griffin and Dan, as Robish stepped back, glowering with yellow eyes up the stairwell.

Eleanor must have read the thought in Dan's mind before he was aware of it himself. "No," she whispered, clinging to his arm. "No, Dan."

At the head of the stairs there was no movement. The whole house seemed locked in unnatural stillness after the snarls and cries. Finally, Glenn Griffin reached out and picked up the revolver. He stood up, very slowly. The soundless pantomime seemed to go on and on. Glenn Griffin reached for his swagger, lifted his shoulders, took a deep breath—but in the breath was a shudder and he closed his mouth. Then his eyes met Dan's.

With a start that made him wonder again whether he had made a mistake by not acting, Dan caught the furious glare of shame: the memory of those few moments of clawing terror and the knowledge that Dan and the others had stood witness to the cowardice. What would this mean? In what direction would it push Griffin?

Behind him Dan heard his daughter take a deep draught of breath. His own lungs burned. Then, breaking the silence, Hank Griffin came down the stairs, stepping quickly, his right arm hanging at his side. He paused on the bottom step, glanced at Robish who stood bearlike and still now, his arms dangling; then at his brother. What Dan heard then was not so much the content of the younger Griffin boy's words as the flattened note of finality in his tone: "Let's go, Glenn."

Glenn Griffin frowned, said nothing.

"This is our chance, Glenn," Hank said, gently, reasonably. "We can't hold them and Robish, too. And maybe the coppers traced Helen, maybe they've got her, maybe they've traced her call here. This is going on too long, Glenn. They're bound to get here sooner or later. They're not dumb."

"All cops are dumb," Glenn Griffin said, and his voice was soft, too.

"Everybody's dumb, ain't they?" Hank Griffin asked. "That teacher. The one the kid slipped the note to. Just because she called back and said she knew it was all a joke, just kid stuff, a game—you think she believes that herself? How do you know there wasn't some smart cop right at her elbow?"

"Don't get scared, kid. Don't be like Robish here. Jumpy."

"I'm not jumpy!" Hank Griffin cried suddenly, and Dan saw his mouth trembling oddly. "But I'm not going to the chair just cause Robish got trigger-happy and you let him. You think the cops ain't working on that right now? You can't knock off everybody comes to the door. Why don't you send him after that teacher now, Glenn? Sure. Shoot up the whole damn city—play safe!"

"Shut up," Glenn Griffin said softly. "Get back to the kitchen and stay shut."

Hank Griffin was shaking his head, and very slowly, very deliberately. "Come with me, Glenn."

143

Glenn lifted his shoulders in that angular and arrogant way. "Tomorrow. After we get the dough."

"What good's the dough gonna do you in the death house?" He was shouting then, his mouth twisting and out of control.

Robish watched this with no expression, only a scornful alertness in his quiet.

"You heard me," Glenn Griffin said then, and he was still quiet, but the anger was there, hard and bitter. "We're gonna stay, see. I'm going to pay off Webb. I got to have that dough for Flick so he'll take care of Webb."

The younger brother stepped down. "Then I'm going, Glenn. By myself."

After that, the silence came back, intensified, deeper.

Finally, Glenn Griffin grinned. "Go ahead, kid. On your own they'll have you back in stir in less'n a hour."

Hank Griffin glanced toward Dan, but his gaze went beyond—to Cindy. "I'm going, that's all." He moved into the lighted living room.

"Goddammit!" Glenn Griffin yelled. "You'll do what I say, you little jerk! I got you this far, both you dumb cons, and I'll get you the rest of the way!"

Hank did not pause until he reached the door of the sun room; then he turned. "Yeh," he said bitterly, low, "you got me this far. And where the hell is that? I'm asking you. We're all headed for the chair, that's where. Only count me out." Then his voice dropped even lower: "Come along, Glenn."

"I oughta——"

Both guns came up at the same instant. Hank Griffin was shaking his head.

"It'd break my heart, Glenn, but I'd do it. You can't stop me. So long, Glenn."

Hank Griffin backed through the sun-room door, turned and ran, his steps sharp on the tiled porch. Dan had seen the sharp glisten of fear in the young eyes, and he wished he had not witnessed the scene, but he could only stand by and watch what was to follow, wondering.

"He's gonna take the car," Robish said.

"Like hell!" Glenn Griffin touched the light switch, plunged them all into total, shocking darkness; Dan felt him brush past, heard him crouching at the window overlooking the driveway, heard that window grind open. "Stay away from that car, you dumb punk!"

Outside, a door slammed. It was strange, Dan thought, that with your senses battered and deadened by too much happening too fast, you could still recognize minute details: the door that closed was on Cindy's coupe. The motor turned over, caught, purred.

Above this sound, though, and closer, Dan heard another. It was Glenn Griffin shouting wildly, a long series of blasphemy and lewdness erupting from the frustration in him as the motor faded down the boulevard.

Hank traveled west four full blocks before he saw the first patrol car. Even in the darkness, he spotted it from a distance because the years had sharpened his awareness and caution in matters of that sort until now his reactions were almost instinctual. He made a sharp right turn, so that he wouldn't have to pass it. A half-block farther on, in the shadow of a dark service station, he saw another. This time there was no way for him to avoid passing it.

He touched the automatic in the pocket of that sweater he'd found in the upstairs closet of the Hilliard house. He'd use it if he had to. If he was going to be charged with murder, why not make it one that he, not that ape Robish, committed? His palms were cold and moist.

As he drove at a normal rate of speed, luckily between two other cars, directly in front of the nose of the patrol car which was at right angles to the street, he knew that he was forgetting something about Cindy's coupe. Something important that made it dangerous. He should have taken the blue sedan despite Glenn's shout. But why? Glenn always claimed his mind was too slow, too blurred with what Glenn called daydreams.

Whatever it was about this car, though, the coppers didn't notice. He watched his rear-view mirror. They didn't follow.

He turned west again, at the first street he saw, and he had gone perhaps two miles, all the while alert, wondering, scanning the shadows along the way, when he realized the significance of those two police cars parked that close to the Hilliard house. He'd been right: the cops were wise. But the triumph wouldn't come. He'd been right, but what about Glenn back there? What was going to happen now to that girl?

Funny, though—now that he was away from her, what happened to her didn't seem so important. There was never anything he could do about what Glenn planned tomorrow after he had the money, anyway. The girl was going along in the car then to make the escape look natural and if necessary, to act as a shield.

Is that why you walked out, Hank?

He knew better. He walked out because he wasn't the dumb jerk Glenn thought he was. He was away from there now, and Glenn, the smart one, the wise one who always had the answers, was sitting in a trap and not knowing it.

Only a few cars approached or passed now, in the late night. He rolled down the window at his elbow. The sharp cold air felt fine.

But underneath the sensation of freedom—he was, he realized, even free of Glenn now—there was this other feeling: the idea that he should turn around, go back, warn Glenn. His brother had been the only human being in the world who'd ever given half a damn what happened to Hank Griffin. His father had been, before he killed himself by it, a cruel and steady drinker, given to wild rages and brutality; and his mother, running from that, had left them all when Hank was so young that he couldn't even remember her face clearly. Glenn had fixed things for him, fought his battles in the alley, then rung him in on the stick-up jobs because he was the best driver and could lose a car faster than anyone else. These memories moved in him now, and he knew that he dare not get lost in them. He had to think of himself. Now. Tonight. Now. A deep frail joy was in him: he was on his own at last. But he had to concentrate now on this moment—not the past, not the future.

Back there, listening to Robish's voice bawling before he came down the stairs, Hank had had a definite plan. Now he couldn't remember exactly what it was. Something about heading west out of town, then doubling back to the Chicago road that he knew would be blocked close in to the city but comparatively free farther north. He could be in Chicago by morning.

He glanced at the dashboard, automatically checking the gauges. There was less than half a tank of gas. And no money. Only the few coins he'd fished out of that desk drawer in the den. That meant he'd have to pull a job—on his own.

This thought, together with the idea of a strange big city like Chicago where he knew no one and the anticipation of the long ride ahead, absolutely alone—all combined, mingled, and made him go weak clear through.

He knew what was coming then; he knew what that quiver in his stomach meant. He wondered if he could drive when that thing hit him.

But he couldn't go back. Those coppers were waiting there, all part of a plan. What was he going to do?

The slow panic settled through him, and he gripped the wheel, taking large draughts of the cold night air. But nothing

147

did any good. The wracking shudders were beginning. The radio had said all roads were blocked. But he couldn't stay back there. He had to get out of that house. Staying there had been sheer torture, from the beginning. The soft rugs, the gleaming furniture, the way those people stuck together, that girl——

They'll have you back in stir in less'n a hour.

He could almost hear Glenn's mocking laugh. But he didn't hate it now. He longed to hear it close, to feel that arm over his shoulder. Why was he here? What was he doing?

You don't even know that girl. Cindy Hilliard. She never said a word to you, hardly. She hates you.

All the while the violence was mounting in him, becoming insistent. He hated this in himself, this sickness or fear or whatever it was. Even worse than the helplessness and the shaking was the black pall of disgust and self-loathing that fell across him. Sickness, the prison doc had called it. Epilepsy. Weakness, Glenn always said.

Tomorrow Glenn would be out of there, with some of the dough; he'd be on his way to Helen Lamar who was in Cincinnati now, waiting with the rest of it. Glenn would find a way to make it, too. Glenn always found a way. He'd handle that stir-crazy Robish, too.

Hell, you and Glenn together, you can take care of Robish.

But somehow he was missing the point. There was something else he had to remember. That he couldn't go back now? That there was no way back? Or something about this car?

Then another car spun past him, traveling fast. And a laugh floated back at him, a girl's laugh, trembling warm and bright as the car flashed past. Then it was gone. But it had brought back that hungry hollowness in him, that same shot-away emptiness he felt when he looked at Cindy Hilliard. His throat clogged and his heart stopped.

Now, he knew, was the time. He would have to stop the car, because his hands were shaking. He searched frantically for an alley, a side street, any place where he could park. But it was too late.

The blackness closed in on him, shut out all thoughts, the shaking inside moved up, spread through him with a sudden and horrible violence. Then there was only the gasping and writhing and shaking until he felt all the parts of his body could not stay together. And, as always, he hoped that this time he would die. In the grip of this paroxysm, which had been a part of him for as long as he could remember, he longed never to waken, never to be forced to return to reality. He wished he could die and never know it. Dying wouldn't be so bad if you didn't know it was happening . . .

The whole house was dark now. It was after eleven. In Ralphie's room, Dan flipped on a lamp and stood blinking a moment at the sailing-ship designs on the shade. He heard his son stir on the bed, and he watched him sit up expectantly, happily, but with just a touch of defensiveness and guilt in his brilliant blue eyes.

Rebellion curled and twisted in Dan. He couldn't do it. They were demanding too much. Was it ever going to stop? So much was happening now, and so fast, that he had not even had time to disentangle its meaning or its threat: Chuck Wright, the parked police cars, the clash between Robish and Glenn, Hank Griffin's departure alone, the uneasy and suspicious realliance between Griffin and Robish. Now this.

Ralphie stared up at his father as Dan closed the door softly. The boy's face still held some of the roundness of earlier years although, at ten years, it had begun to lengthen and harden toward adolescence.

"That Miss Swift," Ralphie said, shaking his head. "Teaches

149

fifth grade, but what a dope. Thought I was playing a game."

"Thank God she did, Ralphie," Dan said, not moving.

Ralphie caught in those words, or in his father's stolid grimness, a hint of threat, and he frowned, startled.

But he was no more amazed at his father's presence than Dan was. Dan could not do what he had been commanded to do. That command from Glenn Griffin was no more than an attempt to reassert his control after his brother walked out. Yes, it was more, too. It was an attempt to placate Robish. But even worse, Dan realized as he looked down on his son, Glenn Griffin was avenging himself on Dan and the whole family because Dan and they had witnessed his cowardice in the face of Robish's gun a half hour or so ago. Mingled in with the revenge, though, was that same twisted sadism that had insisted on Dan's walking all that distance, after disposing of the car.

Junior had to get smart again, see. Glenn Griffin had explained only a few minutes ago downstairs. *While you was out, his teacher comes to call. Just passing by, she says, and wondering about the kid's health cause he missed school today. I'm in the den and your wife, she handles things clever. The teacher don't suspect a thing. Then Ralphie comes down and gives her a book, a schoolbook he says, for her to take back to school. I'm going nuts but what can I do? Then a hour later maybe, she calls up. She's found a note in the book, see. She says she don't believe a word of it. But she thought the brat's mother ought to know the silly kind of games her son plays. Some people, this dame says, might get very upset at reading a note like that, especially with all the awful things that're happening in the world.*

"Ralphie," Dan said now, "Ralphie, didn't I tell you? Wasn't last night bad enough? Look at my head. We were lucky then. We can't always be lucky like that, son. Next time they'll shoot somebody." His voice rose to a cry. "Ralphie, do you want them to shoot your mother?"

"No, no, but——"

Dan stepped closer, the anger stirring in him, the anger that he had been hoping he might feel ever since Glenn Griffin downstairs had said: *You're going up there now, Hilliard, and you're going to make Junior understand we ain't playing games. Some little trick like that could mess up everything. You're going to give him a lacing, Pop. Or I'll let Robish do it for you. You choose. No more funny business from that brat, see.*

"You *say* no," Dan told his son, "but you don't mean it! I've got to trust you, Ralphie. You've got to trust me. I'm taking care of this. Can't you *mind?*"

The rush of his father's words, the rising confusion and fury, brought the boy to his bare feet alongside the bed. "All I wrote was that we needed help. I said we were prisoners. Aren't we?"

"Ralphie," Dan shouted, "do you want your mother to be killed? Can't you understand? Aren't you old enough?"

In sudden bewildered terror, seeing his father's hand lifting, Ralphie squared his shoulders and closed his lips stubbornly, and in the instant Dan realized that he had never been able to control Ralphie in this manner. Gentleness, yes, a reasonable tone, quiet talk—Ralphie understood these and responded. Force only threw up this barrier of stubbornness. This fact adding to his rage and inner bafflement, Dan lowered his hand, grabbed Ralphie's arms and began to shake him.

"Ralphie," he pleaded in a harsh whisper as the violence of his shaking increased, "Ralphie, listen to me, start crying! Cry, Ralphie, *please!* You've got to cry now!" He was thinking of Eleanor's fright, of Cindy's chalk-white face down there, of all they had done so far. "Hear me, Ralphie! *Start crying!*"

But the body was stiff between his hands, only the head snapping, the eyes closed. Dan let go then, stood up, thinking of the delight Robish would find in what he was doing with such pain and reluctance; he lifted his hand, brought it down in a sharp open-palmed blow across the small face, and he heard the sound, saw the eyes pop open, and went instantly sick and empty and stood away.

But the tears came then, and the astonishment and hurt that he had expected. Ralphie was crying, loud, not whimpering; Dan listened with a shock of mingled self-loathing and relief. Then in an abrupt and uncontrollable gesture he reached again, saw the uncertain instinctive dodging of the body, caught his son to him as he kneeled. He felt the boy's hot tears against his own cheek and felt the gusts of breath exploding in wails from the small, convulsed body.

"Cry, son," he was whispering softly, "go on and cry."

And in the words he recognized his own longing, the pent-up frustration and anger. He was holding Ralphie to him, close, and staring into the darkness beyond the windows, wishing he dared give himself over to his own fierce hunger for tears, for any release whatever from the pressures building dangerously in his aching body.

In the morning you'll have the answer, Chuck Wright was telling himself as he drove aimlessly in his father's convertible, the one he had borrowed for the evening because he had felt his own little sports job was too conspicuous. In the morning you'll get the answer from Cindy herself, and you won't take any more run-around.

You must have passed this same corner at least ten times, he thought vaguely, but his mind was not on his driving. His mind was rebelling at the lies and evasions. Let's go back to the beginning. Cindy wanted to know whether you owned a gun. Stick to that point, remember it—it's essential. Then this afternoon, after a morning that made no sense whatever, she and Mr. Hilliard left the office, drove to the eastern edge of the city, picked up a strange man, took him back to their house. To-night, while you were parked down the street a few yards, still trying to puzzle it out, Mr. Hilliard came out of his driveway in a gray sedan you'd never seen before, drove it in a roundabout path to the west, then gave you the slip in a shoddy side street. As if that wasn't bad enough, you spotted him, maybe an hour and a half later, walking, walking like a tired drunk across the river bridge miles from his house.

Then those lies about being a drunkard! That kind of pleased you at first, didn't it? The irony tickled you—the unassailable and conventional man who objected to you turns out to be a secret drinker. Great! Only you didn't quite swallow it, especially after you saw him go plunging homeward without going into the liquor store at all. And he no longer staggered then, he walked fast and steady then, like a man in a desperate hurry.

Desperate. There's the word. Cindy and Mr. Hilliard: they acted like desperate people. But desperate about what? Why?

Why not go back to the club and get a nightcap and go to sleep? You've begun to imagine things now. In the morning you can get the answer from Cindy.

Or you could phone her now. Insist that she come out and talk to you. Or you could go to the house, hammer on the door——

Don't be a fool. Last time you drove by, the house was dark, wasn't it? And Cindy's car was nowhere in sight, probably in the garage. That's another thing. Cindy always parked her car in the driveway and the Hilliard car was always in the garage. Yet last night and again tonight——

At this point, the irritation and confusion working in him, he caught a red glare in his rear-view mirror. There was no siren blast but a dark prowl car eased alongside him, edged him to the curb, in silence. The red light went off. Chuck Wright, frowning, feeling a single catch in his heart, sat waiting. He lit a cigarette.

Jesse Webb was glad for any excuse for action. He had been fighting down his own pressures in the last hours, and with some success. But Helen Lamar had apparently dropped out of existence in or near Columbus, Ohio. And while Jesse had one certain piece of knowledge now—that Griffin was in or near the city, or had been around noon today when that unidentified man wrote the anonymous letter—the knowledge added up to very little as yet. Until someone made a move. He was hoping that the report he had just received meant that someone had made a move.

"Bring him in as soon as he gets here," he instructed a uniformed trooper. "And keep those cars out of sight best you can. Damned if we want anybody getting the idea the police are holding a midnight convention in the kitchen of an eat-joint." As the trooper went out, Jesse glanced with a small apologetic grin toward the aproned owner who stood, lost in curiosity, near the enormous coffee urn.

"I call it a joint myself," the little man said with a delicate shrug. "But it's a clean one, Sheriff. You want any more coffee?"

Jesse stood up from the wooden chopping-table and took his cup to the owner. "You expect any more customers tonight, Joe?"

"Maybe yes, maybe no. Handful of kids on dates. You want me to close up?"

"We'll buy the rest of your coffee. And Winston's trying to reduce again, so he'll take one of those sweet rolls to keep up his strength. I'll have one, too, Joe. You douse those lights out front."

"Anything for the police," Joe said. "Help yourself. There's meat in the icebox. Joe wants to oblige. Pardon me, Sheriff."

"Now," Jesse said, returning to his seat with coffee and rolls, "now Tom, what's so suspicious? A guy's driving a convertible in the neighborhood. Is that against the law?"

"Why should he drive round and round in all kinds of

circles?" Tom Winston picked up a gleaming knife and cut the rolls into neat wedges. "Here? Tonight?" He speared a wedge and lifted it to his mouth. "It's worth asking."

"Tom," Jesse Webb said, wrapping his long lean legs around the table leg again, "why don't our wives divorce us?"

"Mine threatens it, every time we get a case like this. I wish she meant it."

Jesse ignored this reference to Tom Winston's unhappy home life. Eating, he was remembering his own good-night telephone call to Kathleen who was now asleep, he hoped, in his mother's house. No reason now for those precautions, probably. But why take chances? Against a mind like Glenn Griffin's. He only hoped the man who wrote that letter understood that mind. And this thought plunged him again into the unnerving concern he had begun to feel—almost a personal responsibility—for that man and his family. Again Jesse Webb became sharply aware of the trap in which he sat, helpless, while somewhere, possibly in one of those houses within a stone's throw——

"Here he is, Jess."

Jesse Webb looked up into a young face: mid-twenties, gray, questioning but unfrightened eyes, steady, bold, maybe even a little defiant. Tweed topcoat, expensive; dark gray flannel suit; no hat.

"Having a good time?" Jesse inquired laconically.

"I don't follow."

"Been drinking?"

"No."

"Wonder why I'm asking questions?"

"Sure."

"Any idea?"

"No."

Jesse sighed. "Let's have your driver's license."

Without hesitation or fumbling, the young man took his license from his wallet, laid it in front of Jesse on the meat-stained block of table.

"Charles Wright," Jesse read aloud. "Business?"

"Attorney. Hepburn and Higgins. Guaranty Building."

"Anything else?"

"Anything else what?"

In a swift and unreasonable wave of irritation, Jesse Webb untangled his legs and stood up. "Look, Mr. Wright, we're not in court. Let's not be cagey. It makes me suspicious. I've got things to find out. Play ball. I reckon you can't get in any trouble unless you got something to hide. What have you been up to the last hour? Let's have it."

"I'll play ball, Deputy," Charles Wright said then, "but I don't want to be used for the ball. I've got nothing to hide. But I ought to know what this is all about."

"It's none of your business what——" But Jesse heard Tom Winston clear his throat in warning, and he broke off, his voice dropping. "Okay, okay. Your firm handle criminal cases, Mr. Wright?"

"We're strictly corporation law. You haven't answered my question, Deputy."

"Don't get fresh," Tom Winston put in mildly. "What Deputy Webb is asking is whether you'd take on a criminal case, maybe try to help some rat for a fancy fee."

"What rat are you referring to?"

Jesse Webb took over again. He spoke evenly, and his voice was hoarse now. "We're referring to three rats who broke out of the Federal pen in Terre Haute yesterday morning. Don't you read the papers, man? Don't you listen to the radio?" As Charles Wright shook his head, Jesse caught—or wondered whether he caught—a certain quick alertness in the gray eyes. "Well, we have reason to believe these men are in town, or damn close to town. The fact is, Mr. Wright"—and Jesse was leaning forward on his fists—"we have some reason to think they might be in this neighborhood, maybe in one of the houses around here. So when someone starts cruising around——" But he stopped then, certain for a second that a change had

156

taken place on the face before him. "What's up, kid?" he asked curtly, and in his stomach something turned completely over.

"Nothing."

"You know something?"

"Of course not."

"Suspect something?"

"No."

"Damn it, don't lie to me!" Jesse barked. "Your face looks like I just kicked you!"

"Well, it is a kind of shock, I guess. I just never—thought of anything like that."

"What were you doing in that car, Mr. Wright? What's the deal?"

Charles Wright smiled then, a tight sort of smile that never reached the grave eyes. "Well, it just happens that my girl friend lives around here, that's all. And I got the crazy idea just now, when you said——"

"What's her name, Wright?"

There was a slight pause then, a pause that Jesse Webb didn't like.

"Her name's Allen," Charles Wright said then, and very firmly and convincingly. "Constance Allen. But I saw her go into her house just a little while ago. I'm sure she's all right, Deputy."

"You *saw* her go in? You brought her home?"

"Well, no. Y'see, that's the pitch. I might as well tell the truth. She was out with another guy tonight. That's why I've been hanging around. Connie and I are almost engaged. At least I thought——" He shook his head and the smile came again, but still it didn't rise into the steady gaze. "It's just one of those things. I guess I ought to be ashamed. Being jealous, I mean."

"What's her address, Mr. Wright?" Jesse asked wearily as he sat down again.

"I don't see that——"

"Where does she live, Mr. Wright?" Jesse drawled.

"I don't know the exact number," Charles Wright said, and the smile had vanished. "But she works in our office downtown, and of course I know the house. I could look up the number, if you like."

"On the boulevard?"

"Just off it. On Oxford."

"Okay," Jesse said slowly, heaving a sigh and reaching for his coffee. "I reckon we can look it up. Go on home now, kid, and go to sleep. Forget this happened, hear? Forget it."

Charles Wright turned to the rear door, but the deputy's voice stopped him.

"One more thing. Just in case you might think about talking about this, Mr. Wright. I want you to read this letter and then think about the way this guy feels, the one who wrote it. Maybe then you won't be tempted to talk this up anywhere tonight, some bar—or tomorrow in your office."

Jesse Webb watched the younger man read the letter. He saw the face lift afterwards, and he saw going through Charles Wright the same feelings that he himself had experienced and continued to experience every time he even thought of those pitiful words on that sheet of white paper.

"Don't make any more fuss about starting your car than you have to, Mr. Wright."

"But . . . even if you did know the house, Deputy——"

"Yeh?"

"I guess it'd be pretty dangerous to try to close in, wouldn't it?"

"Dangerous for those scum," Jesse Webb said grimly, angry that the young lawyer had put his own feelings into words.

"I was thinking of——" But Charles Wright didn't finish; he turned on his heel and opened the door.

"Stay away from here now," Jesse called after him. "That's an order." Then he took a long swallow of coffee, emptying the cup.

"The boy's got a good question there, Jess. What *do* you have in mind? If they were nice and cozy in that Allen house on Oxford Street, let's say."

"Let's take a look at that map, Tom."

"Here we are. But I've been thinking about that off and on myself all day, Jess. What would we——"

"We're not at that point yet," Jesse snapped. "Did you get the rest of the names filled in on the map?"

"Most of them are there. But you can't be sure, Jess. We haven't had time to do all the cross-checking we should. And you didn't want us asking too many questions. People move in, move out, names change. No directory's up to the minute, Jess. You can see——"

"Oxford Street. Kessler. Here we are."

They studied it together, heads bent over the table. Finally Jesse stood up and took his cup to the urn, stood with his back to Tom Winston. "I don't see any Allen on Oxford, Tom," he said, very slowly, placing the cup under the spigot.

"No, but——"

"Now, Tom, you've got something to do. Find out where that kid lives, who his girl friend really is, where she lives. If nothing breaks around here by morning, I might want to talk to young Mr. Wright again. Also, check his story about that law firm. And I wonder if we could get hold of a city directory."

"Jess, I told you this map can't be accurate. There's no way in the world——"

"Move your fat can, Tom," Jesse said easily, suddenly grateful for Tom Winston, glad to have him along on this. "Anything's better than sitting waiting for the bomb to go off."

Tom Winston shrugged hugely and shambled toward the swinging door into the front of the restaurant. "This keeps up, we'll be suspecting each other," he said. "You're not a cop, you bastard, you're a bulldog."

Jesse laughed then. There was a fresh excitement in the sound.

Behind the wheel of the convertible again, Chuck Wright drove, waiting for the dazed blankness to thin in him. Until it did, no feeling stirred.

You've got it now, he kept telling himself over and over; you've got the whole picture and it's worse than you imagined, much worse than anything you could have dreamed of. But these words didn't seem to reach him. Or the idea, either.

He drove south to his father's house, parked the convertible in the garage as his father had asked him to do. He saw himself doing these things, but he did not seem to be a part of them. He was remembering, as he climbed into his small black car, the way he'd lied to the police. In that split instant of time, while he was still rocking with the blow of actuality, incredible and unreal after all the shadowy suspicions, he had recalled the look on Cindy's face last night and he had known what it meant. The cold coherence of his lie amazed him slightly now: it had leaped full-formed and detailed to his lips, complete with the name of Constance Allen, who worked with Cindy in the office but lived on a farm south of the city. He had lied, he realized now, with the same instinctual cleverness and cunning that had prompted Mr. Hilliard to invent that story of his drunkenness.

Now he started the motor, backed into the street, fully intending in the back of his mind to drive downtown to his club. That's what the police had advised. Then the numbness began to wear away, to slacken off.

Cindy is in that house. Now. Cindy is in that house with those three men.

He brought the car to a halt, hearing again Cindy's words, *Do you have a gun, Chuck?* He jumped out of the car, walked up the front steps of his parents' house, opened the door, climbed to the attic. Only Mattie, the maid, was there and she stood by watching, question marks all over her old and querulous face. Chuck came down in about ten minutes. It had taken him that long to find the rather odd-shaped Japanese automatic he had brought home from the Orient, a war souvenir. When he climbed back into the car, he had the gun in his hip pocket, loaded.

But before he could swing the wheel about for a U turn on the wide and pleasant street where he had spent his childhood, he remembered, phrase by phrase, Mr. Hilliard's anonymous letter to the police. He didn't make the turn; he headed south, away from the Hilliards' home. Take it slow now, Chuck, he was warning himself. Cindy doesn't want the police to know. Mr. Hilliard is desperate that no one know. No one will thank you if you try to play hero here and something goes haywire. Cindy will hate you forever if you pull something wild and reckless now, something that could end in bloodshed. And not necessarily the bloodshed of those three, either, but of the Hilliards. What could you do, anyway? If Mr. Hilliard had wanted help, yours or anyone's, he would have asked. And Cindy—Cindy didn't care what you thought, Chuck, just so long as you didn't think the truth. Trust them. Trust them both. They're desperate people.

But Cindy is in that house.

He trounced on the gas and the car shot forward; he whipped it in a careening turn, going nowhere, aimless again, his body burning, his throat closed and dry.

The police should be told. He was not doing the proper or legal thing in working against the police. But he couldn't help recalling various stories he'd heard, or read. The police is not one man, a predictable human being; the police includes all sorts of human beings, each with his own ambitions and fears and nerves and courage. Take that lanky deputy in the restaurant. *Dangerous for those scum,* he had growled venomously. No thought òf the Hilliards. His was a job to do. That job was to capture or kill those three wanted men. Probably the man was bucking for a promotion.

Still, he showed you the letter, didn't he? To keep your mouth shut, to make you realize the desperation of Mr. Hilliard. Perhaps then the deputy *was* capable of comprehending what Mr. Hilliard was up against. Perhaps——

The decision is not yours, Chuck. It's Mr. Hilliard's. It's his family. Certainly nothing has happened so far in that house, nothing final or fatal; that's what Mr. Hilliard's working against. He has his own ways. And he is determined that the police not come into this.

Still, if they knew that the fugitives were holding hostages in the house——

Hostages. Chuck slowed down. The word brought back a quick memory of war. And with it the thin edge of an idea: perhaps he *could* do something, after all. He himself. Working cautiously and alone. He recalled a certain wartime detail on the edge of the jungle in the Philippines. He recalled the way the Japs had held three officers hostage and the way——

The car was crawling now. Would it work?

No! Cindy is in that house, Chuck. Cindy is there with those three men. Cindy whom you love.

He stepped on the gas again, turned the wheel about and brought the car to a halt in front of the club. The garageman came forward, nodded. Chuck went inside, picked up both the evening papers at the desk, took the self-service elevator to his room. He opened the papers, paged them swiftly and found in the *Times*—on page three tonight—the pictures of the men. A poisonous bitterness rose in him until he tasted it in his mouth as he studied the three faces. Then, in one sudden violent motion of his hand, his fist crashed into the floor lamp, sent it spinning across the room, against the far wall. The bulb exploded. The room was plunged into abrupt darkness. He stood panting, helpless, legs apart, the savage violence still unspent in him.

That's it, he told himself harshly, that's fine, Chuck. Smash up the furniture. Go to pieces now. That'll help a lot. Cindy didn't crack up. Her father has taken more than you'll ever know and he's hanging on, hanging on and fighting in the only way those beasts have left him to fight. Look at the man. He went back into that house tonight, empty-handed, determined, alone.

Chuck was looking at the man Dan Hilliard and he was beginning to breathe more steadily. The picture of Mr. Hilliard brought a slow but expanding respect that was almost a physical emotion in Chuck Wright now—and with it, something quite different, too. That something was shame. He remembered the way he had looked upon Mr. Hilliard and his life— conventional, dull, empty.

A man doesn't fight like that for an empty life. He fights for what is precious and vital to him, the way you are going to fight, by doing nothing, for someone who is precious and vital to you.

You are not going to do a thing, Chuck. Nothing.

He took the gun from his pocket and placed it on top of the bureau in the dark.

You are going to be quiet and calm and you are going to forget any ideas about going near that house until those men have gone.

All the thin and stupid thinking that had built up for Chuck Wright such a phony and childish picture of Dan Hilliard, and other men like Dan Hilliard, now seemed to have been a part of his nature a long time ago. He knew, however, that he had left such thinking behind—and with it a part of his youth—in the space of the last forty-five minutes.

Without turning on the overhead lights, Chuck began to empty his pockets, glad to be able to fall back on routine. But there was something about Mr. Hilliard's letter that, so far, he had not taken into consideration. So far, he had been concentrating on the four people at the mercy of those three men in the house, but now he realized, abruptly and with a heart-freezing shock, that he had not thought about what would happen when those men left. Mr. Hilliard was taking precautions, such as they were, against that moment, but——

163

What if they took Cindy along?

Before the full impact of this possibility reached him, Chuck came across a foreign object in his pocket. He held it and examined it with his fingers for a full minute before he recognized it by touch. It was the key he had forgotten to give back to Cindy in the office today, the key to the rear door of the Hilliards' house. He held it tight in his wet palm now, as though it were a part of the girl herself, and at the same time his mind shot ahead. Was there some way in which he could make use of it?

One o'clock came. Dan Hilliard was gazing at the illuminated dial of his watch on the table beside his bed. Eight and a half more hours until the mail brought the money. Then——

He used what he thought was the last strength in his will to bring his thoughts veering away from that time. Then he slept again, but it was not really sleep because he could not plunge himself far enough below the surface of consciousness. No matter how his body ached and yearned for the peace, he remained alert in every fiber, like a jungle animal in his lair. They've brought you to this, Dan thought. You've entered their world fully now. They've turned your house into a jungle, a wilderness of snarls and clashes and brutish fear. Every motor that passed became, until it was gone, danger, a threat— the police. Every faintest movement downstairs where Robish and Glenn Griffin remained sent a stiffening through him. Always in his mind was the sharp awareness of Eleanor in the other bed, of Cindy and Ralphie in Ralphie's room together, behind the locked door across the hall.

His plan, which he had not really devised but which had come to him in that half-awake dreaming state, was complete now. It amounted to little more than a threat, but it was the best he could invent. It might give Glenn Griffin pause if he did decide to take any of the family along tomorrow. In the morning Dan would carry out the details of that scheme. With that much out of the way, Dan wanted to fight against other thoughts that crept through his mind, the nightmarish memories of the evening just past. But he could not keep his thoughts rigid and marshaled now as he had been able to do earlier. He had passed a certain point, still another one, and he was a different man. The will didn't crack; it weakened, grew soft, flexible.

A hopelessness had worked its way inside, and there was nothing he could do about it. Before, it had been helplessness, which was something quite different; held in the grip of that, he had proved it wrong in some small ways. But this despair that had spread through him, rendering his mind as weak as his body now, was like a dark and powerful drug. No matter what happened, he didn't have a chance. Oh, he'd go through with it all. He'd do what he had to do, and as carefully and thoroughly as possible; but in the end, in the pay-off tomorrow, his whole life, the life of his whole family, would be changed. He didn't dare let himself think in just what way, because he didn't know and it was probably better that he didn't.

You never know anything. There are so many factors involved. Not just fate, not just accident, not just character—but these and also a million other factors that are unfathomable and totally unpredictable. Who would have thought that the rebellion and departure of the younger Griffin would produce in Glenn Griffin that awesome quietness? He was not the same at all now; he had become a different person—the arrogance thin and unconvincing, the swagger an empty gesture, the cruelty more pronounced. Dan recognized—and faced—that quietness for what it was: the thin ice-crust over hysteria. Glenn Griffin then, the leader, on whose cold intelligence of a sort Dan had come to rely, was now crushed and driven by the absence of the brother whom *he* had dominated. During the evening Dan had caught the withering stare of contempt that Glenn Griffin had turned on Cindy. Was that warped mind beginning now to blame her for what Hank had done? And if so, what would this lead to?

Dan knew that he should now, given the opportunity of these few hours, line up in his mind all the factors, examine them thoroughly, and attempt to divine the threats inherent in each of them. Robish's surly defeat, for instance: would he stick by Glenn in the showdown? Was he still intent on his own revenge on Dan? Or on Ralphie?

But there were too many elements. Too many, too many. And his mind was tired, hazy. Sleep hovered under it, beckoning, inviting. Dan wanted to plunge into the dark well of nothingness, knowing that he needed the rest more than any of these circles-within-circles of spinning thoughts.

Then, as it had done ever since he came up the stairs that last time, his mind turned again to Ralphie—lying in there staring at the ceiling, not comprehending his father, bewildered, lost. Perhaps crying silently. Would he ever understand?

Dan twisted about and his muscles protested. The one thought he had so far successfully avoided came lancing at him then, swift and sharp and direct. There were more than eight hours till that money arrived and in that time the police could catch or shoot Hank Griffin, trace his clothes, which were Dan's, or the car, which was Cindy's——

Dan sat up, and heard Eleanor stirring in the next bed.

"Dan? What is it, darling?"

He sank back. "Nothing, Ellie."

"Do you want another aspirin?"

"No, dear. Go to sleep. You need your sleep."

"It won't be long now, Dan. Please don't worry so. It's such a short time now."

"I love you, Ellie," Dan whispered, his throat parched.

He felt her get up, heard her cross to his bed; she was beside him, holding him, not crying, very still, clinging to him.

"I love you, Dan. Always, always."

The words should have made him feel young again, should have carried him back to the time when they had both used those phrases with the same intensity. But he barely heard them.

He barely heard them because it had come to him that, no matter what happened, the police would have a hard time tracing the coupe back to Cindy Hilliard. It would take hours, perhaps days—perhaps enough time to allow him to receive the money from Columbus. It would take a long time because several hours ago Dan himself had removed the license plates from that car and placed them on the gray sedan. Attached to the sedan, they were now at the bottom of White River. But Hank Griffin, possibly unaware of it, was driving a car without license tags. There was an awesome inevitability about it all that shook Dan completely, now that he realized it, and at the same time he was struck again with the terrible and mysterious interweaving of character, fate and accident that determined the outcome of this and perhaps everything else in life.

The thought was simply a thought to him, though—complex and abstract and dreamlike—neither alarming nor reassuring. He closed his eyes, wondering.

Hank Griffin always emerged from those paroxysms with a feeling of purged happiness, of light-headed confidence. When the trembling and quivering and blackness had faded tonight, he found himself on a deserted street, under a street lamp, in a black coupe; and it took him a few minutes, sitting there limply behind the wheel, to realize where he was, and why.

Then, although his mind seemed to have nothing to do with it, he had reached a decision. The decision had been made for him, somehow, and he was helpless to do anything but act on the basis of it.

He had started the car then, eased it forward, his bones aching with the cold; he continued driving west even though his decision, which was not yet clear to him, had something to do with the Hilliard house and the Hilliard house lay some miles behind him.

Now, half an hour after his return to reality, he was on the western edge of the city, dropping south on a back road, heading toward the main east-west highway, U.S. 40, which cut straight through the city. He had caught sight of a clock back there, the lighted dial reading fifteen minutes to 2. If he had been able to calculate time, he might have figured out just how long he had sat back there, writhing in that blankness. But his thoughts had one direction: to get in touch with Glenn.

He was beyond panic, past fear. He knew what he was doing and all he had to do was carry it through and everything would work itself out. The drug stores and gas stations were closed now, except maybe in the center of town and he certainly didn't intend driving there; but he had to reach a telephone. So there was one place, and only one, that he could think of: an all-night restaurant. Where were the all-night joints? On the highways. So he was sticking to his original plan, to head west, get out of town. Only this time, instead of cutting back to the Chicago road, he would call Glenn. He would warn Glenn. He would suggest that Glenn meet him, that they go to Chicago instead of Cincinnati, and then send for Helen Lamar.

All the way, though, he kept saying to himself: You must have been nuts. You must've been loonier than Robish to turn on Glenn like that.

Well, he'd been right about the coppers; they were wise to something all right and parked near the Hilliard house for some reason. But Glenn would know how to handle that. Like taking Mrs. Hilliard and that girl along in the car, the way he'd planned all along. Maybe then no coppers'd get suspicious; or if they did, they'd think twice, maybe hold their fire completely, before giving chase. Glenn had all the angles figured.

After Hank made his call, all his worries would be over. He'd admit now that he wasn't as smart as Glenn; his mind didn't click that way. Then let Glenn make the decisions, let Glenn dope it all out. A surge of joy lifted in him now, pushing back the early-morning chill.

In this mood, he could see everything sharp and clear. Everything. He was even able to think about that girl—and what was going to happen to her if the cops should start shooting and maybe even if they didn't—in a different, more sensible way. *You want a woman,* Glenn always said, *take her. Don't moon about it.*

He'd been mooning. And to hell with it. Maybe he should have taken her, right there in the house. That's what it came down to, all any of it ever came down to—wanting and taking. All the rest was a lot of silliness. He'd gone soft, like Glenn claimed. It must have been that house that did it, that house and the girl. Being in that house had been torture. What right did they—those Hilliards—have to a joint like that? Who says they should have it and not him?

He was nearing the highway now; he could see the passing headlights and the shadows of trucks, their roar deadened by distance.

You got to watch out for roadblocks, though, he warned himself. Not that anybody's going to take a second look at you in this car, and alone like this.

Why did he have to keep thinking about that damn girl, even now? She was just like the rest, like all of them. A slow anger was burning in him. He felt that, somehow, he had been tricked. He didn't know how, in what way. But his thoughts turned savage. He touched the automatic in the sweater pocket.

He was cursing in a low steady mutter of sound above the purring motor. He hated all girls like that Cindy Hilliard, always had. They never looked at you, they passed you by, their eyes were always ahead of them. Too good for you. Too good, hell! What about that boy friend, that lawyer guy? If you were in their class, if you ran around with those gals on dates, they weren't too good for *anything!* But guys like you—scum. His contempt for Cindy Hilliard mounting, Hank was able now to think with a certain pleasure of what was going to happen to her. Glenn wouldn't take her along and then just let her go. He'd push her body out somewhere, hide it so it wouldn't be found for days, maybe weeks. And Hank'd be right there and seeing it happen and it wouldn't hurt him; it would mean nothing to him; he'd even enjoy it.

But he wasn't just sure of that, either. Here he was now, getting mixed up again. *Damn her!* And damn that tough old man or hers! Hank had even come to admire the bastard a little.

Why do you always have to be so mixed up? Always, all your life!

He was approaching the highway with caution now, pushing his thoughts aside as the tension returned and mingled with the baffling conflict that seemed to rage in him forever. Nothing unusual, no concealed cars in either direction. He made a right turn, heading west. The thought that now he was actually traveling in the direction of Terre Haute and the prison he had left almost two full days ago sent a shudder of apprehension and fear down his spine. He remembered the cell, the guards, the routine, the food, the smells; he remembered it all and went sick again, the quiver threatening to come back, low in his stomach. He had forgotten his driving and the car was crawling along. In the back of his mind he knew that once he was talking to Glenn and Glenn was telling him what would be the smart thing to do——

A huge truck charged past, sending vibrations through the

coupe. Hank spat an oath and trounced on the gas again. Then, in front of him, the truck nosed off the highway to the right.

Hank had to whip the wheel to the left to avoid hitting the rear end of the trailer, and he was twenty yards beyond the diner before he realized the reason for the truck's stopping. He had almost passed the phone. He jammed on the brakes, pulled the coupe onto the shoulder of the road at an angle—what difference did it make?—and climbed out, his rage directed now at the driver of that truck.

The air, raw and windy, struck him full across the face. He walked then, with just a suggestion of his brother's jauntiness, along the pavement, then across the parking area, up three steps, into the metal-gleaming and steamy interior.

There was no booth. Almost at once he saw the black phone box attached to the tile wall near a side door in the rear. Scowling at the truck driver who was just sliding onto a counter stool, tipping his hat back from a seamed and ugly face, Hank went to the phone, took into his hands the directory that was suspended from a chain on the wall. He hated looking up names. The alphabet confused him. His nerves were jumping. He shouldn't be here now, anyway. What the hell was he doing here?

Unable to find the name Hilliard, even though he was positive he had the right page, Hank felt a swift ugly impulse to give that truck driver a working over. He could feel his muscles leaping. He could feel his fist crashing against the bone of that guy's face, and his legs working in that way Glenn had taught him, and his arms swinging like pistons, so fast guys twice his weight didn't know what was happening to them. Yeh, that was the one thing he could sure do. But the thought meant nothing to him. There was a taste in his mouth, the dry taste of utter bone-melting weariness.

What difference did it make? Any of it? Where was it all leading anyway?

But he had the name now. He tried to fix the number in his memory and then dial, but he failed; an operator's voice inquired briskly, "What number are you calling please?" He hung up; then, with the directory propped against the wall with his left hand, letting the earpiece dangle, he dialed slowly, his eyes on the numbers one by one. Then, while the phone rang, he remembered that he had only a little change left in his pocket and certainly not more than enough to buy one gallon of gas. He must remember to tell Glenn this, so Glenn wouldn't set up a meeting place too many miles away.

When he heard the voice at the other end of the line, Hilliard's, he spoke sharply, "I'm calling Mr. James," remembering in time the last name Glenn had told Helen Lamar to use in her call last night at about this time.

Then it was that he caught the flash of dark blue in the doorway of the diner, across the shine of counter. He recognized the wide-brimmed hat and his eyes dropped down the uniform. The trooper was young, his face had a weathered look, and he was leaning across speaking to the counterman as Hank heard his brother's voice on the other end of the line, low and hard: "Hello, Hello? Who is it?"

"Hank," he said, but he had gone stiff and helpless, and the word was a whisper.

It was all he said, because the blue moved around the corner of the counter toward him. Hank replaced the earpiece and took one step, waiting, remembering in a flash that it was a murder charge this time, and that meant the chair. The broad bony face blurred before his eyes, and he dropped his hand carelessly into the pocket of Dan Hilliard's sweater.

"That your black coupe out there, mister?" a twanging voice asked, but not unpleasantly. "You know you don't have any license plates on her?"

Already, though, Hank's hand was moving, and too late, with the gun in mid-air, he realized that there was no cause for him to fire. The trooper hadn't recognized him. But by then the trigger was snapping and the explosion thundered in the small room. In the echo, there were exclamations of terror and amazement from the direction of the counter, and the trooper himself bent forward, his head twisting sideways and his hand clawing at his holster.

With the acrid smell of the gunpowder slapping back at him, Hank fired once again, higher, missing; he heard the bullet smash into the plate-glass windows. Then, for the first time fully realizing what exactly was taking place, he whirled, lunged out the side door, and ran.

The cold air took his breath. He saw a parked truck, made for it, expecting each instant to feel the bone-smashing slam of bullet against his spine. Behind the body of the truck, he stopped, crouching. The coupe was in the opposite direction, beyond the diner. There was a flat fenced field, but no cover, in front of him.

Glenn, his mind cried. *Glenn, what now?*

A spotlight flicked on in front of the diner, roamed uncertainly over the truck, throwing a grotesque reflection beyond. Hank saw all this without grasping it for a long dead stunned moment. The other trooper, his mind said then, but the warning came from a distance. The other trooper in the car! Hank began to curse again. How much time passed he didn't know. The automatic was still clutched in his hand, warm now, and heavy. But useless to him because he didn't seem to have the strength to move. Vaguely he knew that they'd close in if he continued to stand here, but he was thinking, with shock, of the face of the man he had just shot and he was remembering Glenn's words: *They'll have you back in stir in less'n a hour.*

Then a bullet struck the earth by his foot, dug in, spurting gravel that stung against his leg. They were firing at his legs, firing under the truck.

Glenn!

Wildly then, because his normally slow mind was working with a desperate sluggishness, he turned and ran. He had no idea in what direction he was going, but he was afraid of the flatness of field beyond the fence and he could only think of crossing the highway, finding cover behind a thicket or in a woods on the other side. Even then, though, he knew that he was not going to make it. Despair dragged his heels, slowed his working legs. His shoes hit the pavement as a bullet whined past his shoulder, and then he felt the blinding blast of the spotlight on him as he half-stumbled, half-ran to the middle of the highway. Somewhere deep inside the familiar wracking shudders were beginning, and he knew that this time he would die. *Dying wouldn't be so bad if you didn't know it was happening to you.*

But he felt the lance of pain even as he saw, reeling, the spurt of blue flame from in front of the diner. The pain leaped scalding up his leg from his calf and he stopped, without going down.

This isn't right, he thought. You shouldn't have to know.

Then he saw the truck charging along the highway, the world-sweeping glare of lights. Rooted there, and with the pain reaching upward hotly to his brain, he heard the roar of motor, the hiss of airbrakes. He stood upright, frozen in the blast of horn, saw the rocking square image behind the lights swerving to his left. He kept expecting to hear another thunder of gunfire, but instead the motor sound deafened him as the fender brushed safely past at an angle. Then the spotlight beam caught the solid mass of silver-colored trailer that swung flatly at him as cab and trailer buckled. Everything then was intense and terrible and in detail. He knew every second of it, saw it all, realized its meaning, his mind still feebly whimpering that it should not be so. The blinding, glimmering wall of trailer took forever to reach him, its sidewise progress slowed interminably by the rubbery protest of gripping tires.

Then it was upon him, and the moment of death itself brought amazement: it had happened—and to him.

6

6

At about 2:15 in the morning, a time when Chuck Wright normally slept the deep and restful sleep of the young, he was roused from a shallow semi-consciousness by a knock on the door. He reached for the lamp that was not in its usual place; then he stood up, hearing the insistence of that rapping, padded in bare feet across the small bedroom and flipped on the overhead lights before he opened the door. By the time he stood looking into the quietly inexpressive face of Deputy Sheriff Jesse Webb, Chuck was alert and cautious, the great balloon of tension expanded in the area of his chest.

"I couldn't sleep, Mr. Wright," Jesse drawled and stepped in; his glance did not miss a thing, including the fact that Chuck still wore shirt and trousers, not pajamas. "I reckon you couldn't, either." Jesse stooped down, righted the lamp that was now a tangle of smashed shade and twisted wires. "Rough stuff, Mr. Wright? Marines, wasn't it?"

"You know. Why ask?"

"Now that's what a man likes. Friendly co-operation, middle of the night." He sat down on the edge of the bed. "We're slow,

Mr. Wright, but in time we get it. You could save us time. And my hunch is those people up there only got a certain amount of time to spare. You follow me, Wright? You know what people I refer to?"

Chuck Wright picked up a package of cigarettes from the seat of a chair, shook one out. "No. You think I should?"

"Goddammit," Jesse said with slow disgust, "I know you *do* —not should—*do*." And Chuck, lighting his cigarette, watched the blood drain from the lean, leathery face. "Stop stalling around, Wright. You're a lawyer; you know you can't cribbage around with the police like this. Listen to me now. There's no one named Allen lives on Oxford, not from one end of the street to the other. And this Constance Allen—who is *not* your girl friend at all, or anyone else's because she's been secretly married for six months—does work in your office, but she lives on a farm out of town. *South.* Now while that don't help me one damn iota, it kind of puts you in a fix. 'Cause if you don't start talking now, Wright, I'm gonna slap a charge against you —aidin' and abettin'; you know the fancy language—and you can get that law firm to go to work for you. But before they can do one damn thing, I'm going to get the name of those folks up north, one way or the other, badge or no badge."

"Stop rubbing your knuckles, Deputy," Chuck Wright said easily, but not angrily. "I don't bully——" But he hesitated then, seeing a look in the other's eyes.

His attention attracted by an object on the top of the bureau, Jesse Webb stood up, strolled over, picked up the Japanese automatic, gave it a thorough examination, even checking the clip. Then he simply stared at Chuck Wright, waiting.

"I've got a permit," Chuck said at last.

"Permit be damned!" Jesse Webb barked. "What'd you have in mind for this, Wright? And don't take me around any more curves, boy. I've been around too many today. Now!"

"I don't want to have to use it," Chuck Wright said then, and very slowly, his gaze meeting the deputy's.

Jesse Webb lifted his brows once, fumbled in his shirt pocket for his own cigarette, lighted it with a wooden match cupped in his palms. "You had me going for a little while," he conceded, blowing smoke. "You're not fronting for those bastards, are you, boy? You want to kill 'em just as much as I do." When Chuck said nothing after that, when he didn't move at all but his helplessness tempted him, just for a second, to trust this tall, laconic character, Jesse added, almost too casually: "What's her name?"

"Maybe it's my own family," Chuck said, stalling, cautious again.

Jesse Webb smashed his right fist into his left palm, and the violent impact cracked like a pistol shot in the small room. "I said let's not play! Your folks came home an hour ago from the Meridian Hills Country Club, and you yourself were in their house earlier. That's how you came by that Japanese gadget, isn't it? Now let's have it, Wright. What's her name?"

Chuck Wright took such a deep breath that his shoulders heaved. "All right, Deputy. You've got it right—so far. But I'm not going to give you the name, and I'll tell you why. You'll get it soon enough, way you work, and you were right when you said those people needed time. They've gone to a lot of trouble —God knows how much—to keep this from getting to the police."

"What the hell do you think I'm going to do when I find out?" cried Jesse Webb, all the weariness and confusion there on his narrow face. "What kind of idiots do people think the police are? You think I'm going to blow up the house to get those rats?"

"What *will* you do?" Chuck Wright asked.

The question riled Jesse Webb, because of his own uncertainty in this matter, and Chuck saw his knuckles whiten as he pushed back his coat and clutched at his belt, planting his long legs. "I'll be ready for them, that's what. They can't stay in there forever."

179

This brought Chuck Wright around full, sharp and flush against his basic fear, the fear that carried his reluctance: "There can't be any shooting when they go, either. You read Mr. —— you read that letter."

Jesse Webb shouted, "I know that, too!"

"But there might be. You can't control that completely, can you, Deputy? State Police, FBI, deputies, maybe the city cops —one guy, just one man, has to get the wrong idea, be tempted to try to pick one of them off when they come out." He reached out involuntarily and took hold of the deputy's arms with both hands. "You must have been in the war, Deputy. You don't have the control we had then, and even then, by God, it didn't always hold them when they got jumpy. There can't be any bloodshed." He was speaking in a low, hoarse whisper and shaking the taller man with both gripped hands. "There can't be any blood—because it won't just be those vermin who get it. You know who'll be killed, don't you? You *know*. If you don't, damn you, what am I wasting my breath for?"

After that, there was a long silence. During it, the tall man removed Chuck Wright's hands, but without any suggestion or hint of anger now, or of annoyance. Shaking his head, he pushed the boy down to a sitting position on the bed and stood above him, saying in a soft, almost gentle manner, "There's going to be blood, boy. I reckon you better get that straight right now." He was a man arguing with himself, sharpening his conclusions for someone else so as to get them clear in his own mind. "Glenn Griffin's not going to take anybody along for a ride and then just drop 'em off and thanks for the pleasant company. If you think that, kid, you don't know the guy the way I do. So what are we going to do? We're going to take the opportunity, when and if it comes, to get as many of those three as possible without sacrificing anyone else. What else can we do, boy? What else is there for us?"

"I couldn't make that decision for *them*. I can't tell you, Deputy. I'm sorry."

Jesse turned abruptly away and stubbed out his cigarette. "Okay. Okay, kid. I honest-to-God don't know whether you're making a mistake or not. I honest-to-God don't know what I'd do if I was in your shoes. But I'm in mine, and I got a job. So that's the way it is. If I make a mistake——"

The ringing of the telephone cut across his words. Without so much as a glance at Chuck, he picked it up. Chuck Wright stood up, a coldness in him now, a terrible certainty, as he heard the deputy say, "H'lo." Then: "Speaking." The tall man listened, his eyes swinging slowly to rest on Chuck but his face impassive. "Dead?" Again he listened. "Damn! What about the trooper?" He nodded automatically. "Fifteen minutes, Tom."

Chuck's voice had frozen in his throat.

"Put on your shoes, boy. You're not sleeping anyway." Jesse Webb involuntarily dropped his arm against the holster under his shoulder. "I'm going to take you for a fast ride. Show you the kind of filth you're letting this girl of yours take chances with." As Chuck drew on his shoes, Jesse Webb, at the door now, continued: "It may be good news, kid. One of 'em's dead."

Dead seemed to Chuck Wright a flat and inadequate word, hardly the truth at all, when applied to the thing at which he stared, along with Deputy Webb, only eighteen minutes later. The siren still wailed in his brain. And the flashing bleakness of the city streets caught in the red glare, together with the sensations of terrific speed and intense cold, and now the sight of this under the blanket that the fat deputy was displaying so casually, all came together in him and he was sick. Hot, flushed and faint. He turned away, took a few uncertain steps along the edge of the highway, his eyes seeing in an unsteady flash the overturned trailer truck, the harsh white illumination of spotlights, the oddly white faces of the curious spectators, and above, that still dark and motionless sky. He was reminded again of the war, and with the memory a little of the heat that scalded his flesh faded away and left him standing, off from the others a little, listening, hearing but not quite comprehending.

"You sure it's him?" Jesse Webb was asking, and even *his* voice sounded stunned and dim with nausea.

"It's the young one all right, Jess," the fat deputy said.

Another voice caused Chuck to turn, to watch them there, all three figures edging away from the blanket now: Deputy Webb, tall, bent forward at the waist, hands in pockets, the fat deputy with his hat shoved back, and this third man in State Police uniform. This man was small and he had a hard, crisp look to him, and when he spoke, his voice reflected this: "MacKenzie didn't even know the slob had a gun, didn't even suspect it. Well, son, you ready to treat this thing seriouslike now? Two killings enough for you?"

"Don't start riding me again," Deputy Webb warned in a whisper. "One of 'em's dead, isn't he? Don't ride me, Lieutenant Fredericks. I didn't plug your man." With this he prowled away, inclining his head slightly toward the fat man. "What about the car?"

But Lieutenant Fredericks followed, and Chuck could hear him speaking, sharply and curtly, while he took off his hat and wiped the silver-gray stubble of hair: "No matter who did it, Mac's on a operating table, son. If we'd been moving all day 'stead of playing around——"

Jesse Webb whirled, and Chuck frowned, listening: "Look, Lieutenant. I'm no superman. Where's Carson? He's been playing it my way, too. I don't think knocking down some doors would have saved your man MacKenzie. I think ringing doorbells and flashing red lights might have killed *other* people, though. I've tried to get the Sheriff back here, but he's a hard man to reach when he's hunting in the woods, hear? If he comes, he can take over. Meanwhile, you've got one dead Griffin and one wounded trooper. God knows I'm sorry about Mac, but you stay away from my throat, Lieutenant. I've got enough on my mind."

At this Lieutenant Fredericks replaced his hat on his head, swiped the handkerchief over his small, hard-edged face. "Personal grudges," he said, "got no place in police work."

"Personal grudges, hell!" Jesse exploded. "Let's get on with this investigation. Who does the car belong to? Where'd he get the car?"

"Easy," the fat deputy said, and as Chuck turned and walked slowly along the edge of the highway, making his way toward a car some distance away, parked at an odd angle on the shoulder of the road, he heard behind him: "Damnedest thing of all, Jess. It's gonna take some time to trace that car 'cause there are no plates on her. No identification of any kind. If it wasn't for those plates missing like that, MacKenzie wouldn't even have stopped in the diner. We can't check the clothes labels till the stores open in the morning, but I've roused Bonham out of bed to start work on the motor serial. That'll take forever. Then there's the gun—*if* it's registered at all, that is. Nothing else in the car to help. Only it looks like it might belong to a woman. Few hairpins——"

Chuck, with the man's voice fading behind him, was paused five yards from the small black coupe. The sight of it, more than the shocking evidence of violence all along the highway, reached him with the impact of a blow. He had no idea how long he stood there, limp and suddenly cold again.

"Well, kid?" Jesse Webb's voice asked near his ear. "Well, you know who that belongs to? Save us a lot of time."

"Maybe the other two have gone, too," Chuck said without turning.

"Possible. Let's you and I drive by the house and find out."

But Chuck only shook his head, a haggard, negative movement that choked off the hope before it could take root. Give the name and address to Deputy Webb and let that hard-nosed State Policeman back there get hold of it, he was thinking, and then what? Sirens, spotlights, tear gas and a machine gun set up on the Hilliard lawn? No thanks.

At Chuck's refusal, Jesse Webb swore under his breath and passed him; he threw open the door of Cindy's coupe, probed about inside with a flashlight. The familiar appearance of the car might have done it; whatever caused it now, an idea returned to Chuck Wright, an original idea, one he'd had a long time ago now, when he first learned what was happening. His mind darted in its original direction again. Perhaps there *was* something he could do.

He turned and walked back to the shadowy circle of spectators, found the man whose cap he had noticed earlier, stepped up to him. "Your cab here? You want a fare?"

"Yes, sir," the taxi driver said, beginning to shamble toward his cab. "A man's stomach can only take so much, huh."

Chuck climbed into the back seat, sat down stiffly, and gave the driver the address of the club. With the key to the back door of the Hilliard house hard in his palm, Chuck said, "Just step on it, and no talk. I'm tired." But that was a lie; he wasn't, not in the least now. "We'll read all about it in the morning paper."

"Ernie," Jesse Webb was saying, hunched over the counter in the diner twenty minutes later, waiting for the coroner's preliminary report, "Ernie, look, I can't explain why, but this can't get in the paper, especially not in the morning paper. Believe me, I've got reasons."

Carson, the FBI man, who had arrived while Jesse was

searching the black coupe, nodded. "Make it an accident. Unidentified victim."

Ernie, who was young and muscular with a blond crew cut, unbuttoned his trench coat. "I'll pass the request along to the city editor, Jess. It's the best I can do."

"Damn!" Jesse rasped. "You'll do more than that. You'll do what Mr. Carson said. Unidentified victim, accident. It don't matter to you, but we got a case on our hands, and we can't let this guy's brother know we got him."

"Why?"

"I can't go into that. Can't you newsboys ever take a cop's word for anything? It's important, Ernie."

Ernie inclined his pockmarked young face and thought with pursed lips. "Jess, look at it this way. You've got a job. That's one thing. I've got one, too, and that's another. This is a story, a helluva big one and you know it. You're asking me to sit on it and then the afternoon papers'll blow it sky-high and I'll be left up a creek."

Patiently, then, very slowly, Jesse said, "There are human lives at stake, Ernie."

"Who?"

At this Jesse smiled. He liked men who knew their jobs; he liked men who did them. And he envied the straight-line, uncomplicated thinking of those men, like Lieutenant Fredericks, however much their methods annoyed him. "Stick with me, Ernie. There's a story breaking, believe me. It's bigger than this. If you use this one, if Glenn Griffin gets hold of this and gets scared——"

Ernie held up a flat palm. "I said I'd try. I'll talk to Roland. But I got to write it."

Jesse Webb nodded. He had the feeling then that all these precautions, plugging one hole after another, were all so much waste motion. After his talk with Chuck Wright, after he'd clarified all the potentials for himself and could find no way out for the people, whoever they were, he had begun to give in to this sense of hopelessness. Strange thing, too—he had, in the last few hours now, almost forgotten Uncle Frank and whatever personal reasons he might once have imagined important in this case. What concerned him now—and on a deep, personal level—was the plight of that family, the man who wrote that letter. As yet, he hadn't even reached the question of what Hank Griffin's actions tonight—why was he alone in that car? —might mean in relation to those people and to the other two convicts. Jesse would get to that, though. He had, it now appeared, plenty of time—since he was working his way to the name of those people in the most laborious, tedious and roundabout manner; since, dammit, that Wright boy had disappeared after taking one look at that black coupe.

As it turned out, however, Jesse had no time at all. Before he could believe it, although he didn't waste any time on amazement now, the long wait was over. In the completely casual and matter-of-fact way that one never expects vital matters to reach a climax, the anticipated moment arrived. He looked up from the counter, saw Tom Winston half-turning from the phone, motioning to him with one beefy hand. He slipped off the stool, telling Ernie again to try, please, to keep the death of the kid dark for a while, and then he walked along the counter, turned and joined Tom Winston at the same phone Hank Griffin had used over an hour ago now, somewhere around 2 o'clock. Tom's wind-reddened globe of face looked up at him, and a grin that held no amusement leaped along his full lips as he spoke, whispering so that none of the others at the counter could overhear: "Come outside, Jess."

They went out, using the door through which Hank Griffin had plunged just before his death, and then Tom Winston touched Jesse Webb's arm—a very unusual gesture for Tom Winston. "The gun," he said. "Jess, the little black automatic Griffin used on MacKenzie. It's registered. It's in the name of Hilliard. Daniel C. Hilliard."

That was all there was to it. After all those hours, it was as simple as that. Jesse's mind didn't stumble; it did not have to swing slowly and uncertainly backwards, examining the list of customers that had been found in Mr. Patterson's house by the dump; it did not have to go over, one by one, the names of the people who had written checks to Mr. Patterson yesterday morning. The name *Eleanor Hilliard* leaped sharp and clear to the foreground of his thoughts. Nor did his memory exert any special effort in crawling over that map of the neighborhood north of the city limits, pinpointing the exact block involved. He had it all, it once, and there was in him no explosion of joy, no violence of excitement, no particular triumph. Only a slow cold something stirring far down inside. And still more questions now, the inevitable ones: What now? Where do you go from here?

Then Jesse Webb began giving more instructions, in a very low and controlled voice, his eyes concentrating on the puffs of steam leaping from his lips as he spoke in the cold air.

Forty-five minutes later—it was almost 4 o'clock but the sky would not brighten even slightly before 6—Jesse Webb, driving a dark brown car whose appearance could in no way be associated with the police, was approaching the Hilliard house from the west on Kessler Boulevard. He didn't like the knock in the motor of Ernie's car, which he had borrowed, but the reporter had called after him that it wouldn't give out on him if he didn't have to give it the works. In a very short time now, he would have a complete report on Daniel C. Hilliard and family, but he could already judge a few things for himself: good income; typical sort of life; excellent neighborhood, not upper crust but middle-class comfortable. Also, he had taken the responsibility of not informing Lieutenant Fredericks of what he had learned.

If it came to a showdown, he'd have to take the matter over
Fredericks' head and let someone else, perhaps Carson or Carson's superior in the Bureau, make the decision. Until such
time, he'd do it his way—and hope. Winston would give the
information to Carson, of course, and further action would be
decided upon at 4:30 in the kitchen of Joe's restaurant in
Broad Ripple. Meanwhile, four patrol cars had been alerted,
their positions shifted to cover, still inconspicuously, the possible exit routes from the Hilliard house. But they had no specific instructions, as yet, as to what to do in the event Griffin
and Robish attempted to escape in the company of the Hilliard
family. This unresolved and therefore doubly dangerous state
of things was what that kid, Chuck Wright, feared, and Jesse
wished he could blame the boy for holding back the name
which Jesse now had, anyway.

Slowing down, Jesse held the car to a steady pace because as
he passed the house, which would be on his left, he wished to
give himself sufficient time for observation and at the same time
he felt that too slow a speed or any abrupt change in it might
call attention to his presence. His first impression of the house
was that it was rather large, set off by itself, flat fields to the
west of it, and two or three vacant and wooded lots to the east.
The windows were dark, and there was a certain reassurance in
this natural-appearing fact.

In the driveway, there was a long, recent-model blue sedan
with its nose pointed toward the street. Jesse recorded this,
understanding its meaning; then twisting about only slightly,
he let his eyes climb from window to window. Nothing. Darkness. But they were still in there—one, perhaps both.

Then he was passing the woods, coming abreast of the closest
house. Walling, his memory reminded him, Ralph Walling. On
his right, across the boulevard from the Hilliards, there were no
structures of any sort, only an expanse of meadow with a realtor's sign advertising lots for sale.

They chose well, the bastards, he said to himself in grim

silence, wishing that he had had more time to study the exact locations of the porches, garage, doors. But he had a fairly accurate picture now. At the first street he made a left turn, intending to pass all the way around the four sides of the block. But he remembered from the map that it was not an ordinary block here; there was no cross-street or road behind the Hilliard house—that is, north of it—for perhaps a quarter of a mile. It was this area behind the house in which he was particularly interested as he turned left again on the graveled back road that paralleled the boulevard.

If a man made his way through the woods that extended rather densely from the rear of the Hilliard property to this road on which he was now traveling west, and if he could approach the house unseen from behind, especially in the heavy darkness now——

But this was, he concluded swiftly, the sort of conjecture that could lead nowhere really because the point you missed, when you began to figure this way, was that the back door of the house would be locked tight and alertly guarded from inside, especially now that young Griffin had gone. His brother was smart enough to realize exactly what danger was involved in this.

Jesse's job now was to find a place for a lookout, a place where a man or preferably several men could keep watch on the Hilliard house. Considering the flatness and low underbrush of the fields to the west and across the boulevard from the house, it would be a tough job, too. This was what he was working on, arranging it in his mind for presentation to Carson and Fredericks, when he caught sight of something which caused him to come to a complete halt on the road a quartermile behind the Hilliard house.

What he saw, at first, was a gleam in the woods, the woods he had been studying. But when he walked back to investigate with his flashlight, what he examined was a powerful low-slung foreign sports car enveloped in the trees, off the little road but not quite completely concealed. He dismissed at once the idea that it might be another getaway car: too conspicuous, too small, despite its power.

The upholstery was leather. The glove compartment contained a book of instructions, in English, on the repair and care of the motor car, a few packages of cigarettes, a discarded fountain pen, a bottle opener. He picked up from the seat and examined a small cardboard box, which was empty. On the lid there were three Oriental-looking symbols in a vertical line; they meant nothing to him. He was about to replace the box when it occurred to him to smell it. The odor was distinct: acrid and metallic—the smell of gunpowder. And then he remembered the odd-shaped automatic on the bureau top in Chuck Wright's room at his club.

But what Jesse Webb was thinking then was so ridiculous and impossible that he refused, for a second or two, to give credence to the suspicion. Finally, though, he fixed the number of the license plate in his mind and drove, rather swiftly now, to the restaurant where Tom Winston and the others were waiting.

Time seemed to stand still now for Chuck Wright. He lay on his back, watching the tops of the trees, not wishing, even in darkness, to expose his head around the corner of the Hilliard garage any more times than was necessary. The darkness had been, of course, in his favor; but he was looking forward to dawn. Now, while nothing moved in or near the house and no sound reached him except an occasional car passing on the boulevard, he could not see well enough to know whether either man was keeping watch out the rear windows.

Twenty minutes ago, when he had seen the blue sedan still in position in the driveway, he had known that the two other men remained in the house. Before he dared make any move at all now, he had to know pretty well where those men were. With no lights in the house, he would probably have to wait till morning and hope then that he could make out in which room or rooms the men were staying. Until that time, he could only lie here, flush against the rear wall of the garage, and consider all the possibilities of his position.

The principal idea was to slip inside, unseen, silently, through the rear door, using the key that Cindy, in her excitement, had accidentally left in his hand the night before last. Once inside, the arrangement of the small back hall was in his favor; it gave him access, through the kitchen, to the downstairs area of the house; the rear stairway offered a way to the second floor; and the steps leading to the basement provided a place for him to conceal himself if he decided to wait and listen inside the house.

At any rate, with any luck at all, he'd be in there and only the two against one and the advantage of surprise on his side.

But there was gnawing in him, a sense of reluctance. Cindy and her father did not want this.

They're going to take someone along, Cindy, he argued in silence. Maybe you.

The tall deputy, that Webb, had convinced him that Glenn Griffin would not leave the house without taking every precaution for himself; this was the meaning of Mr. Hilliard's letter, too. The realization of this, not as potential but as certainty, had caused Chuck, after seeing Cindy's car, to go back to the club, change into tight slacks, sneakers, a sweater; all the while, too, he had been thinking of that State Police lieutenant, the one with the hard-as-nails voice whose impatience to act had pushed Chuck further along toward his decision. And there was the chance, too, that Webb's superior might return, might reverse Webb's caution in favor of the State Policeman's approach. By now, Chuck guessed, or very soon now, the police would have the name, the address, everything. If they did start to move in, somebody had to be inside that house to see that nothing happened to any of the Hilliards.

Chuck examined his watch: 4:17. Not more than two hours, perhaps less, until the sky would begin, slightly, to whiten. Then another two and a half hours before, normally, Cindy and her father would leave for work. Would they let them leave the house today? Would they still struggle to keep up that appearance of a normal routine?

The thought of the Hilliards in there now—sleepless like him and wondering whether they would ever again be able to look forward, without dread, to anything—moved him strangely. It was the first time in his life that outrage and compassion had made him feel a part of something. He felt involved now, one of them. And he wondered about this feeling, letting the idea occupy the vast stretch of empty time that lay ahead.

He realized, lying there, that he had never given himself time to think, to figure out anything: what he had, what he wanted, what he needed. But it came to him now, at this most unlikely time, that he had never really felt a part of his parents' life; he hadn't blamed them then and he didn't blame them now. But he recognized his loss for the first time, and began to understand, faintly at first and then in a vivid rush, that the fast driving, the footloose girls, the drinking and general rebellion, the desperate filling in of time, all had been his feeble attempts to conceal from himself the aloneness. Because he did not have it, he had scoffed at Mr. Hilliard and what he had—involvement, love.

Cindy. Would he ever be able to tell her? Were there words, after all, to describe the brilliant illumination that was in him here in the darkness, on the damp ground, behind her garage?

The strength grew in him, not the strength of the Marine who really hadn't cared much one way or the other there in the jungle, but the solid knowing determination of a man who knew that he was not going to allow anything to happen to the people he loved. Yes, love. The word had scared him once, in that far-off time when he was too blind and stupid to realize its meaning. He was going to see to it that nothing happened to Cindy or to any of the people who, by his own secret and mystifying adoption, had become his family. He loved them all with a deep and certain love that was like an ache in him.

It was a slow murky dawn, and it came well after 6 o'clock; the winter chill explained why. By this time, Jesse Webb was ready for it, for anything. As ready as he would ever be, since it had been determined, at the low-voiced meeting in the restaurant kitchen, with Carson making the decision after a telephone call to his office, that they were not to shoot if Glenn Griffin and Samuel Robish came out of that house with any member of the Hilliard family. They were to hold fire and wait. Lieutenant Fredericks had insisted, with some vehemence, that this was stupid because those filthy killers would not let their hostages live anyway. So the situation was utterly impossible, from any point of view, and it was his idea that one life sacrificed now— although of course every reasonable precaution should be taken not to sacrifice it—could not be weighed against the people those two might kill if they bluffed their way out of this trap. But the decision was against him, with Carson leaning to Jesse Webb's view that there was always the chance that Griffin wouldn't want another murder rap hanging over him: he might let the hostages go once he felt he was safe.

"You're putting a tool into the hands of every felon in the country," Lieutenant Fredericks had said, biting at the words.

And Jesse Webb had sat there, knowing it, acknowledging the truth of this and beginning to wonder in what direction his responsibility really lay. Here was an immediate human situation, and all your training had not really prepared you to deal with it. Why? Because once you brought theory down to reality, this is what faced you: that on one side there was a vague sort of allegiance you owed to society in general, the unknown human beings who might suffer at the hands of these men if they got away; and on the other, the more immediate and sharply defined obligation to these few specific people who might live or die because of your actions within the next few hours.

But the decision had been made, and now all precautions had to be taken, nothing overlooked. Given a chance, the police had to be ready to capture or kill the fugitives. Jesse himself mounted a ladder on the east side of the Wallings' house and climbed carefully, in the first light, over the peak of roof while Tom Winston and Carson showed their badges and explained to the startled people inside what was taking place, although not completely why. From the front corner of roof he ascertained, without standing up even then, that a man placed here could command, over the trees between, a view of the Hilliard residence, including the side door, a small section of side yard, and that length of driveway that lay between the blue sedan and the boulevard. From higher, it might be possible to see more.

An hour later, therefore, one state trooper and one man from Jesse's office were seated in a television installation-and-repair truck, wearing the coverall uniform of an established dealer, and waiting for their signal to appear at the Walling home, there to set up, innocently but as slowly as possible, a television antenna on the Wallings' roof. The truck was three blocks away. That was at 7:35.

At 7:50, in the attic of the Wallings' home where a police radio apparatus was being assembled, Jesse Webb received word from the State House that the license number on the plates attached to the small foreign sports car he had discovered back there in the woods had been issued to Charles K. Wright, Jr. Jesse's guess on this had been right, as had been his earlier certainty that the black coupe which Hank Griffin had been driving belonged to one of the Hilliard family. Bonham at the license bureau had confirmed this, with details. The coupe was owned by Cynthia Hilliard, age nineteen.

Thinking then of his wife, Kathleen, who was probably waking up at his mother's house, far across town, safe now, never really threatened, Jesse understood young Charles Wright, Jr., comprehended his reluctance to talk and also the impulse that had now brought him back to this area. But where was the boy and what was he doing? Didn't the young fool realize that he could snarl up everything now if he startled or frightened those caged animals in there? Where was Wright? *What was he doing?*

Jesse paced the attic, bent low, his head narrowly missing the studs. He was smoking. He hadn't shaved. He felt tired and excited and on edge. It was almost ten after 8, and he was still angry at himself over another report he had received several hours ago, this one from the telephone company. Since Wednesday morning—in the two full days since the three had escaped—one long-distance telephone call had been received at the Hilliard home. This had been a person-to-person call, collect, with charges accepted, to a Mr. James from a Mrs. Dixon. It had lasted four and one half minutes and had been placed from a pay-station phone in a bus station in a town named Circleville, Ohio—which town, as Jesse had quickly ascertained, was twenty-six miles south of Columbus. Trust those rotten clever swine! Helen Lamar was too smart to place a call from Columbus; it was almost as though she had looked ahead, in her desperation, to the list that Jesse had spent so many fruitless hours checking and rechecking. She had bought her car, probably from some fence dealing in stolen automobiles, and she had traveled south, not spotted now, no longer under surveillance, and had called Glenn Griffin and made arrangements of some sort. What these were, Jesse Webb did not know, yet, but he had hopes along that line, too.

This hope was based on the interesting fact that at 3:22 this morning, barely an hour after Hank Griffin was killed, someone at the Hilliard number had placed a prepaid person-to-person call to a Mrs. Dixon in Cincinnati, Ohio. Did this mean that Glenn Griffin knew or suspected that something had happened to his brother? Did he want to make sure that this Mrs. Dixon —who was undoubtedly Helen Lamar—was still waiting, that she was carrying through with her part of some scheme? Whatever the answer to that, Jesse Webb now had hopes that the FBI and the Cincinnati police would soon have Helen Lamar under arrest.

He stomped down the attic stairs of the Wallings' house, then down another flight and into the kitchen. "Would you mind if I made some coffee?" he asked Mrs. Walling who was at the stove.

Mrs. Walling, a plump woman with large, soft brown eyes, still puzzled at the sudden invasion of her house by police who kept entering with great caution from the east, turned and looked at the tall deputy. What she saw made her shove a kitchen chair in his direction and say, "I have some made, Sheriff. My, you do need it, don't you? You look almost sick. Why don't you lie down on the sofa a little?"

But Jesse was unable to finish the first cup before Tom Winston pushed in from outside and leaned against the table. "A man and a red-headed girl just left the house, Jess. They're walking along the boulevard, toward the bus line probably. The man has a big freckled face and he looks worse than you do—which is saying something. The girl's a beauty and she looks sore at the world."

"That would be Dan Hilliard and his daughter, Cynthia," put in Mrs. Walling.

"Cocky, aren't they?" said Jesse. "Letting 'em out of that house even now. Getting real cocksure now, aren't they, the——" He stopped. "Pardon me, Mrs. Walling." Then to

Tom Winston: "That leaves the wife and the little boy, huh? I reckon they figure that's enough. And I reckon it is, too."

Chuck Wright also witnessed the departure of Dan and Cindy Hilliard on foot at 8:30. He crept, his muscles stiff, hugging the wall low, around the far side of the garage and watched them walking down the driveway. *She's* not in there now, he said to himself, with a lifting in his chest. Now there're only two Hilliards in the house, and the two men. The sight of Cindy's slender back and the defiant swing of her shoulders sent a warmth charging through him. Now, he thought, if you can get both of those guys to the front of the house for half a minute or so——

On the bus ride downtown, Dan Hilliard noted without interest that the day promised to brighten; a crisp golden sunlight occasionally appeared, then vanished. It was four minutes to 9— after a long ride in almost total silence, their closeness intensified by that silence—when Dan stepped off the rear door into the early morning crush, held his hand for Cindy. Then, on the sidewalk of Monument Circle, with the shoulders jostling them from all sides, Cindy continued to clutch her father's hand as though she were reluctant to let go of the reassurance it held for her.

"About Chuck," she whispered, her head thrown back and the wind sharp against their faces, "about Chuck, Dad: don't worry about him. I know exactly what I'm going to tell him now. He'll believe me."

Dan only nodded, a haggard sort of agreement with no heart in it because he had almost, but not quite, forgotten his encounter with Chuck Wright last night. Then Cindy rose up on her toes, and Dan was astonished to feel his daughter's lips on his. He was aware that several heads turned, grinning, and while he would normally have been embarrassed by such a public display, he found that instead he was grateful. Grateful and humble and shot clear through with the despair that had been growing in him all night.

Walking along the familiar streets in the direction of his office, Dan tried to look at everything with a keen but unemotional eye. He knew that panic was his enemy; and as 9:30 moved slowly closer, he had to force himself to look ahead and yet to let the numbness inside—or hopelessness—deaden his emotions. The long night had worked a narcotic spell on him in that sense, and he felt fortunate this morning.

On the corner he stopped, out of habit, and bought a morning paper from the blind newsdealer. He went on, rolling the paper and placing it in the pocket of his coat. The plan he had devised in those sleepless hours now seemed a shadowy impossible figment of his sickened imagination. The scheme was a form of blackmail, really, but its success depended on something that, through the night, had disappeared: the cold, cruel but fundamentally rational mind of Glenn Griffin. After the stupefying metamorphosis that had taken place in Glenn Griffin after his brother's desertion, could he be expected to comprehend the meaning of Dan's threat in those last frantic minutes after the money was in hand and he was ready to leave the house? Dan still intended to use the idea, for what it was worth. *Look, Griffin*, he would say then, *you are not going to take anyone along with you in that car*. And when Glenn Griffin grinned at this, with his gun pointing, after he imagined that he had won a point and that Dan had nothing more to say about it, Dan would go on: *"Then you had better take me, Griffin, and only me, because I'm the one who can set the police on the man you're paying to kill that policeman."* Would the grin flicker, fade? *"I know both the killer's name and the name of the policeman now, Griffin. You let them both slip out last night when you were yelling at your brother. None of the others will remember those names, but I do. And if you take anyone but me on this ride, I'll put the police on the killer, and then all your sticking around here will have been for nothing."* Would that do it then? Or would Griffin insist on taking someone else along, too? In that case: *"All I have to do is speak the two names, Griffin, to whoever stays behind, and you can't take all of us."* What Griffin could do then, if he dared risk the noise, was to kill Dan Hilliard outright and do whatever he wished with the others.

Dan turned into the side entrance of the department store. The killer-to-be was named Flick, the man to whom Cindy, a half-hour from now, was to deliver $3,000 of that money that was even now approaching this building in the 9:30 mail. The policeman, whom Griffin was set on murdering in this manner, was named Webb. Last night, in that nightmarish scene between the brothers, the two names had lodged in a corner of Dan's retentive brain.

But as he rode up on the elevator, Dan was disturbed by the coolness of his own thinking. In view of the altered facts of the day, it didn't seem to make good sense. Yesterday, the threat might have forced Glenn Griffin, out of fear that his warped revenge would not be carried out, to do as Dan insisted. But today the cool intelligence was gone from the young man. He appeared to be cracking up. There was a blurred look about his eyes, a harsh red line on his underlids, a loose wetness about his lips. His brooding wildness this morning threatened, given the proper stimulus, to become more unpredictable and violent than Robish's.

Dan was at his desk now, sitting as he sat yesterday morning, waiting for the hands of his watch to reach 9:30. He was recalling, though, the way Glenn Griffin had snatched the phone from his hands last night—it must have been 2 o'clock—and the way he had spoken into it, with mounting alarm, over and over: *Hello, hello, who is it?* But there had, apparently, been no answer from the other end, and as Glenn Griffin replaced the phone, his eyes a great distance from that hallway, Dan had realized fully that he was then, and from that point on, dealing with another and quite different young man.

This realization, in focus now, frightened him; he felt some of the numbness wear away and he could feel his heart hammering at his ribs. There was also that other telephone call last night, much later, the one placed by Glenn Griffin to someone in Cincinnati. Griffin had made that call himself, the crazy desperation reaching such proportions that he risked snarling and cursing at the operator. After the conversation, which Dan had not been able to hear, Glenn had shouted from the front hall to the den: *Hey, Robish! She's still there. She's waiting. There's someone won't let a man down. Hear me, Robish?*

Twenty-one minutes after 9.

Dan stood up and dabbed at the wetness that had gathered under his chin. He went to the files, stood uncertainly before them, knowing that there was work to be done, people to interview today, orders to be given. But he couldn't seem to move. Standing there, his eyes fell on the morning paper in the pocket of his topcoat. He reached for it, flipped it open, and looked directly into the face of young Hank Griffin. Over the photograph were the words:

FUGITIVE KILLED: TROOPER WOUNDED IN GUN BATTLE

There was a knock on the door; it seemed to come from a great and hollow distance. Then Dan Hilliard's bluff and middle-aged secretary said, "Letter for you, Mr. Hilliard. It came Special Delivery during the night. The night watchman signed for it." She broke off, frowning. "Mr. Hilliard, if you ask me, you're catching the flu. Why don't you let me cancel appointments and you go home to bed?"

"Do that," Dan said, accepting the envelope, which was

surprisingly light in weight. "I'll be leaving for a while. After I've taken care of some business at the bank I'm going home."

"If it's something I can——"

"No."

"Yes, Mr. Hilliard."

The door closed gently and Dan made it back to the desk with difficulty. He leaned there, slack and spent, remembering one more astonishing fact about Glenn Griffin, the one that explained the others: he had spent much of the night with his ear close to the radio. Glenn Griffin knew then—and had known all morning—what had happened to his brother. And it was this knowledge that had turned him into the hysterical stranger who was beyond reason. And in the house now with Eleanor and Ralphie.

Dan slit open the envelope and counted five one-thousand-dollar bills and one five-hundred-dollar bill. He slid three of the one-thousand-dollar bills into a plain white envelope from his drawer, carefully placed both envelopes in his breast pocket. The action brought back some of the numbness, and as he stood up, he was grateful for that. But his thoughts remained with Eleanor.

Eleanor was upstairs with Ralphie, at 9:30, acutely aware of the time. While she played rummy with the boy, she could hear what was said below. There was the steady hum of the radio, and then, above it, Glenn Griffin's voice—higher now, different somehow: "Robish. Stick to the window but listen. There're a couple of guys up on the roof of the house next door."

Robish swore heavily from the direction of the den, where he was watching the side and rear yards. "Coppers?"

"How the hell do I know? They got on yellow coveralls. They're working on one of those television things."

"Then what you crying about?"

"Who's crying? You just can't tell, that's all. You had more sense, you'd know that."

"I got sense," Robish replied from the distance. "Me, I got more sense'n you think, Griffin. No gun, but a lot of brains."

"That supposed to mean something?"

When Robish didn't answer at first, Ralphie said, to his mother, "Your play." But she held up a hand, straining to hear.

"Means," Robish called at last, "that your kid brother got his last night cause he got scared, that's all. You been gettin' jumpier ever since. An me, I figure the heat's off us for a while. All depends on Hilliard now."

"Hilliard?"

"You think that big bastard's gonna——"

"Hilliard pulls anything now——"

"Now I guess you're wishing you'd let me keep that there gun, huh, Griffin?"

Above, Eleanor sensed, rather than concluded, that in this brief and broken exchange she had heard the command shift from Glenn Griffin, who possessed the only gun, to Robish, who had none. It was the Griffin boy who was nervous and unstrung this morning, Robish who remained calm and sure of himself, as though he were making his own separate plans now. All this Eleanor realized without being able to grasp the meaning this shift might hold for her and her family.

Glenn grumbled again, on a lower key: "If that Hilliard tries to pull anything. If he ain't doing just what I told him——"

Dan Hilliard, at this point, was doing exactly what he had been instructed to do: he was handing over to his daughter, Cindy, an envelope containing $3,000. They were in the corridor of the building in which she worked, speaking together quietly in one corner while the old elevators groaned up and down.

"Careful now," he said quietly, his eyes holding hers.

Then he walked down the three flights of stairs, and at ten minutes to 10 he entered his bank, where he was well known. He carried a leather brief case, empty now. He spoke to a teller who had served him for ten years.

The teller complied without question, but after Mr. Hilliard, whom the teller had had some little difficulty recognizing this morning, had left the bank with the brief case bulging, the teller examined the two one-thousand dollar bills, which were quite good, and allowed himself to wonder where a man like Mr. Hilliard had obtained them and why he would need that much small cash.

Three minutes later he was wondering even more because in that time he had spoken through the grilled window to a fat deputy from the Sheriff's office who simply asked him to place those large bills aside until he received further instructions regarding them.

Less than five minutes later, Tom Winston was speaking by radio from his office to an FBI agent, not Carson but a new man who had appeared this morning, in the cold attic of the Wallings' residence. This agent, whose name was Merck, went downstairs and outside and motioned to Deputy Sheriff Jesse Webb from the lawn.

Jesse was on the topmost rungs of a high ladder placed

against the front of the structure and in clear view of the windows in the Hilliard house; the ladder was much taller than the highest peak of the Wallings' roof, and Jesse, wearing a yellow coverall with printing across the back, seemed to be measuring the upright antenna and giving instructions, with gestures, to two assistants who stood off to one side, their backs turned carelessly to the Hilliard home.

Actually, Jesse was studying the Hilliard house and garage—he could see it all from this vantage point—and in this way was working off some of the tension that was eating in him steadily like a hungry, vicious animal he could not control. He was thinking, too, of the long-range rifles with telescopic sights and of the binoculars that must be kept out of sight.

He descended the ladder and walked into the side door of the Wallings' house with the man Merck, nodding as he listened. In the side hall he tore off the coverall and reached for his trench coat, aware of Lieutenant Fredericks' eyes upon him from the dining room where three troopers and Carson sat in a huddle. But what Jesse Webb was considering was not the information just received—although the money angle explained why the two men were staying in the house—but of a movement he had seen behind the Hilliard garage while he stood on that ladder. He hadn't dared use the binoculars then, but he had his own idea as to what that movement was. And he was not sure there was anything he should, or safely could, do about it.

Shortly after 8:30 Chuck Wright had become aware of the activity atop the Walling house—long before Glenn Griffin, inside, had noticed it. Chuck, behind the Hilliard garage, had hoped then that this did not mean that the police had found out and were setting up a way to attack. But he knew, below the hope, that this was very likely. It wouldn't take that Webb long, he admitted grudgingly.

Now, at six minutes after 10, stiff with the waiting, he was bristling with impatience. He had been hoping that if one of the two men in the house spotted the activity on that roof beyond the trees, the man who was at the rear window, in Mr. Hilliard's den, would go to the front of the house to investigate. This had not happened. Chuck Wright decided that he would have to find a way to create the diversion that would leave the rear of the house free for the very brief space of time it would take him to let himself into the back hall.

He was prodded, too, by the certainty, mounting in him with the minutes, that Cindy would return to the house. Perhaps that's what they were waiting for in there. If so, and if those police were planning to close in, Chuck intended to be inside, with his gun. As a matter of fact, it occurred to him that the one way now in which no member of the house would be killed or injured was for the police to keep those two inside occupied in an attack from without; their guns then would be turned on the police, the family forgotten, and if he was inside at that point, he gave himself a chance, a slim one, but well worth taking when you considered all the odds. He left behind all hesitation and doubt.

But where was Cindy now? Did she intend to return to the house? When? And what was she doing?

It was a long, narrow room with a bar along one side, booths along the other. There was a raw whisky smell about it and an atmosphere that added to Cindy's sickening apprehension. Behind the bar a man wearing a plaid vest over a once white shirt

looked her over, and she turned abruptly away and crossed to
sit in the first booth, to sit very straight there with her hands on
the table, her eyes fixed. Presently a waitress appeared at her
elbow, a spindly girlish-looking woman with fuzzy dyed hair
and tired, defensive eyes. Cindy ordered an old-fashioned, the
thought of it stirring the nausea in her. With the glass before
her on the nicked table-surface, she looked at her wrist watch.
10:29.

Chuck had never come into the office this late. Mr. Hepburn
had asked about him several times, but neither Cindy nor
Constance Allen could tell Mr. Hepburn why he had not appeared. And Cindy did not know what his absence meant. She
didn't dare let herself conjecture.

She could only think of the man who was to meet her here in
one minute, at 10:30, in this shabby and deserted bar on a
dead-end side street alongside the stage door of a motion-
picture theater. She knew what the man wanted, why she was
meeting him; in a sense, she was committing a murder. Certainly she was aiding in the crime. But these accusations had
attacked her before, and there was one answer, itself a question: What else could she do?

The anger was still in Cindy Hilliard, and it rose chokingly
as she watched the little man who entered now, glanced carelessly around, his dim and very pale eyes sliding over her. The
waitress had disappeared, and the man in the vest behind the
bar had his back turned. Cindy sensed all this, her eyes meeting those of the newcomer; she knew that she could not control
the contempt and disgust in her glare, but the little man who
approached frightened her. She couldn't say how; perhaps it
was only her knowledge of his mission, of what he was going
to do for the money she was about to give him.

"Mind if I sit a spell, miss?" he asked.

Cindy felt her head shaking, inviting him to do what he did
next: slide into the space opposite her, across the table.

"You know my name, miss?" he asked.

Again she shook her head. She did not know it, or want to know it. She wanted to get away from him, to get back to her father's office, to get into the taxi with him and to return to the house, as they had been told to do. She couldn't quite believe, though, that this innocuous-looking man—small, with a smooth, rather rounded face atop a short, thin body—could be a murderer. A paid killer. He looked and spoke, too, more like a salesman, a bill collector, a clerk in the store where her father worked.

"Turning cold," the man commented, and his pale eyes, which she saw were blue, remained on her face as he straightened his rather flashy tie and pointed to the glass on the table. "You're not going to drink that?"

"No."

"Thanks, miss."

He drank delicately, almost smiling, but those depthless pale eyes remained on her. She did not know what she was to do now. She was not sure, suddenly, that this was the man; perhaps he was only a traveling salesman trying to pick her up.

"I'm a messenger," the man said then, finally. "You have something for me to deliver?"

When he said that—perhaps because it appeared so transparently true—she knew that he was lying, that he was the man, that those same hands now resting flatly and without nerves on the table would pull the trigger, killing another man whose name she did not know, either.

She opened her purse, drew out the white envelope. The man took it, nodding, placed it in his pocket without so much as glancing into it. She watched him and the actions of her own hands like a person viewing a motion picture when the sound apparatus has broken down. This dreamlike quality seemed a part of her whole life now.

Then, without warning, an enormous shadow fell across the table, and she looked up. She saw the man across from her glance up, saw those unnaturally faded eyes meet those of the big man standing there, saw them half close in disinterest.

"What you got in your pocket, Flick?" the big man asked, and his voice was hoarse and ugly but somehow gentle. "What'd the lady give you?"

"A letter, Sergeant," the one named Flick replied.

Cindy noticed that the big man, who was evidently a detective, had not removed his hands from the pockets of his coat. And in the back of her mind a voice whispered, *This can't be, this isn't happening.*

"Come along to the station," the detective said. "And you can hand over the envelope, Flick."

The astonishment in her broke then, the rage took over, the blank rebellion. *This can't be. They can't do this! They're ruining everything now!* She stood up.

"You can't——" she began.

The big man only looked at her out of very dark but not unfriendly eyes. "I'm only following orders, miss. They didn't say anything about bringing you in, but I'm doing it to play safe, understand. If you've done nothing, they won't hold you long."

"No," she said, trying to slip past his hulk of body.

"I'm sorry, miss," the big man said, and the anger gave way to hopelessness in Cindy Hilliard then.

"Am I under arrest?"

"Not yet. Not technically. Unless you refuse to come to the station like a nice girl." He looked down on Flick, who was finishing the drink. "I hope they don't judge you by the company you keep, miss."

Tears came to Cindy Hilliard, tears for the first time since it had begun. Tears of rage and frustration and despair. It was over now, all of it; in the little she had been asked to do, she had somehow failed. What would happen if she didn't return to the house before 11:30, as Glenn Griffin had insisted? What would happen then to the others?

By now Dan Hilliard was back in his office. He was waiting for Cindy. He, too, was recalling Glenn Griffin's insistence that Cindy return to the house with Dan. Griffin made clear that his reason for this was that he wanted to be sure, when he left, that his man—the one Dan knew was named Flick—had already been paid for the job he was to do. But Dan mistrusted this explanation as he mistrusted every word that came from those lips. He had about decided that Griffin would attempt to take Cindy and Eleanor with him, on the theory that two women with two men in a car that was not known would be the safest way to get out of town; Dan was aware also that Griffin possessed no better tool with which to tie Dan's hands. In that way, Griffin and Robish would have all the time they needed. And Dan was inclined to think—in that deadened cool way he had now—that with that setup the four of them could probably get by those patrol cars that he had seen in the neighborhood last night. And then what?

It was not going to be that way. Dan was going to see to it. At that point, the value of living dropped into nothing. He realized now, sitting behind his desk, that there is an ultimate juncture at which the question of living or dying loses its meaning and importance. At that juncture, you still fight to live— that's probably automatic—but your success is measured then not by whether you survive but by what greater catastrophe you prevent.

And there you have it. That's where all of it had carried him, down their criminal depths and then up the steep ascent toward the only conclusion that a decent human being could reach. Now he had only to wait, and without impatience, although the sound of his own watch ticking cut into his flesh, through nerves, into the marrow of his bones.

When the door opened, he stood at once, knowing it was his daughter, that it could be no one else. But the man who entered was very tall, with a narrow head under a battered, water-stained hat, with bloodshot eyes and a slow but definite manner as he crossed to stand in front of Dan Hilliard with his hands jammed down into the pockets of his trench coat. The man looked at Dan Hilliard for a long moment, and Dan's blood chilled. The man flipped back his coat and Dan caught a quick glimpse of badge, of leather holster, of gun butt.

Very slowly then, Dan sank back.

"Morning, Mr. Hilliard," the man said. "My name's Webb. Deputy Sheriff, Marion County. I received your letter, Mr. Hilliard."

Dan threw back his head, feeling the remnants of pain all through his body, and thinking, stunned: This is the thing you've worked against, lied against, fought against. It can't go like this now, now with the money in your pocket. "I don't know what you're talking about, Deputy."

It appeared then that Jesse Webb lost his temper. He pulled his hands out of his pockets and rested on them, with the palms flat against the top of Dan Hilliard's desk, the lean body hunched forward. "Look," he said in a hoarse, cracked voice. "Look, Mr. Hilliard, I wouldn't be here if I didn't have it, hear? It's taken a long time, I started from scratch, but I'm here, and we don't have time to waste, do we, Mr. Hilliard? So let's have the rest of it now, straight, from the beginning. Then we can decide what we're going to do about it. Goddammit, start talking, Hilliard!"

Whatever he saw on Dan Hilliard's face then stopped him; he straightened, taking a deep breath, and looked past Dan Hilliard, out the windows. "Sorry," he mumbled. And then in a much softer, gentler tone: "But what are we going to do about it? That's the question now. What do we do, Mr. Hilliard?"

It was going on 11 o'clock! You can't wait all day for something to happen, Chuck. He was crouched now behind the shrubbery at the corner of the garage, concentrating on the head that appeared, was gone, then inevitably reappeared behind the transparent curtains in Mr. Hilliard's den. The feeling persisted in him, for some reason that he couldn't explain, that if he waited too long for an accident or impulse to draw that man out of that room, he might never make it inside in time. He no longer considered the danger; if he used his training and was cautious, he might be able to help. If it came to endangering any of them, he wouldn't act at all. But that decision could only be made when he was inside the house and knew what was going on, what was being planned.

You've got to create your own diversion, he told himself with savage calm.

He had selected and then rejected various possible methods. Whatever he chose must serve its purpose by alarming them slightly, alerting them even, but not to the point of action against Mrs. Hilliard or the boy, not to the point of panic. He finally hit upon a way that could be explained, perhaps by Mrs. Hilliard inside, as a perfectly natural occurrence, especially after the wind of the last two days. Whether the two men would respond to the sound itself or, later, to a logical explanation of it—well, that was one of the risks, but comparatively a small one.

He placed the gun carefully in his hip pocket. Then he took the small key into his left hand and picked up the two-foot length of dead bough that he had been studying for some time. The wood was rotten and crumbling; perhaps it would not make sufficient noise. And it was not as heavy as he would have liked; it might not travel all the way over the pitched roof and strike against the top of the front porch or in that general area where it would have to fall to draw the man from the rear of the house. But if it did, it would certainly be easy to explain. Branches often dropped onto the roof from the large but dying oak to the west of the house. Chuck remembered one night in the living room when this had happened, startling him so that Cindy laughed for minutes. With the sound of that laughter still in his mind, he planted his legs, drew back, and let go.

The branch twirled and looped far up over the roof, cleared the top of the inverted V by inches and dropped out of sight. Then Chuck fell flat and waited, listening. The sound came— first a thud, then a scudding as the broken bough tumbled and bounced down the far pitch of roof. Chuck's eyes were on the window. The thin but transparent curtains flew back; but he couldn't move. He saw a square block of unshaven face appear, the eyes darting about. Then the curtain swished down and the head disappeared completely.

It was his chance. He had to take it, knowing, as he ran, in long silent glides, that a bullet might stop him now that he was upright and in full view. He reached the porch, crouching now, not yet breathing hard.

He slipped the key into the lock. In the distance, deep in the house, he heard two men's voices, then a woman's. He edged the door open. There was one small but rather sharp crack of sound. He closed it behind him, made sure it was locked again.

The back hall was dim, very small. He paused, still listening. He was beginning to breathe heavily now, as he heard footsteps lumbering through the house, coming to the rear. Chuck, moving very slowly in the semi-darkness of the basement stairs, crept down one step at a time. The damp odor of the Hilliards' basement struck at the hunger in him. He glanced hastily around in the comparative brightness.

Above, from the direction of Mr. Hilliard's den, the thunderous steps halted and a deep voice said, "All clear here, Griffin."

Farther away, a lighter one—a strangely high-pitched voice —called, "Okay. We take the woman's word for it. This time."

"Who's jumpy?" the first voice shouted, and a mean, ugly laugh was mixed into the words.

Chuck took up his position directly under the stairs so that he could cover anyone coming down the steps. He rested against the musty-smelling wall, trying to quiet his breathing. The Japanese automatic had already begun to feel natural in his right hand.

7

7

It didn't take Dan Hilliard long, perhaps five minutes, to give Jesse Webb the facts, some of which the deputy gestured aside, indicating he was aware of them, some of which he leaned forward to hear with particular intentness. He interrupted only once, to question Dan Hilliard closely about his daughter, Cynthia, and exactly where she had gone, and what the idea behind that could be.

At the end of his explanation, Dan said, "This man Flick is going to kill you, Deputy. He's going to do it for the $3,000 my daughter's giving him now."

"So that's the way of it," Jesse Webb said, rubbing a hand over his shadowed, unshaven face and glancing around Dan Hilliard's office for no reason at all. "So that's the way he was doing it."

"We had no choice, Webb."

"Who said you did?" The deputy sounded angry. "We'll take care of Flick, Mr. Hilliard. There're ways of handling scum like that." He brushed it all aside then, a short downward handstroke of impatience, but he heard what Dan Hilliard was saying.

"I wrote this letter a while ago, Deputy. Another anonymous one, but you would have known who wrote it in time, after——" That he didn't finish, but pushed the letter across the desk.

Jesse Webb read it quickly, then let his eyes drift to Dan Hilliard's worn and haggard face. "Thanks, Mr. Hilliard. With those two names—mine and Flick's—I reckon we could have prevented it. Nice thinking. Even now, huh?" Then he twisted the sheet of paper in his hand. "Even at a time like this, huh?"

It was Dan Hilliard's turn for impatience. "What else could I do? Let that killer shoot you in the back some night? Plant a bomb in your car?"

The anger in Dan Hilliard's voice made Jesse Webb smile, but only a little and a trifle wanly. "If your daughter went to Flick," he said, "he'll be picked up. There's a city detective following Miss Cynthia Hilliard right now."

At this Dan stood up, his knees caving slightly. "You fool," he cried. "You damned idiot!"

"All right, all right, let off steam now, Hilliard. Take a swing at me. I've been wanting to sock someone for two days myself. How did I know? I was trying to protect your girl. How did I know what they'd send her into?"

Dan Hilliard subsided, but he did not sit down. He looked ashamed now, behind the new sharp intentness springing into his face—ashamed of the violence. "I've been waiting for her, that's all. It's late. Those fellows are going to get anxious, Webb. You might not know what that means. I do." He was climbing into his coat. "I have to get back up there now. Without her, I suppose." He pulled his hat down low and hard.

"She'll be all right, Hilliard. Don't worry about her. I swear she'll——"

"Swear," Dan said in a low ironic whisper. "What can you swear to? That they won't somehow get word of this, those two, that their man Flick has been picked up? That they won't jump to the idea that I caused that? Or Cindy? Can you swear they won't shoot my wife or my son, thinking I double-crossed them? Swear! What can you swear to?"

"To this, Hilliard. That if there's one less Hilliard in that house of yours, there's one less innocent person might be killed in the next hour!"

Dan picked up the brief case and moved to the door, turned. "Thanks, Webb. I'm sorry I blew up."

"Why be sorry? Look, Hilliard"—and he took two long strides toward him—"look, nobody blames you. Not for anything. Get that, hear? Nobody in his right mind can raise a voice against what you've done. I'll see to it. *I'll* see to it!"

Dan Hilliard met the tall young deputy's gaze. There was a brief moment of silence, during which the two men understood each other and found that understanding a warmth between them. Both felt they had known each other for a long time, and it was a strange but not disturbing sensation, coming at such a time—oddly satisfying.

"There's more to it than that, though, isn't there?" Dan Hilliard asked, glancing at his watch, which read seven minutes after 11.

The other nodded. "There's this. That story about the young Griffin kid shouldn't have broken in the paper this morning. I tried to stop it, but somebody had a job to do. They did that job. I've got a job, too, Mr. Hilliard, same as you have. Only mine's a little different, hear? It's to keep those two from getting away, killing whatever hostages they take along and then go on to kill others some place else."

Dan looked at his watch again. "You're saying you've got them now and you're going to see they don't get away, no matter what."

"I'm saying," Jesse Webb went on in that dry, cracked voice of his, "that I don't want to see anyone killed any more than you do, but we're both going to have to decide the odds when the time comes. There's no way to predict, that's all."

219

Dan Hilliard's shoulders slumped, but only slightly, and he said, "I'm not blaming *you*, either, Webb."

Then Jesse Webb cleared his throat. "If there's any way to get them to come out alone, of course, on the run——" But he broke off. "You want a lift?" he asked briskly.

"I'm supposed to take a taxi."

"Oh." Then: "How about a gun?"

Dan hefted the brief case and gave his head a negative twist. "They search you when you come in?"

This time Dan Hilliard nodded, but in the middle of the movement, while his hand reached to the doorknob, he went very still and quiet all through.

"Good luck, Mr. Hilliard," Jesse Webb said.

"I've changed my mind. About the gun."

"You want one?"—a touch of surprise there, an edge of caution.

"Yes."

"So they can have another one in there? You said they had only one now. Listen, Hilliard—if there's any shooting, we're coming in."

Heavily then, a decision made: "May I have it?"

Jesse Webb reached into his coat and handed over the .38 from his shoulder holster. The gun was heavy in Dan Hilliard's tired grasp, heavy and unwieldly and unnatural. He fumbled with it a moment, but only a moment, shifting the brief case under his arm, finally breaking the gun; he shook the steel-jacketed bullets into his big palm. He crossed to the desk again.

"Are you crazy, Hilliard?" Jesse Webb demanded.

"Possibly. Only a crazy man'd go into that house with an empty gun, wouldn't he? Griffin doesn't think I'm crazy, deputy. That's a very, very long shot, but I don't have any short ones in sight. Do you?"

Jesse Webb shook his head, and as Dan Hilliard crossed to the door again, the deputy said, "One more thing." It was too late then to stop, but a sense of fairness drove him on anyway:

"There's one more card I haven't mentioned. It's face down but this is it. A young fellow named Wright. Charles K. Wright——"

"Yes?"

"I can't be sure. I don't know. But there's a strong chance that he's hiding near your house somewhere."

"Good God," Dan Hilliard breathed, stunned, surprised too that anything was capable of adding to the solid weight of shock and anguish and fear in him now.

"As I say, I don't know. I just thought maybe you ought to have the whole picture."

"Thanks, Deputy," Dan Hilliard said, turning to the door, with all the weight showing in his heavy sloping shoulders and plodding gait as he disappeared.

"The poor sonofabitch," Jesse Webb muttered, but with a kind of sad and strange reverence that shone in his own tired eyes.

Under the basement stairs, Chuck Wright was trying to make his own decision. When do you go upstairs, Chuck? How long do you stick down here listening? His watch read 11:30 now, and above his head this particular time seemed to have, for the two men, a certain importance. The disadvantage of his position, Chuck had decided, was that he could not hear all the conversation that occurred up above, even though most of it was in loud snarled whispers between the dining room and den; and it was hard for him to make any accurate judgments on the basis of what snatches he could decipher.

By 11:30, he gathered, the young-voiced man toward the front of the house—that would be Glenn Griffin—had expected to receive a telephone call from a man whom he seemed careful not to name. Perhaps he named the man, but Chuck didn't hear it. At any rate, his voice was shaking now in a way that Chuck didn't like at all.

"Didn't that gal give him the dough? What's happening? Robish, what you figure's happening? Why don't he call and say it's fixed like he promised?"

"I don't know the guy," Robish replied from the den. "Wouldn't catch me paying that kind of dough for a job I could do myself. I'd a-done it for you, Griffin. Give me a gun."

That was, Chuck Wright decided then, the second time the man referred to a gun in that way. Did it mean that he didn't have one? That there was only one gun up there between the two of them?

No rushing it now, Chuck reminded himself. No mistakes now. Take it easy. You can handle them both, and easy too, if they have only one gun. But you can't be sure what would happen to Mrs. Hilliard or the little boy if you tried it. So take it easy and stay where you are for a while.

But the sound of the younger man's high-pitched voice continued to work on Chuck's nerves. It reminded him of something or someone, but he couldn't remember what or whom.

If you could flush them out, both of them, from behind, while Mrs. Hilliard and the boy were still upstairs——

He began to think of this, listening to the steady pacing in the front of the house now. Those steps were not swift; they reminded Chuck Wright, in their slow, steady rhythm, of wild animals he had seen in cages. And with the memory came the picture of those sad, bewildered but steadily ferocious eyes.

All at once then, when he heard Glenn Griffin again— *"Where's Hilliard? Why ain't he back here?"*—Chuck realized what the blurred vehemence of that voice recalled to him. The thought struck him with a smashing impact and he felt a renewed urgency tighten through his body. He remembered then, not a wild animal, but a man who resembled one, a certain Sergeant Thomas, one of the toughest, hardest men he had known; he remembered Sergeant Thomas's hardened sun-baked hulk of body writhing on the jungle floor and those glassy eyes, without recognition in them, and the lifted carbine that seemed a part of the berserk man's arm. Chuck Wright remembered all this, and the report that had drifted back after Sergeant Thomas was shipped, unknowing and marble-eyed, to a stateside hospital: the sergeant's condition was improving but he had bashed in the head of a guard in the mental hospital. It was the only time Chuck Wright had witnessed the crack-up of a human being, but he recognized now in that trembling voice upstairs the same tremor, the same uncertain inward terror.

The thought left Chuck Wright a little faint, his mouth dry, his palms moist. It left him knowing, though, that he had to get upstairs, all the way up to Mrs. Hilliard and the boy. And he could wait no longer.

The basement steps were solid, and he could see clearly now. In the back hall, he heard, beyond the door leading into the den, the older man moving about. Chuck kept his gun on that door, twisting to back slowly up the rear stairway, one step at a time, not tense, his muscles responding automatically to his desire that he should be alert, ready, but not stiff with tension. In this way he moved until he felt safe to turn fully and continue up.

The upstairs portion of the Hilliard house was not familiar to him. He crept down the hall, keeping his back close to the wall. A floorboard squeaked occasionally, but he disciplined himself not to stop on this account. He came to the open door of the front bedroom, the one on the southeast corner of the house, across the hall and stairwell from the one in which he judged Mrs. Hilliard was staying with the boy.

He backed into the bedroom, recognizing it as Cindy's, having no time for the surprise to reach him. With the gun held in front of him, he used his other arm to search behind. There was silence downstairs now and that quiet took on a sinister meaning in his mind. His hand found a door, then a knob. He edged the door open very slowly until he judged that he could step back and inside the closet. All the while his eyes remained on the bedroom door leading into the hall. Even when he was in the closet, concealed between the dresses with the faint perfume scent that was familiar to him, he kept his eyes and the gun on the hall door.

He had not been there, silent, listening, for more than ten minutes when he heard that frightening voice from below, this time rising and falling in a savage sort of relief and glee and banked-down anger: "Here they come, Robish. There's a taxi stopping out front."

From the top of the Wallings' house, Jesse Webb had seen the taxi approaching from some distance. He wore again the yellow coverall and he had to keep busy, tightening the guy wires, stepping back to survey his work, returning to it. But he was conscious, with his stomach twisting, of the men deployed on the edge of the woods below, of the patrol cars down the street in both directions, of Carson across the roof surface from him, the studious young face watching him; he was aware, too, of Lieutenant Fredericks down below, eaten with that impatience of his, striding up and down the side lawn. When he spotted the taxi, Jesse glanced to make sure that the rifle was within reach on the far side of the pitch of roof. He called down the three prearranged words, and he could feel the alertness come into the others. Lieutenant Fredericks stopped walking, peered up at him. He was not scowling now. He even smiled once and lifted his hand in a sort of salute to Jesse Webb, a gesture that said, silently but crisply, *I'm with you now, son. The decision's made. Let's hope it's the right one. We're in it together. Let's get at it.*

224

Watching the cab, Jesse wanted to explain something to Lieutenant Fredericks, something that was strange and mystifying to Jesse Webb himself: that there was no personal grudge involved now, that he had not even thought of Uncle Frank's withered arm for some time—although he was determined that this time Glenn Griffin would not shoot first and then be allowed to surrender—and that in some inexplicable way his sense of responsibility had shifted to this family of strangers in that house, to the man stepping out of the cab now, brief case in hand.

Dan Hilliard stood with his back to the house, paying the driver. Then, with no hesitation whatever, without a heaved sigh or any discernible reluctance, he walked toward his own side door. Hilliard was, Jesse noted, a larger man than he had thought, big of shoulder, those shoulders square and set now, not sloping, no longer with that haggard droop in them. Hilliard paused, knocked. The door opened. The house swallowed him.

Jesse could not see the Hilliard garage from his position, so he decided to mount the ladder again, bringing himself higher above the roof where he could command a view of the entire Hilliard house and yard. First, he moved the rifle within reach of his right arm. And as he stared down now at the silent ordinary-looking house, and the wind whipped at his face, cut through his body, he felt a throb as of an old wound. Here he was now, at the time and place he could not have pictured but toward which he had looked forward ever since the first report came two full days ago. Here he was and he was not thinking of Uncle Frank's arm or even of Kathleen now that she was safe and out of it, but of the look on Dan Hilliard's face in his office when Jesse Webb introduced himself. Silently he cursed the men who had brought that expression to the face of another human being. They would not get away with it. You couldn't let them get away with that.

The longing to know what was happening, what was being

said and done in that house at this moment, made him grip the rungs of the ladder and bring his long body full against it, made him feel the effort to pry his eyes away like a twist of pain behind his forehead. What were they doing? The girl wasn't with Hilliard. He had the money, but he also had that empty gun. What the hell was going on in there?

Here they come, Robish. There's a taxi stopping out front. Chuck Wright wondered then if he had waited too long. When he heard Mrs. Hilliard moving in the bedroom across the hall, heard her mumbled instructions to Ralphie, heard that bedroom door close and the lock turn, Chuck came out of the closet, stepped to the hall door, then paused, listening to the swift muffled flutter of Mrs. Hilliard's footsteps descending the stairs. She was down there now; he was no longer between the men and the family. The family was split up now and he had allowed it to happen.

They, Griffin had said. That would be Mr. Hilliard and Cindy. Cindy, too. The urgency pulled at his leg muscles but a sick shrinking inside now answered his question: He should have acted when the two men were down there alone.

With a savage inward gesture, he pushed all that aside and stepped, with extreme caution, to the banister. There was still the chance that, if they started to move too fast, he could go down the back stairs, use the one weapon, surprise, that could mean as much as the gun in his moist palm. Whatever he did now, though, he must do in one headlong spurt without too much careful thought.

Down below then, the high-pitched and oddly empty voice: "Where's the redhead, Hilliard?"

Struck with disbelief, Chuck took a breath, held it. He

226

couldn't hear Mr. Hilliard's low-voiced reply—it was a mutter —but a gladness sang in Chuck Wright, deep down, under all thought and tension. At once he was ashamed of it, but he couldn't stifle it. It didn't seem possible, but Cindy was not in the house. Chuck tried to dry his palms on his trouser legs and then took a firmer grasp on the automatic.

"He's lying," Robish said. "It's a Goddamn trick."

"The dough's all here," Griffin announced, and he sounded bewildered, or surprised, at the feel or sight of it. "Too late for tricks now, Pop." And some of the light-hearted excitement returned to his tone. "We're on our way. Only just one more thing, Hilliard. I don't like the way you're staring at me. Lay off, see. Put your hands up. *Up!* Let's see what you're carrying."

Chuck Wright, straining, listened. Easy now, he told himself again. Not yet, not yet.

With his hands lifted, legs apart, eyes dead ahead, Dan Hilliard felt Glenn Griffin's gun working and probing cruelly along his sore ribs while the other hand went through his pockets. He didn't jump when the gun muzzle found the sore spot. He didn't flinch when, with a low whistle of amazement and narrowing of rage in his anxious eyes, Glenn Griffin stood back, the deputy's .38 in his hand.

"You bastard," Glenn Griffin said then, and the tone made Dan Hilliard wince inside with an ironic satisfaction. In his astonishment and anger, Griffin was not examining the gun.

Dan saw the gun going up then, swinging high and sideways; he heard Eleanor's stifled shriek at his side; then he felt the muzzle across his cheekbone. It took a long moment for him to taste blood. He still had not moved. A tooth began to throb. He could feel the muscles of his face leaping.

"*Say* something!" Glenn Griffin shouted, and the tone brought the sweat cold to Dan's leg and arms under the coat. "Don't just stand there! What'd you expect to do with this thing?"

Still Dan Hilliard didn't answer; he felt the blood along the cheek, inside and out, and he felt Eleanor leaning slightly against him, not weeping but small sounds escaping her. Those sounds, more than the leaping pain, caused Dan Hilliard to keep his eyes on the unloaded gun.

"Give me that," Robish said, stepping in. "Give me it and let's blow. You got the dough. What're we waiting for?"

But the gun Robish wrenched from Glenn Griffin's hand was not the one Dan Hilliard had brought into the house. Robish held the loaded gun.

"Griffin, snap out of it!" Robish bellowed. "We gotta move!"

In the hallway above, having heard the ugly smash of metal against human flesh, Chuck Wright had to grip the banister with his left hand to keep himself from plunging down the stairs. The gun's on Mr. Hilliard, he growled silently. You can't move. Hold it. That's an order.

At the same time he felt caught in the grip of his own helplessness, uselessness. No matter what he did, or how, one of those guns—for there were two now—would be turned on one of the Hilliards.

"Get the kid," Griffin said. "Hilliard, the kid and your old lady are going for a ride. Any objections?"

"Yes," Mr. Hilliard said, and Glenn Griffin laughed shortly.

But he listened, too, as Mr. Hilliard explained why—in a low murmur, steady and cold, which Chuck Wright could not make out—and then Mr. Hilliard's voice rose a notch: "If you don't want that to happen, Griffin—if you've got enough sense to see that I can put a damper on everything for you and get that hired killer nabbed—you'd better take me. Only me."

"Listen who's telling us what," Robish snarled, with a terrible impatience behind the words.

"Wait a minute, Robish," Griffin's voice said anxiously. "Maybe the guy's got——"

"Nothing! That's what he's got. Tell him to stuff it! What the hell do I care what happens to your cop? It's my skin now. We're wasting time. Christ, those woods out there might be full of Feds for all we know. I'm moving. The kid and the woman!"

Chuck Wright realized, not quite too late, that Robish was lumbering toward the stairway. He wheeled, stepping in three long strides into the room, Cindy's room, across the hall from the locked door. He brought the Japanese automatic up and stood flattened against the inside wall of the room as the heavy feet pounded up the carpeted stairs.

Now? Now, when his back's to you and he's trying the door, twisting the knob angrily? One of them now, and fast, and take your chances with the one downstairs?

But they're not your chances, Chuck. They're Mr. Hilliard's. And his wife's. The helplessness was a dead weight in him now while he heard Robish's low mutter of rage and insistence, and then behind it, in the bedroom, the faint but definite voice of the child, crying. Those sobs came to him above the other sounds.

Then Robish stopped. Chuck took one chance. He eased his head around the door frame, took a look at the heavy head sunken between the steady rise and fall of massive shoulder, the enormous body facing the closed door with indecision.

229

What are you waiting for? All you have to do is tighten your finger, pull that trigger, but be careful now to aim high because of the boy beyond. What are you waiting for, Chuck?

He heard from below a few more words: "Had it all doped, didn't you, Hilliard?" And now a current of amusement ran liquidly under the voice: "Thought we could make a deal, did you, Pop? You're getting pretty brave, ain't you?" Then the tone dropped, changed: "Maybe you better tell me what's happened to Flick then, Pop. Why he didn't call me this morning? You better tell me now, Pop, 'cause pretty soon you're not going to be talking, see? See?" There was a small screech-sound at the end, betraying the fright.

Pull the trigger, Chuck! Mr. Hilliard's going to die anyway unless you can——

But Chuck Wright was not prepared for what happened then. He watched Robish step back, the shoulders still heaving, and he saw him lift his foot.

Although the jolt of the kick shook the whole frame of the door, the lock held, the hinges held. Behind the door the boy's sobs stuttered off into whimpers. Spitting an oath then, Robish stepped back and kicked again. This time the wood cracked like the report of a rifle. The violence of the sound seemed to stir the big man, and then he was kicking again and again, a low laugh exploding deep in his bowels, and the wood splintered and shredded and broke with deafening reverberations through the house.

"Robish!" Griffin shouted from below. "Robish, you God-damned fool! No noise! No racket now!"

The last words were spoken as Glenn Griffin himself tore up the stairs. The handsome head appeared before Chuck Wright could draw himself back into the room, but Griffin did not see him because he kept screeching at Robish in that high-pitched and terrible voice, "No noise! You want to wake up the neighborhood? No noise, you dumb sonofabitch!"

Now Chuck was safe behind the door frame. But he couldn't

wait. The men, both of them, were upstairs. Both of them, facing each other at the head of the stairs. It was the break he'd been hoping for, and now that it had come, he wasted no time whatever. He thought, as he shoved his head around the door, that he heard the front door open and close. He couldn't be sure of this, but the wonder of it—and the incredibility—held him rigid there a moment before he fired.

It may have been that split second of time that defeated him. He saw Glenn Griffin's gun coming up at him, and he swung his own gun to the right, just a little, and fired, expecting to hear the explosion from Glenn Griffin's gun, but feeling only the jolt along his own arm. The dry stench of gunpowder reached him, and he was in the jungle again, sure of himself, all thought erased, only the moment here and now, immediate. He saw Glenn Griffin dropping or flinging himself down on the stairs. Chuck brought the automatic up again, all very fast now, all sudden and precise, but not quite precise enough because the big man's mind worked slowly but his instincts were sure. Chuck saw the spurt from Robish's hand, saw it even in the brilliant sunlight, and he fired once again himself, at the big man, knowing in the thunder that, for some reason, he had missed this time. The reason came to him then as he felt himself clawing at the wall, heard his own gun clattering to the floor, and felt, for the first time, and with surprise, the impact of the bullet against his chest. As yet, even when the first wave of blackness broke over him, there was no pain, but he knew the pain was coming. It always came.

Even then, slumped down inside the room, wondering a little at the wetness around his chest, he knew what would happen now, knew that the big man would step into the room and finish the job. This didn't seem so important, though. It was really strange. There was something so much more important. He had failed. He hadn't even hit the big man. Everything had gone wrong and it was his fault.

He heard then—from an echoing distance—what he took to

be footsteps descending the stairs. But this was not possible. He didn't believe this.

Then the burning came, as he knew it would, blanking his mind, forcing him to concentrate on the searing fire deep inside until the black wave broke over him and carried him down.

Robish plunged down the stairs, tripping over Glenn Griffin but not falling, muttering fiercely. In the hall he brought himself to a halt, his little yellow-green eyes wild. Dan Hilliard waited, the despair packed solid in him now, knowing that his impulse of a few seconds before had saved Eleanor but that Robish would kill him and that Ralphie was still upstairs.

When Glenn Griffin had rushed up the stairs to stop Robish's attack on the bedroom door, Dan Hilliard had seen his chance, perhaps the one chance left to him, and he had unlocked and opened the front door; without a word, he had pushed Eleanor through it. She was no sooner outside than the three shots exploded above, and she had paused, turning instinctively, breathing one word: "Ralphie." Dan had shouted at her in the echoing thunder: "It's not Ralphie, it's not Ralphie! *Run!*" The very savagery of his reassurance had sent her running, but when Dan himself had closed the door and started toward the stairs, he had been sure that, up above, one of those three shots had killed his son. The sight of Glenn Griffin slumping slowly down on the stairs above had stopped him, held him in the hall; he expected to see the figure slide down the steps, but instead it was Robish who stepped over the fallen man and came tripping and cursing and lunging down like a great maddened bear.

Finally he made out a few of the words that Robish muttered to him: ". . . wise sonofabitch . . . got the cops, anyways . . . smart double-cross . . . bastard . . ."

Dan listened, his eyes on Robish's clutched gun, not understanding the words. What had the police to do with what had happened up there?

Then, like a swift jolt of electric current up and down his whole body, he heard a voice, from above, a tentative but uninjured voice, no pain in it: "Dad? Dad?"

"Stay there, Ralphie," Dan called. "It's all right!"

"All right," Robish echoed hollowly, but he did not move; he seemed to have no idea how to move. "You sneaked a copper in——" The words seemed to give him the impetus; Dan saw the idea seep upwards in the man, finally reach those opaque eyes. Robish charged to the front door, flung it open heedlessly, driven by fear and rage.

"Any more of you out there?" Robish bawled into the cold air. "I got one of you upstairs! Who wants it next?"

Seeing the man in the half-open door, blind to Eleanor's absence, senseless in the grip of his own terror, Dan Hilliard edged closer, slowly, without sound.

"Any more of you out there?" Robish was bellowing in the echo of his first words, when no answer came. "I still got Hilliard and the kid. They're alive!"

Those words roused in Dan Hilliard the same savage atavistic fury that had caused him to smash Robish that first night, but the instinct was refined now, controlled by caution, thought. He was very close to the man's back.

In one sudden movement then, before Robish could shout again, he grabbed the door, his fingers inches from Robish's heavy breath, whipped it open, crashed his shoulder into the man's back, then stepped back, lifted his foot and plunged it into the man's spine. All the coiled rage in him drove his leg, and it sent the hulk of body across the porch—a few spraddled-legged steps at first, then a headlong plunge off the steps onto the grass.

233

Robish rolled as he struck the ground, lifting the gun. The explosion thundered up and down the street, but the bullet dug into the solid wood of the closed door that Dan Hilliard had snapped shut and was already locking from inside.

Dan turned then from the door, expecting the barrage of police gunfire outside as he started up the stairs, his arms loose at his sides but his large, lined face clenched like a fist. He was surprised when no sound came from outside.

And when he was halfway up the stairs, he stopped, stunned. Glenn Griffin no longer lay on the stairway.

When Jesse Webb, clinging to the ladder that was propped against the front of the Wallings' roof, saw a woman emerge from the front door of the Hilliard house, he stiffened, lifting his hand automatically to give the signal that the men below had been expecting. But the woman was alone, hesitating on the porch a moment, and Jesse did not bring his hand down in the prearranged signal. There was that moment of suspense and then three shots rumbled; in rapid succession, muffled in the Hilliard house but clearly discernible even at that distance. Jesse recalled his own warning: *If there's any shooting, Hilliard, we're coming in.* But he saw the woman turn from the house then and begin to run, and this action—the lithe, swift desperation in her retreat toward the safety of the trees—stayed his hand. His long fingers flexed convulsively as he thought of the rifle.

Why not? Why not now?

Still, he waited, hoping for some answer. It came shortly, after a few seconds that seemed an eternity to Jesse Webb, in the form of a hollow shout from the direction of the Hilliard front door. Jesse couldn't make out the words, but he recognized the furious, frenzied defiance as that of a trapped man. He did not know whether the words, whatever they were, were being shouted after the woman or at the police in the woods.

He had no time to get a report on the content of that bull-like cry, however, because at that moment a brawny man with a huge head came charging out the front door as though propelled from behind. He fell twisting onto the grass, and Jesse Webb then reached for the rifle. In the second he turned, though, he heard another shot, this time not muffled, and when he lifted the rifle and sighted over the trees, he saw the black glitter in the man's hand. He brought the man into the dead center of the telescopic sight, followed easily and smoothly as the man lumbered, trying to run, but hobbling a little as though he had injured a leg, toward the blue sedan. He had him now. This was Robish, and he had him.

But Jesse Webb clamped his lean jaws together until the pain climbed his jawbone and entered his teeth. He couldn't. Not this way. Whatever the shooting inside the house had meant, there was still the chance that Griffin was still alive. What would happen to Hilliard and the boy if Griffin were startled now, if he realized the police were outside, if he had that other gun——

But the other gun was empty. Robish had fired. The gun in the house then was Jesse Webb's own .38 and Hilliard himself had taken the bullets from it.

"Tom," Jesse Webb said through cracked lips; and then when a familiar voice responded from the attic window, he went on, although the rifle still lay along his arm: "Hold fire. Robish is leaving in the Hilliard car. He's armed. Get him three or four blocks from the house. No closer. But get him."

Tom Winston moved in the attic.

There was no way out for Robish now. They had him.

What held Jesse Webb, what caused him to lower the rifle and let the others take over while he refused to give the signal to close in, was the one other unknown element that clogged

235

his mind: What had become of that kid, that Charles Wright, and that funny-looking automatic of his? It was Jesse Webb's hunch—and he still played hunches when they were this strong —that that gun was also in the Hilliard house.

If Hilliard wanted him, Hilliard would call. That is, he would call if he was still alive.

Jesse looked down, only for a moment then, to see Carson leading Mrs. Hilliard from the woods into the Wallings' house; the studious-looking young man had one arm around her. But Mrs. Hilliard was not crying.

Get in there, now, Jesse Webb ordered himself furiously. And then he answered himself, just as furiously: Let Hilliard try it his way.

Because Jesse Webb had already begun to suspect that it was Dan Hilliard who had pushed the woman from the house. What that meant exactly, he didn't know. But he decided then, arbitrarily, to give Hilliard another five minutes. He would wait at least until Carson had Mrs. Hilliard's report of what was happening in there, until he had a report on what Robish had shouted out the doorway.

Dan Hilliard mounted the stairs, his tread heavy and deter-mined, hearing instead of the police fusillade he had expected, the motor of his car grinding over outside. As he reached the head of the stairway, where Glenn Griffin had been lying a few moments before, he saw a streak of blood on the carpet and heard, outside, the spit of gravel and the mounting roar of motor that receded toward the street. He paused.

But only briefly because, while he heard Griffin's voice on his right, behind the smashed door—"In here, Hilliard"— he saw something in the door of Cindy's room that drew him there instead. He looked down, with the ugly bleakness returning in him, into the gray face of Chuck Wright. His whirling mind took in the dark stain on the floor, the twisted and lifeless-looking body, the blood-spattered and odd-shaped gun. In one fluid movement, Dan Hilliard stooped, picked up the automatic, the blood warm against his hand, and turned to cross the hall. It flickered through his mind that Robish had taken Chuck Wright to be a policeman; this had brought him downstairs in terror. Dan Hilliard thanked Chuck Wright silently and stopped in front of the splintered door of his own bedroom.

He knew what he was going to do now. Before the police came in, before anything else, he was going to do it. It was simple, really. But the thought of Ralphie in that room made Dan Hilliard slip the gun into his coat pocket, with his hand closed over it. He would shoot through the coat. He would empty it into Glenn Griffin, and that then would be the end of it.

He stepped into the room. Ralphie was on the bed, huddled in one corner, and in the corner behind him stood Glenn Griffin. His dark, unnaturally bright eyes turned from the window and fixed glassily on Dan. But Dan was looking at the icy-white and frozen terror on the face of his son.

It would not be so easy. The boy's eyes returned at once, in sickened fascination, to the muzzle of the gun that Glenn Griffin kept fixed on him. The gun was empty, but still it was not going to be so simple.

"You got to get me out of here, Pop." But the insolence was gone; the attempt at arrogance thin and worn. "That copper over there nicked me. You got more of 'em outside?"

Dan saw, with a twist of pleasure that he did not like, the blood-edged furrow along the side of Glenn Griffin's scalp, and he realized that Chuck Wright's first shot had stunned but not seriously wounded the convict. Well, he'd finish the job, now. He, Dan Hilliard.

First, though, he had another job. One more. "Ralphie," he

said quietly, his voice a dry whisper, "Ralphie, look at me. Listen."

"No time now, no time!" Glenn Griffin cried, licking at his lips, and he moved his gun closer to the boy's head.

Dan Hilliard became aware of something else then, recorded it, worked around it. He couldn't startle Griffin into lifting that gun, bringing it down in desperate frustration on the boy's skull.

"Son," Dan said slowly, very low and definite, the word spreading a hypnotic effect over the quiet room, "listen to me. Nothing's going to happen to you. That man is not going to shoot you. Do you hear me?" Ralphie nodded, but a flicker of uncertainty appeared in his bloodshot eyes. Dan's heart twisted. "He's not going to shoot you, Ralphie, and I'll tell you why, son. Believe me, because——"

"Lay off, Hilliard! You don't lay off, I'll get it over with. You got to get me out of here, see!" The frantic note was clear, and it was this that Dan feared.

Dan's hand was on the butt of the automatic, his finger looped over the trigger. Ralphie was between him and his target. "I wouldn't lie to you. Have I ever lied to you, Ralph?"

The boy's head shook, once.

"*Christ!*" Griffin screamed. "Will you stop it! Are there any more cops out there, Hilliard? Why didn't they knock off Robish? There ain't any more, are there? They'd be in here by now!"

Still, Dan ignored him, concentrating on his son. "Ralphie, that man's gun is not loaded. It doesn't have any bullets in it. Do you believe me?"

He was conscious of the start in Glenn Griffin, the quick grin of disbelief, but he was studying his son's face.

"Do you believe me?"

Then, very slowly, the boy nodded his head.

"What's going on here?" Griffin shrilled. "Hilliard, you

deaf? It's loaded, Hilliard. You wouldn't have brought it back with you if——"

Griffin stopped then, the eyes brightening into a glazed stare.

Dan said, as slowly as before: "Ralph, you're a very big boy. I want you to mind me, understand? I want you to do whatever I say now."

"Stop it!" Griffin yelled. "Stop the talk! My head hurts. I got to——" He broke off, and somewhere in his reeling mind a suspicion took root. He lowered his voice. "You wouldn't a-come in here with a empty——"

That moment of self-doubt was what Dan had been playing for. "Ralphie!" he barked suddenly. "Run!"

The shout brought the boy up off the bed in one bound before Griffin could move.

"Get downstairs and outside!" Dan Hilliard shouted.

And then he saw Glenn Griffin lifting the gun, swinging it after the boy. Dan had to break his first impulse with a great and terrible effort of will that cracked like pain through his body. He kept the automatic in his pocket even when he heard the empty gun clicking, but he was more certain, hearing those frantic fruitless clicks, what he was going to do now. He heard Ralphie on the stairs, skittering down. The boy was gone. He would not see this. Dan had made sure of that.

He watched the dazed bleak horror in the face across the room; he saw the white teeth bared; he heard the faint boylike cry in the back of the young man's throat as he brought the deputy sheriff's gun up to point directly at Dan Hilliard. Dan heard the clicks, over and over, and then, above this, a stranger sound than any: the short explosion of his own laughter.

It was then that he brought the automatic from his coat pocket. The rage was cold in him now, and he continued to think of that gun muzzle pointed at his son's back. He could feel his grip on the automatic climb like a pain up to his shoulder. He was going to do it now.

Whatever Glenn Griffin saw on Dan Hilliard's face then—

239

the pitiless eyes, the set of jaw, the purple swelling of the bruise that Griffin himself had put along one cheek—whatever it was, it caused him to back into the corner, his tongue darting wetly from between his lips. His eyes dropped, but they appeared not to see, not quite to comprehend the meaning of that gun in the white-knuckled hand that moved closer.

Dan Hilliard had no control over what he was going to do now. They had put the people he loved through two days of nightmarish hell; they had beaten and threatened and terrified; they had brought violence and the smell of blood and filth into his home. There was only this now, this one final act, and it would be over.

Glenn Griffin was sliding down against the wall, the saliva dribbling in little bubbles down his jumping chin. His mouth opened and closed and opened again, working loosely, but no sound came. He pleaded with those fluttering hands at his neck. The grotesque pantomime of frenzy did not touch Dan Hilliard's icy intention.

Now. Now. Why don't you pull the trigger? Why don't you get it over with? Why should anything hold you back? Why should you, Dan Hilliard, live by scruples these men never felt? Why should you hesitate when they——

But Dan Hilliard was not one of them. This was his room, the bedroom in which he and his wife slept. This was his home. And down below, his wife and daughter and son were waiting, wondering, not knowing any of this, still trembling with the fear this scum had brought into the house. Across the hall lay the young man who loved Cindy, who must love her deeply; and he, perhaps, was dead now. He needed help, and quick. In the electric brilliance of this moment, Dan Hilliard lowered the gun slowly until the muzzle pointed at the floor. He didn't have the right. He was not one of them.

The quivering mass of animal-being crumpled in the corner before him sickened Dan Hilliard. He turned away slightly, looking out the window.

"Get out," he said softly. He felt dirty all over, as though some of the slime had wiped off on him somehow. "Get out of my house," he said, but still quietly.

Then, staring out of the window, seeing in the distance a man on a ladder against the roof of the Wallings' house, he heard the scrabbling behind him, as Glenn Griffin, whimpering, clawed his way across the bed, staggered toward the hall; Dan heard the quick drum of steps on the stairway and the opening of the front door. Dan tossed the automatic to the floor. He had almost murdered a man; he had almost become one of them.

He threw open the window. "Webb!" he shouted, and a blade seemed to turn over in his throat. "Webb! Get a doctor and ambulance, fast!"

Then he whirled about and strode swiftly toward his daughter's bedroom where Chuck Wright still lay crumpled and unconscious. Dan was bending down, kneeling in the blood, when he heard two shots outside. They seemed to come from a distance, with a whine in them.

Jesse Webb lowered the rifle.

In his mind that slender, dancerlike figure of a young man was still spinning down there on the Hilliard lawn; but he knew, of course, that the figure lay quite still now, quite lifeless. Two minutes before, he had received the report on Robish: the big man had smashed up the blue sedan in the chase and the police had pulled him from the wreckage, badly injured, but alive. Alive for a while, anyway, Jesse thought grimly. Until after the trial.

It's all over, Jesse thought then, and rubbed the back of his very tired neck.

241

But he was remembering, as he climbed slowly down the ladder, his legs aching and stiff, the way he had lifted the rifle when he saw that figure emerge from the front door of the Hilliard house. Griffin had been running at full tilt, arms raised, hands working convulsively, the mouth shouting indistinguishable words. Had those words been a plea for mercy? Across the tops of the sun-tinted trees, Jesse Webb could not hear them. Did he remember then that other time when, after using a gun himself, Griffin had thrown it to the pavement and demanded the privilege of giving himself up? Or was Jesse Webb concentrating only on fixing the head dead center in the crossbars of the rifle sight? He had fired, feeling only the recoil of the rifle, seeing the figure stop, twist, sink to one knee on the grass, remain balanced there until the second bullet reached him. It spun him about and he wobbled upright a moment, but only a moment, and then plunged forward, arms and legs outstretched, face down in the grass.

Jesse was on the Wallings' lawn now, leaning the rifle against the ladder, feeling the heat that remained in the barrel. After violence, he had learned to expect a certain secret shame, an appalling sense of failure that amounted almost to nausea. If matters had to be settled so, someone had failed. He didn't know who, or what. But he wished there was some way to keep that feeling from creeping through him.

He made his way into the Wallings' house, hearing the siren wails in the distance, picturing the confused scene on the Hilliard lawn. He sank into a deep chair alongside the telephone table. He could already hear the soft note of relief in Kathleen's voice, even though she'd try to cover it. And he could imagine, too, the grim, curt satisfaction in Uncle Frank's voice when he phoned him later.

But Jesse Webb did not share the satisfaction. That other feeling, almost disgust, was in him, and strong. Not because he'd killed a man; he no longer looked upon Glenn Griffin as a man in that sense. The feeling was in him because life should not be so. And then, as he picked up the phone, he was glad for the feeling. It set him apart from men like Griffin and Robish, who also killed. He still clung to a hope that someday it would not be necessary to settle matters in this manner. Until then, he had a job, and he had done one part of it in the last two days. Except for some unpleasant but necessary details, that part of the job was over. Somehow, along the way, he'd lost the idea of personal revenge. That, too, was good, wasn't it? Maybe getting over an idea like that, as Lieutenant Fredericks had suggested, made you a better cop in the end.

Jesse Webb didn't know, for sure, and when he heard Kathleen's voice, he forgot it all, completely, until he had replaced the phone two minutes later.

Everyone, including Eleanor, had insisted that Dan stay home. Cindy was at the hospital with Chuck, and there was certainly nothing more Dan could do now. He needed his rest, and his swollen jaw looked terrible. But here he was, sitting stubbornly in the white and sterile waiting room, and Eleanor was beside him, quiet, on the wicker couch. Their hands did not touch, but both were aware of the closeness, a closeness that was not new, really, but newly recognized.

Dan saw the deputy sheriff—the tall, lanky one named Webb—approaching along the silent, tile-floored corridor with a trim nurse trotting soundlessly at his elbow, trying to keep up with the long strides. Jesse Webb removed his hat then, in the waiting room, and he stood there, a trifle awkward, a little shy, with his lean head shot forward.

"Miss Standish here," he drawled, "will give you the details. The kid'll be out of here in two weeks. I reckon that's enough for me. Your daughter's in the room with him, Mr. Hilliard.

243

She just apologized to me about something. It seemed to bother her a lot, that business about carrying the money to Flick. Not that Flick can do much about it, where we got him. Or that she could have done anything different, then. I guess that's all. Now will you go home?"

Dan stood up. "If the boy's conscious, I'd like to see him."

"Room 402," the nurse said, "but——"

Jesse Webb touched her arm and she stopped. A little crookedly Jesse was grinning down at Dan Hilliard. "I want to say something."

"Yes?"

"Now it's gone. Well, no matter. Something about—you ever want a job, sir, just look me up." It was not what he'd intended to say. It didn't even come close, being utterly foolish and meaningless, but it was the best Jesse Webb could manage.

Dan Hilliard was smiling, too, and his eyes made Jesse forget the lopsided shape of the face before him, with the jaw ridged and puffed along one side. The eyes were blue now, just like the daughter's, not black as he had imagined in the time he'd known Dan Hilliard. But there was a warmth in them, a knowingness, that it might take the girl a lifetime to acquire. Embarrassed then, Jesse turned to Mrs. Hilliard: she still wore the housedress, her hair was light, her face small and oval. Mrs. Hilliard's eyes were soft and they seemed to look into him, and he thought of Kathleen.

"The same to you," Dan Hilliard said, and he offered the deputy his hand. "You're stealing my thunder, though. That's my work—handing out jobs. Pretty dull, compared to yours, but——" He shrugged.

"Room 402, sir," Jesse Webb said, releasing Dan Hilliard's thick-muscled hand. "Then listen. You get some sleep, hear?" He said that last a little louder, a trifle more gruffly, than he'd intended. But he grew uncomfortable under Mrs. Hilliard's eyes, wondering whether she could read his thoughts.

He watched Dan Hilliard moving down the corridor, stepping lightly and briskly now, his body upright and confident. And the nurse began to explain to Mrs. Hilliard, in some detail, just what had taken place in the surgery.

It's a funny thing, Jesse Webb was thinking, how you never get said what you feel or think. He rubbed the back of his neck, blinking back the sleep that threatened to catch up with him now. You never seem to say what's in you. He was thinking of a word, and even the word itself sounded odd in his mind. Magnificence. That was the word. You'd never think of applying it to Dan Hilliard, or people like Dan Hilliard and his wife. But it applied. Maybe you didn't think of it normally because the chips weren't down; but when the chips were down——

He saw Dan Hilliard turn into a room far down the hall.

What Dan found in that room was a young, full-bodied man stretched out flat on a bed with a very white sheet drawn up to his blunt-looking chin, his head turned away from the door. Beyond the man, framed in the early afternoon sunlight spilling through the high windows, was a slim, red-haired girl whose shoulders were set at an angry cant.

The young man's head turned slowly as Dan entered, and the gray eyes opened wider.

Dan stepped to the bed.

"You tell him, Dad," Cindy said. "I've been trying to make him see. Wasn't he foolish, Dad? I was nearly crazy in that police station, suspecting he was up to something, thinking he might be in there, too. Tell the man, Dad, so he'll learn not to be such a reckless fool."

Her anger might have fooled Chuck Wright, although Dan doubted even that as he fought down a smile. He noticed the bright spots of color high on his daughter's cheeks.

"You were a reckless fool, Chuck," Dan said. "It came in handy."

Chuck Wright looked very pale, not much like himself at all, but some of the grayness had gone from his face. "I couldn't do anything else, I guess." His voice was weak.

245

Dan cleared his throat. "Yes," he said brusquely. "Yes, I know the feeling." He turned to the door. "Don't let her rag you, son. Make her invite you to Thanksgiving dinner. I understand you'll be out of here by then."

Dan Hilliard closed the door behind him and paused a moment in the hall, struck again by the radiance that he had caught in his daughter's face. His body was tired, but his mind was not. He started down the hall. Had he said what he came all this way to say to Chuck Wright? Probably not. There were things you didn't say, that's all. But there were things you knew, without saying. And there were changes that took place in you without your ever being aware of them.

He reached his wife; she was alone now. She stood up and took his arm. "You," she said, in that same bullying way of her daughter back there, "you're going to bed now. You're going to sleep for three solid days. I mean it, Dan. I mean it, too."

They went down in the tiny elevator and then through the stone-and-marble entrance hall of the hospital.

In the sunlight that poured down on the wide steps outside, Ralph Hilliard was surrounded by three men who looked suspiciously like newspaper reporters to Dan. One carried a camera. Ralph stopped talking when he saw his parents, and he waited for them, very still, very grave, very adult for his ten years. Then he said, out of the corner of his mouth, to the three men: "Only if you tell him I said so, I'll sue you for libel."

Dan didn't inquire what his son had told the reporters. Eleanor, too, said nothing. After the picture had been taken and they were in the taxi, she turned her face to Dan Hilliard and kissed him full on the lips and held him like that, but without any desperation, for a long time. Ralph Hilliard, embarrassed, stared out the window.

ABOUT THE AUTHOR

Although Joseph Hayes has been writing on a full-time basis since 1943, The Desperate Hours *is his first novel. Born in Indianapolis in 1918, he spent two years in a monastery and eighteen hitchhiking through the South, and at all sorts of odd jobs, such as pushing wheel chairs at the Dallas Fair, managing a small icehouse, farm work and warehouse work. At twenty he was married to Marrijane Johnston, and together they worked their way through three more years at a Midwestern university by editing a drama magazine, typing and editing doctorate theses for correct English usage, directing amateur theatricals and radio acting. The Hayeses moved to New York in 1941 and for the next two years Mr. Hayes was employed in the editorial department of a play-publishing house—until he decided that he, too, could write plays. As soon as the first, co-authored with his wife, was published, he gave up employment promptly, and for the last ten years he has been free-lancing successfully. His work has appeared on many television screens and in the national magazines. A play,* Leaf and Bough, *was produced on Broadway in 1949. He now lives in Brookfield Center, Connecticut, with Marrijane and their two sons, Gregory and Jason—with frequent jaunts in as many directions as possible. He is now at work on another novel and has completed a new play for Broadway.*